I raised my hand to touch Van's cheek. "When I looked at my sisters, it took all my control not to attack them...and I don't know how long my control can last. Just say goodbye and let me walk away from you, *please*."

"Not this risk-taker, honey." He gave me a tight smile. "I told you two nights ago how I felt about you, Megan. Nothing's changed for me." He tipped my chin up so that my gaze couldn't avoid his.

I tried to smile, but the tears that had been brimming in my eyes splashed over. "I didn't plan to tell you like this, but I think I'm falling—"

Kill him now while he's vulnerable!

The terrible thought tore through my mind with such cold intensity that I reeled backward. I could tell from his alarmed gaze that my horror was mirrored in my eyes.

Dear Reader,

Sisters.

They fight with each other, dis each other and know each other's most secret weaknesses. But when the chips are down, they're there for each other. That's usually the case...but what happens when your sister is under the power of an ancient curse that might turn her into a vampire? And what if *you* might be the sister who's about to turn vamp?

Personally, those are questions I've never had to face with my sis, but it's one that's suddenly disrupted the lives of the fabulous Crosse triplets...and changed their pampered existence of shoe-shopping, dating and partying into a fight against the dark side with their lives and souls on the line. Enter Megan, Kat and Tashya's world of Manolos and cocktails, stakes and vampires...and learn for yourself just how binding the bonds of sisterhood can be.

Harper Allen

Harper Allen

DRESSED TO SLAY

Published by Silhouette Books

America's Publisher of Contemporary Romance

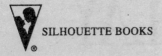

SILHOUETTE BOOKS

ISBN-13: 978-0-373-51423-6
ISBN-10: 0-373-51423-9

DRESSED TO SLAY

www.SilhouetteBombshell.com

Printed in U.S.A.

Books by Harper Allen

Silhouette Bombshell

HARPER ALLEN,

her husband and their menagerie of cats and dogs divide their time between a home in the country and a house in town. She grew up reading Stephen King, John D. MacDonald and John Steinbeck, among others, and has them to blame for her lifelong passion for reading and writing.

To the members of the Syracuse,
New York, chapter of RWA

Prologue

It's one of those questions that yank me back from the edge of sleep: was there any way things could have turned out differently? If Angelica Crosse had lived long enough to pass on to her daughters some of the knowledge that had been drummed into her from birth, would it have helped? Or if she hadn't wanted so badly to give the three of us the ordinary life she'd been robbed of that she'd left instructions in her will for Grammie and Popsie to have custody of us, would that have changed anything?

Problem is, once you start playing this game, there's no good place to stop, leaving a girl slathering on way too much Bobbi Brown concealer to hide the bags under her eyes when her alarm goes off in the morning. Or in my case, simply resigning myself to the possibility of needing my first mini-facelift before I hit the ripe old age of twenty-two. If Katherine and Natashya and I hadn't been triplets. If we hadn't gotten engaged when we did. If Grammie and Popsie hadn't raised us to be indulged, shop-till-we-drop princesses, if—

As I say, no good place to stop; and on those nights, when all this is going through my head and making it impossible for me to get back to sleep, I get the sinking feeling that everything that did happen probably would have happened anyway. Lance and Todd and Dean still would have gone to Dean's stag party, the stripper who called herself Zena still would have shown up, and our cheating jerks of fiancés still would have said yes to getting down-and-dirty lap dances from her.

Which all added up to Kat and Tash and yours truly, Megan, being totally unprepared when the men we were supposed to walk down the aisle with turned into undead creeps and tried to kill us.

As Tash says, don't you just *hate* when that happens?

Chapter 1

"My point is, these days girls are supposed to get a wild and crazy send-off the night before their wedding, like guys do." With a drama-queen toss of her curls as she entered the house, my sister Natashya flounced through the foyer into the living room and plopped herself onto a sofa. "Yet here we are, home before midnight like a bunch of *nuns* or something, while Dean's stag is probably just getting to the smoking cigars and watching X-rated DVDs stage. If I were you, I'd be totally pissed, Megan."

My other sister Katherine didn't pause in the entrance hall, either. "The brat's right for once, sweetie. As bachelorette parties go, yours blew big-time," she drawled over her shoulder as she headed toward the kitchen, leaving me to punch in the Crosse mansion's security code. I don't know if it's because I'm technically the eldest of the three of us, beating Kat in the getting-born race by ten minutes and Tash by half an hour, but that task always falls to me.

"Somehow I don't think breaking out the Monte Cristos and popping *Dick Does Dallas* into the DVD player is Mandy Broyhill's idea of appropriate entertainment." I turned from the security keypad and shrugged at Tash. "Or Lance and Todd's idea of entertainment, to be honest. It's more likely that they took my darling hubby-to-be to a strip club."

"They wouldn't. The only one around is the Hot Box, that sleazy dive on the outskirts of town, and Toddie knows I'd kill him if he ever set foot in there," Tash said dismissively. She frowned. "Besides, there's been some weird stories going 'round about that place lately. I know a girl who says after a couple of her brother's friends went there they ended up calling in sick to work the next few days and the next thing you know, they quit their jobs and just dropped out of sight. I wouldn't be surprised if the police raid that dump and find some major drug-dealing going on. But my point is that even if you don't care if your last night as a free woman is a blast or not, I do. When it's my turn in a couple of months, I want those totally babalicious cowboy dancers who entertained at Brittany's stagette party."

"The ones who stripped down to their six-guns?" Silver-blond hair swinging like satin around perfectly tanned shoulders, Kat returned from the kitchen carrying a pitcher full of something frosty-looking in her right hand, with stemmed glasses wedged adroitly between the fingers of her left. She set the glasses and pitcher on the spindly Sheraton table in front of Tash. "Appletinis, anyone?"

She didn't wait for a reply, but started pouring. I sank

onto the sofa beside Tash and eased off my shoes with a sigh of relief. My middle sister, as languidly elegant as her nickname, can power-shop all day in a pair of Manolo stilettos and dance till dawn in strappy Jimmy Choos, while Tash's idea of casual footwear is a pair of Chanel heels, but I occasionally feel the need to reconnect with my baby toes.

"Right, and when you tucked a bill into their holsters, they said, 'Much obliged, little lady.' What I *don't* want is a dreary little get-together at Mandy Broyhill's without a square inch of naked male flesh in sight," Tash insisted. She was indulging in one of her favorite irritating habits— running the silver cross she wore back and forth along its delicate chain. It was irritating because it always made me want to do the same to the identical one around my neck and I couldn't, because then she'd know she'd irritated me. "Anyhow, I'll bet tonight had something to do with Grammie being voted president of the Maplesburg Reading Club instead of Mandy's mother. I mean, Mandy's the social leader of our set, so she couldn't very well *not* throw a party for you, Meg, but maybe she accidentally-on-purpose forgot to arrange any entertainment, as a kind of payback for her mom."

My irritation turned to annoyance. Dottie Crosse had indulged us, petted us and spoiled us rotten from babyhood after her only child, our father, died. And when three eligible bachelors had popped the question in the same week to her three granddaughters, she hadn't batted an eyelash at the prospect of arranging June, July and August weddings, so I certainly wasn't going to let Tash take out her sulks on Grammie when she and Popsie arrived home tomorrow. He'd insisted on a weekend in New York after she'd exhausted herself planning my big day. I opened my mouth to say so but Kat beat me to it.

"Mandy didn't arrange for half-naked cowboys to show up at the bachelorette because *she* had her eye on Dean before he started dating Megan, and being the social leader of our set, she's also a prime bitch. But if you think tonight was dreary, just wait until your party, sweetie. According to the grapevine, most of your so-called bosom buddies don't intend to show up to give you a send-off—and don't even *dream* of trying to blame Grammie for that, because it won't have anything to do with her." She drained her glass. "Remember Bev Simmons? The mousy little brunette your darling Toddie was about to propose to before you decided you wanted to be a cosmetic surgeon's wife?"

I glanced at Kat. Was it my imagination, or was her drawl just a tad slurred? "Kat's right. You stole a boyfriend and most of our friends are on Bev's side. You better hope that being Mrs. Doctor Whitmore, wife of a rising young liposuctionist, is enough to buy you a committee seat on the Maplesburg Hospital charity drive next spring, because right now, little Tashie isn't exactly the most popular girl in town."

"Not get on the charity committee next spring? But that would be social *suicide*." Tash looked appalled and then annoyed. "You're kidding, right?"

"Not at all," I informed her with sisterly callousness. "Read the rule book."

"Under Boyfriends, other girls', penalties for filching," Kat corroborated obligingly.

Tashya exploded. "If you two knew this would happen, why didn't you *tell* me? I never would have bothered with Todd if I'd thought it would make problems for me! Why *would* I?"

"Uh, because you love him?" I ventured. "Just a crazy possibility, seeing as how you're going to go through the till-death-us-do-part thing with the guy."

"Tha's right. Till death us do part," Kat echoed with a hiccup. "You know, I just realized what a creepy phrase that is. Puts visions of twin burial plots in your mind, doesn't it? Hot damn, girls, I can hardly wait till Lance and I tie the noose, I mean, knot, next month."

She looked away, but not before I saw the flicker of desperation in her eyes. For a moment I was speechless, but then I found my voice. "Are you saying you feel the same as Tash? Because if you are, I've got news for both of you—there's no *way* I'm going to let Grammie get humiliated by—"

"I won't be a no-show at my wedding in August, if that's what you're worried about," Tash snapped. "I wouldn't do that to Grammie and Popsie. And Todd's all right, I guess, even if he is stuck on himself a lot of the time. I just want—"

"You just want the kind of life Grammie has." Kat nodded solemnly. "Same here. When Lance popped the question I had every intention of turning him down. You know me—so many men, so little time..." Her voice trailed off. "Except I found myself saying yes, even though I knew he proposed to me to get in good with Popsie's old golfing buddy Thaddeus Bayer, of Bayer, Schwartz and Dunhill. But I can't complain about being his fast-lane ticket to making partner, not when becoming Mrs. Lance Zellweger's going to get me what I want."

"A life like Grammie's." I didn't make it a question. "Membership in the Maplesburg Country Club, a show-place home, the benefits of living in a pretty upstate town while still being able to make a day of it in the Big Apple for shopping and a show. That's what the two of you want badly enough to marry men you aren't in love with?"

"You should talk, Megan," Tashya shot back. "Or are you going to pretend that just thinking of becoming Mrs. Dean Hudson the Third makes you feel like jumping into your hottest Victoria's Secret baby-dolls and waiting between satin sheets, instead of stifling a big ol' yawn? You've got even less excuse than me and Kat. You're smart enough to get into Harvard, but you don't want anything more exciting than Grammie's life, either."

"That's not—" I stopped in mid-denial, the breath going out of me. "Omigod, you're right," I said unevenly. "Dean's an investment banker who's already starting to lose his hair, and I don't even think I *like* him, much less love him. But I'm going to marry him, for the same reason you're going to marry Todd and Kat's going to marry Lance…because marrying them is the surest way we know to have the dullest lives we can. What's *that* about?"

"I'm surprised you haven't figured it out." Kat squinted at the pitcher. "Enough for one last round," she said. I started to shake my head but she ignored me. "Uh-uh, you're going to want this, big sister. Remember when Grammie was worried about me becoming anorexic and she sent me to Dr. Hawes?"

"Hawes the shrink?" Tash shuddered. "Gawd, everyone at school was whispering that you were going to be shipped off to the nuthouse. That's why Tommy Baldwin backed out of taking you to the Christmas dance that year, wasn't it?"

"And took you instead," Kat agreed. "I always wondered if you had something to do with my appointments with Hawes losing their confidential status, Tash. But I got my revenge."

Slow comprehension filled Tashya's gaze. "You were the one who stuck toilet paper to the back of my dress the night of the dance? It took *months* for me to live that down!"

"Cool it, both of you!" I barked the command sharply enough to get their attention. "In seventeen—" I glanced at my watch and saw it was nearly eleven thirty "—no, sixteen and a half hours, I'm going to walk down the aisle. In the next couple of months, the two of you intend to do the same thing, even though all three of us have just confessed that we're not real crazy about our prospective grooms. You seem to know why, Kat, so dish!"

She sat back. "Okay, Meg. When I went to see Dr. Hawes I found myself telling him about the nightmares we all had when we were little. I told him I always woke up convinced that you and I and Tashya had been in terrible danger."

"Well, duh," Tash broke in. "We were being hunted down in them. Whoever was after us had killed Mom and Dad and wanted to kill us. That *might* be the danger part, no?"

"You remember that much?" Kat turned her attention my way. "What about you, Megan?"

I guess I should explain something here. It doesn't happen so much now, but when we were kids our dreams were practically always identical, even though we weren't. So Kat's question made perfect sense to me, I just didn't have a good answer to it.

"When they stopped coming, I let the memory of them fade. All I remember was they left me terrified."

"They were a bunch of dumb nightmares, for heaven's

sake." Tash shrugged. "I never tried to suppress them, especially after Popsie told me they came from eating cheese before bedtime."

"He told us that, too," Kat informed her. "I guess you were the only one either dumb or logical enough to believe him."

"Maybe both," I added. "Sometimes you scare me, Tash."

Unexpectedly, she grinned. "Sometimes I scare myself."

Once in a while Tash comes out with a flash of humor that makes me wonder what's really behind those china-blue eyes and under that cloud of red-gold curls. I also wonder if it isn't my fault and Kat's that she usually doesn't reveal that side of herself.

My nanosecond of soul-searching ended with her next words.

"So the reason we're all getting married is because of some stupid dreams that made you and Kat wee-wee the bed when we were kids and that made Kat go on an air-and-water diet when she was fifteen. That's the big theory?"

For a moment I thought Kat was going to give one of those bouncy curls a sharp tug, but she got herself under control. "What I learned was that some girls who slip into anorexia are trying to exert control in the one area of their lives they think they can—their body image. And they do it because sometime in their past they've experienced a traumatic event. When Hawes told me that, it all clicked into place for me."

"What clicked into place?" Tash sounded bored. "And what does your eating disorder six years ago have to do with us now?"

"Because this time we're all trying to impose control over our lives," I said slowly. "We're choosing situations where we can pretty much predict what the next fifty years will be like. We're almost certain those fifty years will be screamingly boring, and we'll be spending them with a philandering cosmetic surgeon, a lawyer who'd sell his own mother and an investment banker who probably wears three-piece Brooks Brothers suits to bed, but that's better than—" I stopped.

"Better than what?"

"Better than what used to cause the nightmares until we started wearing these?" Kat flicked a manicured nail at the tiny silver cross around her neck. It was a mirror image of the ones Tashya and I had on, and so much a part of us that I sometimes forgot we wore them.

"Now you've totally lost me." Tash squinted at hers. "I never really liked having to wear this, not even when we were kids, and I always thought it was kind of dumb that it didn't have a clasp. If it hadn't been a present from Grammie, I would have snapped the chain long ago. Now you're telling me that if I had, my nightmares would have come back?"

She reached for the chain around her throat. The next moment she dropped it beside her empty glass.

"Booga-booga," she said complacently. "Guess who gets to wear Grammie's antique pearls at my wedding. And don't either of you dare tell her I broke her chain on purpose," she warned.

When I think back on that night I tell myself that if I'd had any kind of premonition at the sight of Tash's broken chain, I might have saved the three of us from our fate. But I didn't get a premonition—I just got pissed off at Tash.

"Don't worry, if I told Grammie anything, I'd tell her

you broke the only thing you had to remember our grandfather by."

"Popsie?" Tash made a face. "God, Meg, if I needed
anything to remember Popsie by, which I don't since it's
not like he's dead, how about my little Mini sitting outside
in the driveway? Or our sweet-sixteen diamond tennis
bracelets, or—"

"Not Popsie, you birdbrain, Grandfather Darkzyn.
Mom's father." There was a tight feeling in me, as if I
was standing on the edge of a cliff "Grammie once told
me those crosses were a present from him on our second
birthdays, and since he died not long after, I'd say you
just broke your only bequest from him. But if you
thought you'd be the first Crosse triplet to wear
Grammie's pearls down the aisle, think again. I'm the
eldest, so I get them first." I threw down the gleam of
silver chain and the small silver cross I'd just snatched
from my neck.

"You forgot to add nya-nya, sweetie," Kat drawled,
picking up Tash's chain from the table. "And our grandfather's name was Anton Dzarchertzyn, not Dark—"

Okay, time-out here while you try to put yourself in my
place. Remember, I'm talking about Kat, for God's sake—
Kat, whose languid sizzle fells males like trees; Kat, whose
favorite reading material is the *Mr. Boston Guide to Cocktails.* That's what I tried to tell myself, anyway, but as her
head jerked up without warning and her eyes suddenly
darkened to dull cloudiness, the person standing between
Tash and me no longer seemed to be my sister.

Or if she was, someone—or some*thing*—had temporarily done a pod-person number on her.

"One will be the striking talons of the eagle—she will begin the battle." The harsh, guttural voice rasping from Kat's throat was as chillingly alien as everything else about her. "The second will be the far-seeing gaze of the eagle, and she will warn of coming danger. The third will be our wings. She will fly us into the very core of the darkness; we pray she proves strong enough to fly us out again. These are our roles and our duty, and have been for all the unlit centuries of night. Without my presence the circle is dangerously open. I close it and form the three."

Pod-Kat's hand closed over the chain at her throat. With a sudden tug, she broke it free.

"I *get* it, all right?" Tash snatched the chain from her. "Just because I had the idea of wearing Grammie's pearls at my wedding, you and Meg have decided to wear them to yours first. Well, be my guest. The last time she took them out of the safe, they looked like they needed restringing, anyway." She glared at us. "And forget what I said about not wanting to marry Todd. I can't *wait* to get away from your stupid insider jokes at my expense. I'm sure you both think this eagle thing is screamingly funny, but for once your dumb little sister isn't hanging around for the punch line. I'm going to bed."

"Somebody has trouble handling her cocktails," Kat purred. "The punch line to what you call the eagle thing is that we don't know what you're talking about, right, Meg?"

She was Kat again, right down to her languid tone, and from what she'd just said, she'd totally blanked on her eerie little performance just now. With difficulty I found my voice. "Wrong, Kat. Striking talons, far-seeing gaze, core of darkness— Any of those sound familiar—?" I nearly jumped out of my skin as I heard the familiar chimes of the front door pealing.

Kat arched her eyebrows a fraction. "Tash is in a worse snit than usual, you're as nervous as a cat…next time I make appletinis, remind me to cut *waaay* back on the vodka. Anyone planning on seeing who's on our doorstep at this time of night? My money's on a pizza delivery driver with the wrong address."

"I will." The glance Tash shot over her shoulder at us as she sped to the door was suddenly hopeful. She came to a halt in front of the mirrored doors of the French armoire that stood in the hall and fluffed up her curls. "Pizza guy my butt! Maybe that dreary party tonight was all part of Mandy's maneuver to get us home in time to send Meg a totally hot strip-o-gram! I should have guessed she had something more planned!"

Okay. Remember what I said about not having a premonition when Tash took her chain off, and how, if I had, I might have been able to change our fates? Well, the premonition thing finally kicked in as Tash looked through the security peephole. Big whoop, since it was already too late to stop what was about to happen, but of course I didn't know that at the time.

"Don't open the door," I said in a rush. "Those stories you mentioned that are going around about the strip club aren't the only weird things that have been happening in Maplesburg, Tash. The other day I overheard Popsie telling Grammie that the police have gotten more than the usual number of complaints about Peeping Toms in the last couple of weeks. The thing is, more than half of the women insisted someone was standing outside the upper-story windows of their homes. And like you said, there's been a rash of job absenteeism and disappearances lately, not just of young guys, but girls, too. Something's going on in this town. I don't care if Heath Ledger's body double is standing on the front step, it's midnight and we're three women alone. We're not going to open the door to a stranger—"

"Oh. My. *God*." Tash's hand was already groping for the doorknob. As I reached her side she turned towards me with an expression on her face that could only be described as glowing. "If I can't answer the door to a stranger, how about to our fiancés?" she said, her tone oddly breathless. "Because that's Lance and Todd and Dean out there, sis. But there's something—" A flush of pink rose up beneath her skin. As her lashes swept down over the blue of her eyes, she bit her bottom lip, as if to stop it from trembling.

I'd seen her like this once before, when I'd barged in on her and Todd going at it hot and heavy in the cloakroom of the country club the night he'd proposed to her. Except that time I'd been pretty sure she'd been faking it, and this time I didn't think she was.

Her lashes swept dreamily up. "There's something *different* about them," she said in a purr Kat might have envied.

"They're Lance and Todd and Dean," I scoffed. "And we agreed earlier that they don't exactly get our motors racing, so what's with the cave-girl routine?"

"I'm with Meg." Kat drifted up beside us, her hand at her mouth to cover a delicate yawn. "We all know what our hubbies-to-be are here for, don't we? They've just come from a stag party. They're probably a lot drunk and a little frisky—and from one or two unfortunate experiences with former boyfriends, I can tell you that drunk almost always wins out over frisky. If we let them in, we'll be spending the next two hours stroking their—"

"Egos," I said firmly. "So turn out the porch light, Tash. That should send the message they're not getting any tonight."

Tashya's hand slid slowly from the doorknob, the dreamy look fading from her gaze. "I guess you're right," she said in a puzzled tone. "It's not like I want Todd thinking he can have it any old time he wants it. What kind of marriage would that be?"

"You think one day Dr. Todd might regret dumping mousy Bev Simmons for our sister?" Kat mused as we turned away.

"Big-time," I agreed promptly. I hesitated. "Kat, we need to talk. Are you sure you don't remember spouting off about roles and duty and the closing of the circle by—"

"Oh, *merde*."

Her disgusted response wasn't directed at me, I realized as I followed her gaze and saw Tash looking through the peephole again. Even as I headed grimly back to the door, Tash's fingers flew over the security keypad to disable the alarm.

"I can't help it, Meg," she said in the same breathy voice as before. "I mean, *look*—have you ever seen three hotter males in your whole life?" She flung the door open as she spoke, and I skidded to a halt. Two feet away, just over the threshold, stood Lance and Todd and Dean.

I tried to swallow, but my throat was suddenly too dry. Tash was right, they were different.

They were incredibly, sexily, *irresistible*.

Chapter 2

Better take another time-out here.

The thing is, our fiancés weren't irresistible. Lance had a beefiness about him that even his Armani suits couldn't conceal, and Todd had boyishly tousled chestnut curls that Kat and I suspected were the result of a body perm. Tash swore they were natural but even so, his eligibility stemmed more from his tax bracket than from devastating good looks.

As for Dean, the two times we'd done the horizontal mambo together I'd nearly nodded off while he'd sat on the edge of the bed folding his boxers and meticulously cuffing his silk socks into flat balls, as if he were packing for camp. When he'd finally joined me, I'd realized that watching him fold his clothes had been the thrilling part, and for the next five and a half minutes—oh, *please,* every

girl checks her watch when she's with a man like Dean—
I occupied myself by weaving a highly creative fantasy that
included a couple of gorgeous firemen from the Maplesburg FD, a cop whom I'd flirted out of giving me a
speeding ticket the previous day and the sexy mechanic
who'd worked on Popsie's Mercedes the time I'd borrowed
it and done something unfortunate to the steering. They'd
been hot. Dean and Todd and Lance weren't.

Except now they were. Dean's open shirt revealed washboard abs that almost rippled as I looked at them, instead
of the incipient little paunch I was used to seeing on him.
His thinning blond hair was thinning no longer, but swept
back from his forehead in a thick golden cascade that ended
up somewhere around his collar. His cheekbones were
more prominent than I remembered, hard slabs that
matched the new firmness of his jaw.

This last one almost broke through my reverie. Dean's
weak profile had always been his least attractive feature,
even trumping his hair. In the dim recesses of my mind a
feeble alarm bell rang, telling me that if Dean Hudson the
Third had suddenly acquired bone structure a supermodel
would sell her soul for, something was really, *really* wrong
with this picture. Instead of listening to it, I impatiently
shut it off as my gaze strayed south of Dean's belt. I sagged
against the hall armoire.

My boyfriend had a package. I blinked, shook my head
in disbelief, and looked again. It was still there. My boyfriend had a real, honest-to-God *package*, and it wasn't the
kind that came wrapped up in pretty paper and ribbons, it
was the kind that usually came wrapped in a well-worn pair
of Levi's on a bad-boy biker in my daydreams. Dean's

investment-banker suit trousers were straining over the unmistakable bulge, and even as I watched, his zipper notched down a trifle.

I heard a tiny moaning sound, realized it was coming from me and sank my teeth into my lower lip in an effort to get control of myself. Beside me, Tash was making the same kind of low moan.

"So adorable of you boys to drop by." Kat came up behind us, her sex-goddess drawl tinged with regret the way it always is when she's about to puncture a male's hopes. "But you'll have to take rain checks all round, sweeties. You don't—"

Her drawl cut off abruptly. I heard her swallow, heard her moan like Tash and I had, and then I heard her huskily ask Lance if he felt like a nightcap…and just as she did the mute button on the alarm bells in my head suddenly released.

"No!" I turned swiftly to her. "Whatever you do, don't ask them in, Kat! They're—they're—" My protest sputtered off as I tried to figure out why I was making it.

"We're what, honey?" Dean's voice had a sexy note I'd never heard in it before. "A little bit drunk? A little bit horny?" His eyes, their normal pale blue now a glowing sapphire, met mine and again I felt heat lapping over me.

"A little bit…*dead*," I said faintly.

I didn't know where the words had come from. Confusion filled me, and I opened my mouth to begin an apology—but then I stopped.

Because just for a second I saw what was really standing on our doorstep.

Unbuttoned shirts fluttered open around three rotting chests. Lank clumps of hair barely covered brown, parchment-looking scalps. Even as I watched, Dean leaned casually against the doorframe and a chunk of greenish flesh detached from his fingers. They hadn't been dead long enough to have become putrid corpses, of course. I realize now that what I saw in that instant was the *essence* of their deadness.

But the way they looked wasn't the worst part. That came when I glanced down and saw what remained of their feet: Dean's in polished Brooks brogues, Lance's in Italian slip-ons, Todd's in the ergonomically correct German loafers he swore were the only shoes that could stand up against hard hospital floors.

Admittedly, Todd's uber-shoes always made me want to fling my hand across my eyes and cry, "The horror, the horror!" but not this time.

Because this time they were hovering an inch or so off the ground…and so were Dean's brogues and Lance's slip-ons.

And then they weren't. All three of our gentlemen callers were standing on solid ground, and as my gaze traveled upwards I saw everything else was back to normal, too. They shimmered. They were gorgeous. They were walking wet dreams and they were here for the fabulously fortunate Crosse triplets. And even if that wasn't normal, suddenly it seemed so to me.

"A little dead?" Beside me Tash gave a breathy laugh. "Don't mind her, Toddie. Meg's been chugging back Kat's appletinis all evening."

"So how about it, big guy?" Kat looked through her lashes at Lance. "You up for it? A nightcap, I mean."

"And anything else you're offering, beautiful," her

impossibly handsome fiancé growled back. "You inviting us in?"

BING!...Bing!...bing... I firmly shut off the irritating bells that kept fading in and out in my head as Kat replied.

"As tempting as the three of you are, lover, I don't think my darling sisters would appreciate me poaching on their turf. I'll let them hand out their own party invitations." She crooked a pink-polished nail at him, gave him her most smoldering look and began sauntering back into the living room.

Lance looked at Todd and Dean. "The crooking-her-finger thing—unspoken but a definite legal invite, right?"

"Hell, don't look at me." Todd raked strong surgeon's fingers through his chestnut curls, and even as Dean's locked-and-loaded state sent erotic shivers down my spine, I indulged myself in imagining what Dr. Todd's dexterous fingers could do to a girl. "I'm the schmuck who figured if a nurse's aide was batting her eyes at me, I had the green light to hustle her sweet ass into the laundry cupboard and give her my best bedside manner, and we all know how that turned out. Sure, the little tramp was fired, but I almost got hauled up before the hospital board. I'd say the crooked-finger thing's a tease."

"That was a no-means-no situation, Whitmore." Dean saw me watching him and gave me a devastating grin before turning to Lance. "Unlike our groping friend here, Zellweger, you've got nothing to lose by giving it a shot. See what happens when you try to cross the threshold."

I can't explain it. Tash says she can't, either. We both stood there and listened to this conversation, and neither one of us found anything weird about it. All I felt was a kind of dizzy impatience to get Dean alone and out of his clothes, and I couldn't understand why they were still standing there.

Neither could Kat, apparently. "Come on in and help me whip up more appletinis, gorgeous," she murmured as she passed by on her way to the kitchen with the empty pitcher dangling from her fingertips. "Why waste time making nice with the brat and the brain when you could be with the only Crosse sister who can tie a cherry stem with her tongue in three seconds flat?"

"That's my cue, boys." A sharklike grin on his face, Lance stepped over the threshold and into the house. "Think you can perform that trick without the cherry, babe?" he asked as his hand slipped around to Kat's tush.

Kat, who's made it clear in the past that she doesn't appreciate being handled like a melon being tested for ripeness, gurgled sexily. "I can try. Let's find some privacy while your dreary future sisters-in-law are deciding whether they're women enough to handle what their fiancés can give them."

"Women enough? What a total *bitch!*" Tash sputtered in outrage as Kat led Lance down the hall into the kitchen.

My attention was temporarily diverted from Dean. "But being obviously bitchy isn't like Kat. Do you think she's—"

"She could be right." Todd's superheated look at Tash held a hint of dubiousness. "If you're still set on waiting until after the ceremony tomorrow, princess, I can respect that. I think I'll head on back to the Hot Box, okay?"

"The Hot Box?" Tash's gaze narrowed. "Listen, Pookie, whatever my cherry-stem-tying slut of a sister says, I can show you a whole lot better time than some boob-job recipient in a G-string. Get in here and I'll show you."

Okay, the Crosse triplets could never be mistaken for Jo and Beth and Amy of *Little Women*. I mean, even now I was storing away the intriguing tidbit Todd had let slip about Tash rationing out the sugar until she was well and truly Mrs. Doctor. Tash had given the impression that her prowess in bed was so amazing her formerly tomcatting fiancé didn't have the energy to look at other women anymore. But there's a line we don't cross, and both Tash and Kat had just jumped eagerly over it. First off, we never diss each other in front of anyone else—not seriously, that is. Secondly, we don't use what Grammie calls "gutter-talk." *Bitch* didn't quite make that category. *Slut* did. And Kat's slam about us not being women enough was unforgivable.

So, as a panting Tash yanked Todd into the house, I reached out to do the same to Dean…and then let my hand drop. I turned to watch her flounce up the stairs, Todd so close behind her you couldn't have slipped a piece of paper between them.

Weak-kneed lust warred with sisterly concern in me. I credit Grammie's steel-under-marshmallow upbringing with the fact that concern won, at least, temporarily. "I should go after them," I sighed. "If she's been holding out all this time only to let Kat goad her into it at this late date, she's going to hate herself in the morning."

"Sooner than that." Dean's voice was velvet. "Honey, let her and Todd play doctor while you and I occupy ourselves with our own game. Wanna start out on the sofa, maybe move to the floor when things start heating up?"

My mouth went dry and every other part of me felt hot and wet. "The floor?" I repeated huskily.

He held out his hand. "You'll need room to go crazy while

I lick every inch of you. You'll need even more room to go out of your mind when I give you your big present, little girl."

I ask you: who listens to a line like that with a straight face? Okay, all of us, at one time or another, but inside we're doing a mental eye-rolling, if not actually gagging. But gazing adoringly at Dean, I bought into it unquestioningly.

"Big…present?" I extended my hand. His fingers folded over mine tightly enough that I winced, but somehow the pain was exciting. "So what are you waiting for? Come in and let's start unwrapping it." I felt the standing-on-a-cliff sensation shudder through me for the second time that evening, gave his hand a tug—

And felt my bones turn to ice as my sisters' screams tore through the house.

I ripped my hand from Dean's and yanked open the hall armoire's doors. "Hit the alarm monitor beside you!" I shrieked, reaching to the back of the hat shelf. "Someone's broken into the house! Tash and Todd must have walked in on someone upstairs and maybe Kat and Lance surprised someone else in the kitchen!"

Where I came up with the double-set-of-intruders scenario is still a mystery to me, but at the time my *glamyr-*fogged mind seized on it as the only possible explanation for my sisters' screams. My fingers found the objects I was looking for at the back of the hat shelf—Popsie's ancient revolver and the box of ammunition that went with it. A few summers ago he'd insisted all three of us receive qualified instruction on how to handle it, overriding Grammie's objections with the argument that in the time it took for the police to arrive, knowing how to use a gun could save us from being raped, or worse. Bullets spilled to the floor as

I loaded it. "I'll take the kitchen, you go upstairs for Tash! The police should get—"

"You really are as dumb as I always thought you were, aren't you?" Dean gave the armoire a careless push. It gouged its way across seven feet of Colonial heart-pine floorboards before coming to a halt in front of the alarm keypad on the wall by the open front door. The next moment he'd batted Popsie's revolver halfway across the room. "Get the picture now, sweet thing?" he asked in the velvet voice that only minutes ago had been turning my knees to rubber.

I stared at him, my mind not processing the fact that he'd one-handedly shoved across the floor a piece of furniture that had taken four able-bodied men to move when Grammie'd had it delivered. "What's the *matter* with you? We've got to help Kat and Tash!" Without waiting for his reply I ran to the living room, grabbed the gun from where it had landed on the sofa and began sprinting to the kitchen.

I hit the floor so hard that one of my shoes flew off. Pain pierced my left butt cheek as a heart-pine sliver inserted itself through my skirt into my tush. I looked up in shock.

I'd run full tilt into Dean's washboard abs…which was impossible. He'd been standing a good fifteen feet away from me as I'd started my dash into the kitchen from the living room. He hadn't run from the hall to intercept me or somehow leapt those fifteen feet, he'd simply been at the door one moment and in front of me the next. In the split second between those two positions he'd *slid* sideways…not across the floor but through the air, like a chess piece being moved by an invisible hand onto a more offensive square.

As he looked down at me, I saw space between his feet and the floor, but when he spoke, the fact that my fiancé was defying the laws of gravity fell to second place in the creepy sweepstakes.

"Forget your sisters, bitch! Help yourself!"

His voice was still velvet, but now it was dirt-stiffened velvet. It was velvet that had been used as a corpse-cloth and was stained with unidentifiable fluids. And if that sounds as though I was still feeling the effects of the appletinis, all I can say is that by then I was stone-cold sober and desperately wishing there *was* a stiff cocktail within reach to numb my senses. All five of them were telling me stuff I didn't want to know, and my sixth sense had gone to Def-Con One with the alarm bells again.

"Uh-uh." From my seat on the floor, I forced the words past my stiff lips. "You can't be. They don't exis—" Dean's canines, razor-sharp and gleaming, lengthened past his bottom lip and I couldn't deny the evidence any longer.

My fiancé was a vampire. And if he was, then it was perfectly possible that Lance and Todd were, too. Kat and Tashya were still screaming, but even as I decided to make it a triplet thing, Dean lunged.

He hadn't been a vampire for very long, as I've since learned. Maybe his newbie status was the reason for his coordination being off just enough that I had the chance to roll out of his way. I cracked my kneecap a good one against the Sheraton table in front of the sofa, scrambled backwards on my splinter-stabbed butt, and suddenly realized I still clutched Popsie's revolver. I cocked it and fired.

If any goth-types reading this are thinking, *God, how stupid can this chick be not to know vampires can't be killed with lead?* I have two things to say to you. One: I hoped the books and movies were wrong on that; and two: a couple of black dresses are admittedly a good starting point for a wardrobe, but at a certain stage, why not consider adding a few pale neutrals?

The books and movies weren't wrong on the lead bullet thing. Dean looked down at his six-pack torso where the entry wound was already closing up. "It's all true." His voice had gone back to sounding sexy, but it wasn't working on me anymore. I glanced frantically at the Sheraton table, which in the past I'd dismissed as a fake antique Grammie had paid too much for, but which my newly-appreciative gaze now saw as a flat surface supported by four legs that might just work as stakes. "I've got a ripped body, a full head of hair and I can't be killed. This is the best investment I ever made in my life!"

"Correction—you can't be killed by an ordinary bullet." I jumped to my feet, hoisting the Sheraton table and smashing it against the floor. The table leg I held broke free. "But from all I've heard, a stake'll do the job just fine!"

Not the snappiest line, but the best I could manage under the circumstances. Dean's expression was one of unholy glee, *unholy* being the operative word. His eyes no longer looked sapphire, but black, and the snarl erupting from him didn't sound like anything human.

I plunged my makeshift stake into his heart.

That was the plan, anyway. The problem was that Grammie's Sheraton table turned out to be the real deal and not a sturdy fake. Even as I drove the leg against his muscled chest it broke, leaving me with a stub of worm-eaten oak in my hand.

Dean snarled again and attacked.

I had one quick glimpse of his face, distorted by rage into something out of a nightmare, and then his right palm came blurring toward me. It connected with my cheekbone so solidly that my head whipped sideways and the rest of me followed. I fell onto the sofa, bounced once and tumbled to the floor.

"She said there was a price!" He yanked me up by my blouse. It ripped and he transferred his grip to my shoulder, his fingers digging into me like knives. "We'd get everything we'd ever *dreamed* of in exchange for killing you three and I'm not about to let you screw up my part of the—"

My knee came up instinctively. Here's a tidbit of information you might thank me for one day: vamps react to a kick in the family jewels just the way any human creep would. Dean gave a high-pitched scream and doubled over. I turned to run.

"You bitch!" He grabbed me by my hair. My feet flew out from under me, but as I fell I felt a tug at the back of my head and I was free. I saw Popsie's revolver sticking out from underneath the sofa, and stupidly I reached for it again. It caught on something but I didn't let that stop me.

"What the hell?" As I twisted around to face Dean I saw his rage-filled expression temporarily replaced by one of pure male bafflement. I took in the object he was holding and pure female irritation temporarily replaced my fear.

"It's a hair extension," I said coldly. "I had some woven in for the wedding."

He let it drop, his brief flash of non-undeadness falling away with it. "Maybe they'll bury it with you. Or maybe there won't be enough of you to bury when I'm finished."

He was on me before I had chance to do anything more than thumb back the hammer on the revolver, but as I felt my ribs start to give way under the pressure of his embrace when he pulled me to him and went for my neck, I knew it didn't matter. Gun or no gun, from the moment I'd invited him into the house I hadn't had a chance of getting out of this alive. From the absence of screams coming from the kitchen and the upstairs, Kat and Tashya hadn't had a chance, either.

The thing that had once been Dean Hudson the Third crushed me to its chest, the tips of its teeth poised against the thudding pulse in my neck. I closed my eyes, prayed Grammie wouldn't be the one to discover her granddaughters' bodies, and felt my former fiancé go in for the kill.

Which is when Popsie's old revolver went off.

The explosion was deafening, even muffled as it was by the fact that the gun was jammed between us. Dean jerked backwards, his gaze mocking. "You're supposed to be the smart one, Megan, but you're just as blond as your sisters, aren't you? I already told you, I can't be killed with a—"

Surprise crossed his chiseled features. He opened his eyes wide, looked down at the still-smoking hole in his pumped left pec, and then looked back at me. *"Fuck!"* he said in an aggrieved tone. "I only had eternal life for a couple of hours, damn—"

He didn't finish his sentence because his mouth turned into dust. His mouth and every other part of him, to be exact. For a moment dust-Dean just stood there. Then the dust lost its shape and fell in a greasy heap to the floor by my hair extension.

The only reason I can give for what I did next is that I

was in shock. Instead of fainting dead away or throwing
up or forcing my rubbery legs to move, I bent down to look
at the Dustbuster-fodder my ex-fiancé had turned into. The
thought flickered briefly through me that I should feel
something at Dean's demise, since to quote my earlier
words to Tash, I'd been planning to do the till-death-us-do-
part thing with him.

Except death hadn't parted us. Not even his un-death
had, although his becoming a vamp had definitely widened
the chasm. But if the events of this evening hadn't
happened and we'd spent our whole lives together, there
would have been a big, empty gap where our marriage
should have been. As Kat had admitted about her and
Lance, we'd just been a means to an end for each other. As
I peered closer at what was left of Dean, I realized all I felt
was relief that I'd killed him before he'd killed me.

His remains were as yawn-inducing as he'd once
been—just a greasy pile that looked like something
Smokey the Bear would want you to kick sand over if you
were on a camping trip, except for the misshapen silver
blob capping the lead bullet in the middle of the ashes. The
melted blob was attached to the one of the silver chains
Tash and Kat and I had torn off our necks earlier this
evening. They'd obviously ended up under the sofa when
I'd grabbed the Sheraton table, and one of them had tangled
around the barrel of Popsie's revolver.

I was looking at a homemade silver bullet, I realized
slowly, and somewhere under the sofa were the materials
for two more. If Lance and Todd hadn't sunk their fangs
into my sisters' necks yet, I might still save them.

Even as the wild hope ran through me, I dropped to my

knees and began feeling under the sofa. I snagged one chain, scrabbled farther under the sofa to snag the other and leapt to my feet. The next moment I was racing to the kitchen, dropping the first chain and cross down the barrel of Popsie's revolver as I ran.

"Nuh-uh." The scornful tones of Tash came from halfway up the staircase. "Bullets don't work. Neither does Mace, as I found out. You gotta use one of these, apparently."

She held up a broken length of wood. From the pineapple carving that topped it, I recognized it as part of one of her canopy bed's posts but I didn't waste time with questions.

"Throw it here! I'll use it to stake Lance—"

"Sorry, sweetie, I already took care of him." Kat's drawl sounded a little ragged around the edges and her Alexander McQueen bustier top was destined to join my ruined skirt in the garbage, but she mustered a weak smile as she brandished a broken wooden mixing spoon. "I thought you two might need backup, but it looks like all three of us did good on the vamp-slaying, no?" She made a little *moue* with her lips. "Now *that's* a sentence I never thought I'd ever say. I don't know about you two, but I really need normal right now. Anyone up for a little drink—"

"Foolish!"

The thickly accented rumble came from the doorway. It says volumes for the Crosse triplets' state of alertness that we simply stared at the figure who had delivered it instead of rushing at him with our weapons. Tash recovered first.

"We deny you entrance to our home's threshold," she said swiftly. She frowned. "And that means to our home, too, if you need it spelled out. Like, you can't come in.

You need our permission and we totally withhold it and deny it and—"

"Did you remove holy protections out of vanity? Did you think they were simple *baubles?*" As our unexpected visitor thundered across Tash's babbling he stepped forward and entered the house. "I believed those who bore my blood would have more wisdom, but I was wrong. Your foolishness almost brought you death!"

Whoever he was, since he'd been able to enter without our permission, he wasn't a vamp. He looked to be about Popsie's age or maybe a little older, and his accent sounded Russian. A homespun cloak was flung over his shoulders and a heavy gold ring glinted on his left hand, but the most striking thing about him were his eyes. They were dark and piercing, and right now they were regarding us with less disapproval than when he'd entered.

"However, your courage and skill saved you, so I pray is still hope for you." He swept off his cloak and inclined his head in an oddly formal gesture. "Forgive me, I have not properly presented myself. My name is Anton Dzarchertzyn…but if is easier, you may call me Grandfather Darkheart."

Chapter 3

"And you can call *me* from hell when you get there, creep!"

"*No*, Tash! He's not a vam—" Before I could finish my warning my youngest sister launched her pineapple post in an overhand throw. As I leaped toward the old man, hoping to push him out of the way, I saw the missile slice unerringly through the air at his chest.

Something huge and black blurred across my sight line. I heard a furious growl as the shape propelled itself upward, and then the hell beast was upon me, Tash's post between its slavering jaws. I fell backward, my attention fully focused on the enormous dog standing over me, his teeth no longer clamped into part of Tash's canopy bed but bared inches from my throat.

Wolflike golden eyes held mine. A wolflike silver-tipped ruff stood up around a snarling wolfish face and massively muscled wolflike front legs were planted on either side of me.

"Call off your damn wolf." Kat's voice was steady, but then, she wasn't the one in danger of becoming a canine snack. "This gun might not be much use against vamps but I'm pretty sure it could blow White Fang there to kingdom come."

"Mikhail, release!"

The man who was trying to pass himself off as our dead grandfather gave the command sharply. The animal—I *really* wished Kat hadn't used the *W*-word—let a low growl trickle from its throat. It slowly backed up until it was standing by its master and gave me a final burning glance before bounding out through the open front door into the night.

I got to my feet. I had a sliver in my butt, I'd ruined an outfit and I'd gotten way too up-close and personal with pointed white teeth in the past hour. Add in the fact that my fiancé had made a deal that included him getting turned into a vamp in return for killing me and you'll understand why my party manners were a little the worse for wear as I turned to our visitor.

Doing a good impersonation of a marine drill instructor minus the flying spittle, I shoved my face close to his and pointed at the door. "Your scam's not going to work. We happen to know that our Grandfather Darch…Grandfather Dzark…"

"He said we could call him Darkheart," Tash supplied from the stairs.

I ignored her. "We know our mom's father died years ago, so whoever you are and whatever you're after, you screwed up! You're lucky you happened to catch us in the middle of a situation that puts you near the bottom of our headache list for now, but if you and your highly illegal pet aren't off this property in three seconds I'm calling the police!"

"*And* the dogcatcher," Tash threatened. "Even if you can afford to bail Cujo out of the pound, they're still going to make you pay for the snip-snip operation they give all strays. So if you don't want—"

From the darkness outside came a growl. I cut Tash short. "*One.*" I folded my arms. "*Two.*" The old man stared steadily back at me and I felt my confidence begin to evaporate. He was obviously some kind of kook, dressed the way he was and with a semi-tame wolf as a sidekick. What if he refused to leave? I glanced sideways at Kat and saw from her frown that she was thinking along the same lines as I was.

The three of us had just whacked our fiancés. Granted, there weren't any bodies lying around, but there was definite evidence *something* had happened here tonight. And although Dean's no-show status at our wedding tomorrow might be chalked up to cold feet and Todd's and Lance's absence at the same function as solidarity with his sudden desire to stay a bachelor, eventually an investigation would be launched into their disappearances. Did I really want a report on file stating that the night before the ceremony, the home of the missing men's future brides had resembled a war zone, with said brides looking suspiciously like the survivors of said zone?

"If we call the police we'll have to file a complaint and we won't get to bed for hours, Meg," Kat said with elaborate casualness. "Since we weren't taken in by our visitor's con there's really no harm done. I say we let him leave—"

"One will be striking talons of eagle!" the old man interrupted harshly. "One will warn of coming danger and third will fly into core of darkness! By blood of all slayers before you, including mother, is vital you believe. Battle has already begun and we have no time to waste!"

He didn't know it, but he'd blown it. Halfway through his eagle rant I'd been one wide-eyed gasp away from throwing skepticism to the wind, even though I knew there was a possibility he'd been lurking outside the house and had heard Kat when she'd said those very same words. But by bringing our mother into his little scam he'd pushed the envelope too far.

Grammie and Popsie have always done their best to make Mom and Daddy real for us. But Kat and Tash and I have an unspoken agreement to leave the subject of our mother…well, unspoken between us. When the Russian made the mistake of trying to use her to convince us, my immediate reaction was fury.

And if behind the fury I felt an awakening dread, I didn't bother to examine that, either.

I opened my mouth to tell him where he could shove his eagle, but he spoke first, his glare fading. "I should not blame you," he said heavily. "You know nothing of duties that have been yours throughout all unlit—"

"'*Throughout all the unlit centuries of night.*'" Kat's face paled. "'*Without my presence the circle is dangerously open. I close it and form the three.*' Oh, God, it's what I said just before everything went crazy, isn't it? How could I have blanked something like that out so completely? And how you could you know those words unless—" she swallowed "—unless you really *are* our grandfather. What happened here tonight was connected in some way to our mother, wasn't it?"

"Our mother the vampire killer. Yeah, right," Tash said, her tone dripping sarcasm. "Don't tell me you believe him, Kat. You're probably still on edge from…" Her words trailed off. "From vamp-slaying," she said hollowly. "Omigod…we're hereditary *slayers?*"

"We're hereditary normal American girls, is what we are," I said tightly. "You said it yourself, Kat—Boris here's a con man, using a few scraps of information he somehow gathered about our grandfather to pull a scam on us. We're vamp slayers? *Mom* was a slayer?" The illogical dread I hadn't acknowledged a moment earlier was suddenly as impossible to ignore as a grenade with its pin pulled. Desperately I tried to defuse it. "I'll admit Dean and Lance and Todd behaved like total pigs when they showed up here tonight, and even that we had to fight them off. The rest just couldn't have happened the way we remember." In my mind I saw Dean crumbling to dust, but I thrust the vision aside and grabbed at the only acceptable explanation. "It's more likely that the appletinis we knocked back are making us recall things a little foggily."

"That you try to deny is no surprise to me." The Russian shook his head, watching me closely. "But in your heart you know the truth, granddaughter. You must face it."

"Megan's the Queen of Denial, Grandpa Darkheart," Tash broke in impatiently. She turned to me. "There's a big ol' pile of greasy dust upstairs that used to be my boyfriend, another in front of the sofa over there, and I'm betting there's a third dust pile in the kitchen. I know it sounds crazy, sis, but since we now have proof that vamps exist, isn't it kind of reassuring to find out we're genetically equipped to handle them?" She frowned thoughtfully. "When I snapped off that bedpost and staked Todd, I was like *Yes!* You *go,* Tash! And I totally didn't understand where that was coming from because I'm so against violence usually, but now that I know I've got slaying in my blood, it makes sense."

"No, it doesn't," Kat contradicted. "But given that nothing else that's happened in the past hour does, either, I agree with Tash, Megan. If Grandfather Darkheart's correct and some kind of battle's already begun, you'd better start believing in this triplet slayer business pretty fast, sweetie."

The old Russian's steel-gray eyebrows pulled together. "*Nyet.* Only one of you is true Daughter of Lilith—a slayer, as they say in your American *televideniye* shows. The other two may kill *vampyrs,* but through luck and determination, not because they inherit title from mother."

Something inside me snapped. "*Nyet* to all of it, Boris! Our mom wasn't a slayer, she was a part-time translator at the New York firm where our father worked after graduating from Harvard Law. Two weeks after she and Dad met, they got married," I said, my voice shaking, "and Grammie's told me a million times how happy Mom was in the role of a wife and mother—so happy that it was only at the urging of my father that she agreed to a trip back to her home country. Not as imaginative as your scenario of her being a cut-rate Buffy, perhaps, but that's the way it was."

"She did not want to make journey home?" I had to admit it, the old fraud was good. The rawness in his voice seemed almost real. "She still had not forgiven me," he said in an undertone. "If she had never forgiven, tragedy might not have come so soon."

His fake pain was the last straw. "My parents' deaths are none of your business," I said tightly. "It *was* a tragedy that their car went off a cliff during their visit home, but if you think you can use that tragedy to bolster whatever false claim you're—"

"They did not die from car going over cliff." He gave a firm shake of his head. "That is what everyone was supposed to believe, but—"

"But *nothing!*" I yelled. "She was killed in an accident, not by a vampire, and she was an ordinary woman, not a Daughter of Lilith or whatever you want to call it!" I rounded on Kat and Tashya, but they were a blur, because sometime in the last second my eyes had flooded with tears. "Don't you understand, we *have* to keep believing that! In his version our nightmares were *real!*"

The words were out there and there was no way to call them back. My gaze sought Kat's, hoping for her particular brand of languid reassurance, but it was Tash who broke the silence.

"But in my nightmares Mom died trying to save—" Her eyes widened and a shutter fell behind her gaze. "You're right, Megan, they just can't be real," she said huskily. "They were just nightmares that I can blame on cheese or my imagination or watching a scary movie before bed. That's the only way I can handle them."

"Same here." Kat's fingers went to her neck, as if she expected to feel the familiar silver chain and cross around it and her other hand tightened on the revolver. "I think I'll go with my sister's version, Grandfath—" She caught herself and her voice hardened. "I dumped too much vodka into the mix tonight. You're a fake. There's no such thing as vampires, we're not Daughters of Lilith, and the nightmares we used to have when we were kids were just that—nightmares. Now get out of our house before I'm forced to use this gun."

The three of us were standing shoulder to shoulder. The old man's hooded gaze swept from Tashya to Kat before coming to rest on me, but when he spoke it was obvious his words were directed more at himself.

"There is no strength in blindness, and without strength they will not live through another night. I must do what I had hoped not to do." Before he finished speaking I took a step toward him, but as I took a second step I froze. "It is time, Mikhail." The Russian didn't look down at the wolf that had silently materialized from the darkness outside. "Show them!"

Like its master, the beast stared straight at me, but unlike the man's gaze, the animal's glowed with hatred. "Kat, get ready to shoot," I said tensely, not looking away from the wolf. "I think Cujo's about to—"

Watch!

The one-word command exploded in my head. I looked at the Russian, but his eyes were closed and his mouth was set in an anguished line. My glance darted from Kat on one side of me to Tash on the other, and the chill in me intensified. They were both staring straight ahead, and as I watched I saw tears glaze the china-blue of Tash's gaze. From her parted lips came a low moan of terror. I broke through the paralysis gripping me.

"*Stop* it!" I tugged the revolver from Kat's limp fingers.

Turning back to the wolf, I jammed the barrel between his eyes, my hands shaking so badly that the gun knocked against his skull. His glare on me didn't waver. I thumbed back the revolver's hammer. "Whatever you're doing to my sisters, stop it right now or I'll blast you to—"

My throat slammed shut in midsentence. A giant hand seemed to squeeze painfully around my heart. As if I were in a speeding train rushing toward a tunnel, blackness suddenly blotted out everything but the hypnotically glowing gaze in front of me. From a long distance away I heard the gun hitting the floor, and at the sound I made a last attempt to struggle free from whatever was about to envelop me.

But I was already enveloped, not by darkness, because my vision was slowly returning, but by a thick, homespun…cape?

Instinctively I began to pull the heavy fabric from my shoulders. Then the same moan of terror I'd heard Tash make rose in my own throat. I thrust my hand out in disbelief.

It wasn't mine. It was a man's right hand—an older man's, judging from the veining beneath the work-worn skin. That wasn't all; the shoulders over which the cape was flung were broad and solid, like the rest of the body I seemed to be trapped in, and even my mind didn't feel entirely my own anymore. When I tried to scream, the voice that came out of my mouth wasn't mine, and although I had no trouble understanding the words, they were in a language I'd never spoken.

"*Pridyl slishkom pozdno.*" I have arrived too late. My— *his*—mutter was shot through with anguish. His—*my?*— feet stumbled on a rough path that led to a Hansel-and-Gretel cottage before carrying us up the stone steps to the cottage's half-open door.

As I saw the heavy gold ring on the middle finger of the left hand that pushed the door fully open, any last doubts I had vanished and pure terror sluiced through me.

I was back in the nightmare that had haunted me as a child. But this time I was experiencing it as my grandfather had experienced it....

He was too late.

Bursting through the front door, Anton Dzarchertzyn almost fell over the body of the son-in-law he'd never met. He swept his travel-stained cloak aside and crouched quickly, his fingers seeking a wound he prayed not to find. He rose, relieved that his prayer had been answered, and pushed through the door at the end of the hall.

From the still-smoking spots on the floor, it was evident the young blond woman had killed two of them already. As he moved to her side she smashed a wooden chair against the wall and was left grasping a splintered leg that still had a partial rung attached. Quickly he held out the object he'd taken from under his cloak in the hall.

"Use this!"

If his daughter felt any surprise at seeing the father she'd once angrily thrust from her life standing beside her now, she showed no sign. She spun toward him and snatched the stake from his grasp, turned again to confront the thing rushing at her, and plunged the sharpened yew-wood into its chest.

The *vampyr* was a young woman with short black hair curving onto her cheekbones. Her paleness was an indication she hadn't fed recently, Anton knew, and now she never would again. He turned away. A moment later he heard the rattle of wood striking wood and he turned back.

The stake lay on the floor. A few ashes clung to it, but as he looked they sifted into nothingness, leaving a third charred spot. His daughter grabbed up the stake and faced him.

"I told myself that if I was careful, my family would be safe," she said, her voice ragged. "I let David convince me that even though you didn't approve of our marriage, you had the right to meet your granddaughters at least once. If I hadn't come back here, he'd still be *alive,* damn you!"

Anton shook his head, understanding that her anger at him stemmed from intolerable grief. "Eventually the one who calls herself a queen would have found you and yours, my daughter. While you grieve for your husband, console yourself with the knowledge that you fulfilled your destiny when you sent her to hell." Revulsion swept through him. "God grant that the fiery hair she was so proud of is now truly alight for all eternity."

His daughter's face blanched. "I killed this one and two males. What do you mean, a queen *vampyr* with fiery red—" From a room upstairs came a faint mewling cry, swiftly cut off. Anton read the truth in her terror-flooded gaze a split second before her words confirmed it. "The triplets! *She's with my babies!*"

She pushed violently by him, racing through the hall to the flight of stairs he'd seen as he'd entered the house. He sped after her, his heart a stone in his chest.

Red hair rippled down the back of the queen *vampyr*'s garnet velvet gown as she bent over one of the three cribs lined against the wall of the nursery. That much Anton glimpsed before his daughter pulled her from the crib and the stake in her hand sank into the vampyr's breast. Blood, ancient and black, spilled over the velvet bodice, filling the air in the room with the stench of a charnel-house. Letting the stake fall from her hand, his daughter turned to the cribs.

The Queen of Darkness fell upon her.

"Nyet!" Anton grabbed up the stake. Even as his fingers closed around it his daughter fell backward into him, released from the *vampyr's* grasp. Instinctively he caught her…and then instinctively he recoiled.

"Yes, *staryj vrag.*" The mocking whisper sounded like burning bells on a hell-steed's bridle. Lifting his stricken gaze from the twin trails of blood running down his daughter's neck, Anton Dzarchertzyn saw a smile curve the red lips of the thing standing in the doorway. "I have tasted her, as you see. When the Daughter of Lilith is one of my creatures I will insist her attacks be more on target, but this time her rash aim was to my advantage. Before another night passes she will be hunting with me, not against me." A pale finger touched the already congealing blood high on her breast and was raised to parted red lips. A pointed red tip of a tongue flicked out and the blood disappeared. "Unless, of course, you do what you must to prevent her from becoming mine. I will be waiting to see if she comes to me, old man."

A soft rustle of velvet and she was out of sight. A harsher rustle, like stiff wings unfolding, seemed to come from halfway down the stairs. Anton heard the front door slam shut.

Slowly he lowered his daughter to the floor. As he cradled her to him her eyes, blue and unfocused, met his.

"I missed her heart. I *failed,* Father!" The admission

escaped her in a whisper. "I tried to forget who and what I was, and my skills grew rusty. I have shamed my heritage…but thank God I stopped her before she harmed my daughters."

The trembling of her hand was a sign that the poison was traveling through her and unconsciously his gaze moved to the stake on the floor. He looked back to see her watching him.

"Now I ask you to keep me from further harm, too, Father, and protect me in the only way possible. But first give me your word that my daughters will be safe."

"It shall be done. A home will be found for the little ones here in their mother's country—"

"No!" Blue eyes blazed at him. "They will have the life I once thought I could have—an ordinary life far from the shadows and ancient blood-obligations of the old country! I want my daughters to have the opportunity to live without realizing such evil exists in this world…to live without ever knowing the burden of being Daughters of Lilith! Besides, the queen will anticipate you will keep them here. If you truly care for your granddaughters, deliver them to my husband's parents and stay out of their lives!"

In her agitation she gripped his arm, her clutch upon him weak. Suddenly Anton felt faint strength flowing into her fingers, and from the fear that crossed his daughter's face he knew she understood as well as he did what that growing strength meant. She released him.

"It is beginning," she said flatly. "Do what you must, and do it quickly."

"Yes." His voice sounded like dry leaves blowing across a November landscape, Anton thought. Once it had thundered at her, argued with her, tried to bend her to his will, all to no avail. From childhood she had taken risks that had stopped his heart in fear, shown defiance that had made it beat faster in anger; and throughout all her days she had been the skylark of his mornings, the dancing firefly of his dusks, the glowing star that warmed his world.

Did she understand that? Was it too late to tell her?

"I know, Father." Her eyes holding his, she put the stake into his hand. "Even when the rift between us was as wide as an ocean, I knew you loved me as I love you. I have your vow that my daughters will come to no harm?"

"You have my vow," Anton said. He felt his heart break.

"Then strike the blow and deliver my soul to God," his daughter whispered.

Anton Dzarchertzyn raised the stake. He saw the light begin to fade from the blue eyes fixed on his, saw the dark sickness start creeping across them, and he brought it down in a sudden sweeping plunge toward his daughter's—

"No!" My eyes flew open as the scream tore from me, and I saw that I was no longer in the room where my mother had died twenty years ago. Even better, I was back in my own body again—although from the waves of disorientation passing over me and the fact that I was on my hands and knees on the floor, I'd forced my little astral projection jaunt or whatever it had been to end far too abruptly.

Tash had been right, our mother had died trying to save us. So had our father, but his violent death hadn't been tainted with the fear that those he was fighting had turned him into one of them. I remembered my grandfather's fingers checking for tell-tale puncture wounds on my father's neck, and his relief when he'd found they weren't there.

Comrade Boris was who he'd said he was: Anton Dzar-chertzyn, or as he'd told us to call him, Grandfather Dark-heart. It was no use trying to persuade myself he was a fake anymore, not after the proof Cujo had somehow just made me watch. And if Boris was the real deal, then his assertion that we were hereditary vampire killers was probably—

I jerked my head up in alarm. Where was everybody? My panic subsided as I heard Tash's and Kat's voices mingling with Darkheart's somber tones in the living room. It made sense. They'd gone into the trance before I had, so they'd come out sooner. Now they had questions and Boris—I mean, Grandfather—was apparently answering them.

Which left one member of our late-night get-together unaccounted for. Cujo. White Fang. Mikhail of the glowing golden eyes.

I heard a noise behind me. My gaze fell on the revolver, still lying where it had fallen earlier. I lunged for it and did a sitting whirl on my butt.

The man standing before me was gorgeous. Six-three, at least, and every one of those inches prime, buff male. He was wearing jeans, a ripped white T-shirt and a beat-up brown hide jacket that looked as if there hadn't been too many steps between the cow wearing it and the man putting it on. His hair was shaggy enough to graze his dark eyebrows, but short enough not to do more than brush the collar of his jacket, and its mixture of midnight-black strands tipped with pewter was ultrasexy in a funky, right-out-there kind of way. But everything else took second place to his eyes. They were an amazing hazel shade—sparks of green swirling in a to-die-for golden brown, although even as I let myself fall into them I realized that they were staring at me with the same implacable enmity I'd seen in—

The blood in my veins went from pleasantly heated to chilled. My arms shot out stiffly, aiming the revolver I was clutching directly at the man looking down on me.

"But how… You're the…" I filled my lungs with some much-needed air and tried to form a complete sentence. "Cujo?"

Granted, a one-word sentence, but he seemed to catch my drift. His glare hardened. "Mikhail Vostoroff. I'm an *oboroten*—a shape-shifter. But even when I'm in human form I've got a wolf's reflexes, so I advise you to put the gun down before you get hurt."

God, I hate it when gorgeous guys turn out to be world-class jerks. The shape-shifter thing didn't bother me after everything else I'd experienced that night, but the fact that tall, dark and handsome Mikhail was an arrogant prick did.

Put the gun down before I got hurt? Could the man *be* more patronizing?

"Yawn," I said sweetly. "My reflexes are pretty darn fast, too, Mikey-baby. Us Daughters of Lilith are well-known for the fast-reflex thing, in case you hadn't heard."

I caught the gleam of white teeth before his smile flat-lined. "You should have stayed to watch the whole show. You missed the part where Anton goes to the cribs and realizes your mother was wrong. See, by the time Angelica pulled the bitch-*vampyr* away, she'd already left her mark on one of you—only one wound, not two, but that's enough to pass on vamp blood. Problem was, Anton couldn't find it in him to harm any of his granddaughters…so he kept his vow to his daughter and got all three of her triplets to safety."

"He's telling the truth, Meg." Kat came into the hall from the living room, Tash and Darkheart behind her. They grouped themselves beside Mikhail, and even in my stunned state I was alert enough to realize I was being centered out. "One of us is part vampire. That's why Mikhail's here."

"Shape-shifters can totally sniff out vamps," Tash said with the air of an instant expert. She gave me the same commiserating look she'd used when we were little and I was about to catch heck from Grammie while she escaped scot-free. "Mikhail says—"

"If Mikey-baby's got something to say, how about letting him tell me himself?" I stood up, my stomach feeling like I'd left it down on the floor. "Well?" I demanded, facing him.

His teeth flashed white, but not in a smile. "Your sister's wrong, I can't always tell for sure," he said softly. "But as soon as I laid eyes on you I felt my hackles rising. My money's on you being the one who received the kiss of the queen *vampyr*."

Chapter 4

"I still think my idea of having a flower girl strewing rose petals in front of you would have been totally romantic. It might even have made up for the fact that it's pouring down buckets on your wedding day." Tash leaned closer to the full-length mirror in the church's waiting room and scrubbed a fleck of lipstick from a front tooth before composing her expression into a shyly virginal smile, complete with downcast lashes. "I *do*," she said tremulously, looking up from her bridesmaid's bouquet of star orchids and meeting her own eyes in the mirror. "With all my heart, I—"

"Can it, sweetie," Kat snapped from her position at the window where she'd been staring out at the rain. "Even if the guests waiting in the church right now haven't grasped that the leading man in this farce isn't going to show up, you know this wedding isn't just missing a groom, it's missing the groom's best man and his head usher, as well. Or had you forgotten that what was left of our fiancés last night didn't even fill a vacuum bag when we did our little clean-up job?"

"Keep it down, Kat!" I hissed, squeezing the ribbon-wrapped stems of my bouquet—in my case, white lilac and baby's-breath—so hard that the heads of the pins securing the ribbon pressed into the palms of my lace demi-gloves. I glanced worriedly at the door, outside of which I assumed Popsie was pacing and looking at his watch, as he had been since four o'clock had come and gone a half hour ago. "We've got to appear devastated when we learn we've apparently been dumped by the men we love."

"Don't keep saying that!" Tash protested. "Toddie didn't dump me, I *staked* him. I wish there was some way I could let people know, instead of going through the humiliation of—"

Kat was off the couch and in front of Tash in three strides. "Are you out of your tiny mind?" she demanded furiously. "If one whisper gets out about what really went down last night, I'll stake *you!*" Her frown deepened. "I don't believe it. You're wearing Grammie's pearls, you little weasel. With everything else that's happened, you borrowed them for a wedding you know isn't going to take place. That's pathetic, sweetie."

"As pathetic as the flask tucked into your garter that you've been taking nips from whenever you think no one's looking?" Tash shot back. "If any whispers get out, they'll probably come from you after a few more slugs of whatever you've got sloshing around in your handy little booze-carrier!"

A weird feeling of déjà vu swept over me. Then I realized why the scene playing out in front of me seemed so familiar. I'd seen it before in any number of heist movies—you know, the kind where the criminals make a daring score and get away with the diamonds, only to fall out among themselves and shoot each other up afterwards. I stepped in.

"We won't have to worry about whispers if the two of you keep shouting insults at each other. Tash, borrowing Grammie's pearls *was* weaselly. Kat, what's in the flask?"

"Vodka martinis." She arched an eyebrow at me. "No tell-tale smell. Want a nip, sweetie?"

I waited while she lifted her lemon satin bridesmaid's dress, revealing the matching pale yellow garter encircling her thigh and the slim silver flask secured there. She handed it to me. I uncapped it, took a healthy swig, and turned to the partially open window beside us.

It was screened with rain-drenched cedar bushes. I dropped Kat's little pick-me-up into them and closed the window.

"Damn you, Megan, I needed that!" Her voice was jagged with anger. "This waiting around is getting on my nerves!"

"It's getting on mine, too," I said sharply. "But unless we want to end up in a holding cell, we have to go through with this charade. We all agreed on that last night, remember?"

"Was that before or after we learned you were a vampire, sweetie?" she retorted sharply.

"After," Tash butted in. "First Mikhail did his mind-thing with us, then he and Megan got into a big argument in the hall, then Grandfather Darkheart went all Carpathian on their asses and they shut up. *Then* we sat down and talked about how we were going to handle this whole situation."

"Meg, I'm sorry." Kat's expression was stricken. "I don't usually shoot off my mouth after a couple of drinks. You were right to toss the booze."

"Especially since if she *is* a vamp, you don't want to get her pissed at you," Tash advised. "Just joking, sis," she added over her shoulder to me as she turned back to the mirror.

"Don't blame the martinis, Kat," I said coldly. "I've seen you tipsy a time or two. I even recall holding your hair back when you got up-close and personal with a toilet at the country club the night of our engagement parties. Alcohol might loosen your tongue, but it's never put words into your mouth you wouldn't think of otherwise. You've bought into this whole stupid Kiss of the Vampire crap that our long-lost grandpa and his mangy sidekick shoveled at us last night. Has it occurred to you that it might be total fantasy?"

"Like I've said before, the Queen of Denial," Tash mumbled at the mirror as she blotted the fresh lipstick she'd just applied. "So we're back to the our-fiancés-didn't-really-turn-into-vamps-it-was-just-the-appletinis thing again?"

"No," I conceded, "I accept that they were vampires and we staked them." I tossed my bouquet onto a small side table and sat down on the sofa. Folds of tulle rose up on either side of me like frothy surf and I beat them down, feeling overwhelmed. "I'm even willing to accept that Boris is our Grandfather Darkheart and our mother was a Daughter of Lilith or a vampire killer or whatever. What I *can't* believe is that one of us is going to turn into—"

"Yoo-hoo, ladies, it's show-time!"

Without warning, the door opened and Grammie Crosse burst in, her plump and powdered face beaming at the three of us. Even at such an inopportune moment, I felt my heart swell with affection for her, and I wished I could spare her the upset that my ruined wedding was going to cause her.

Unfortunately, my wish immediately came true with Grammie's next excited words.

"I just got the word that a car with three tardy males in it has pulled up to the curb, darlings—*such* a relief! Not that I ever doubted they'd show, of course. Megan, dear, let me straighten your veil. Kat, shake out the creases in your sister's dress. Your grandfather was all set to march outside and give Dean a piece of his mind for almost making us think he'd stood you up but I said, Edward Crosse, in a couple of months when all three of those young men are your sons-in-law, you can ream them out all you want. Megan, love, you look like an angel. You *all* do, darlings. Oh fudge, I *promised* myself I wouldn't start crying before the ceremony!"

She was wearing a periwinkle-blue mother-of-the-bride dress with a chiffon overlay that floated around her as she flitted from one to the other of us. Abruptly, she stopped flitting and the chiffon stopped floating. "Oh, dear," she said in a suddenly non-fluttery voice, looking at us.

I could understand why she was staring. Beside me, Kat looked the way she had the night at the country club seconds before I'd caught back her hair and she'd gripped the porcelain rim of the toilet. By the mirror, Tash had gone the same color as the pearls around her neck and I felt as if I'd just stepped into an empty elevator shaft.

"Toddie's here?" croaked Tash. Her tone was thick with horror. "Wha-what does he *look* like?"

"Very handsome, I'm sure. I didn't watch them get out of the car," Grammie said, her gaze still encompassing us.

"But those young men could be Robert Redford and Paul Newman all rolled into one, and I still wouldn't expect any one of you to go through with her wedding if you were having second thoughts."

I was so rattled that I almost reminded Grammie that Redford and Newman, as dishy as they'd been in her day, were Popsie's age and definitely out of the running as suitors for her twenty-one-year-old granddaughters. Then I focused on the relevant part of her comment. "Second thoughts?" My voice was as hoarse as Tash's.

Grammie took a breath. "It's only money, darling, and your grandfather's got oodles of it, so if you're thinking about how much everything cost—the catering, the flowers, the cases of Cristal—then don't. And as for Dean's parents, it wouldn't bother me in the least to tell them my granddaughter's decided their son isn't good enough for her. When they deigned to fly out from Philadelphia to meet us at the engagement dinner, they spent the whole evening making sure Edward and I knew their connection to every important Main Line family. I wanted to tell them that the only good thing I'd ever known to come out of Philadelphia was cheese steak—"

She was on a roll and I didn't like interrupting her, but I knew if I was going to, sooner was better than later. "You think I've changed my mind about marrying Dean?" I asked in the cawing voice that seemed to be the Crosse triplets' new and permanent method of communication.

She shook her head. "I'm simply saying that if you have, tell me. Nothing means more to me than the happiness of you three girls and I don't intend to stand idly by and let any of you walk into something that might take away that happiness."

That's our Grammie Crosse—a slightly stout, cashmere-twinset-and-tweed-skirt-wearing lioness when she thinks her cubs are being threatened. In return, her cubs would do anything to protect her, as Kat immediately demonstrated.

"Meg hasn't changed her mind, darling, and Tash and I intend to go through with our weddings later this summer, too." Her desperate gaze strayed to the window I'd thrown her liquid courage out of, but then went back to Grammie. She gave a laugh that sounded like the noise a rusty cemetery gate might make if you pushed on it. "It's relief you see on our faces, that's all—shaky, *enormous* relief. We were a teensy bit worried that something might have happened to our hubbies-to-be, weren't we, girls?"

"Yeah," I agreed hollowly, "that's it, Grammie. When they didn't show up on time we began to think something terrible had happened. Like a car accident."

"Or like an accident with a piece of wood." Tash caught our glances. "Or a car, like Meg says," she corrected swiftly. "I can see how a car accident would be more likely."

"So now that we know they're okay, we're just…" Kat looked beseechingly at me.

"Relieved," I ended unoriginally. I gave Grammie a smile that felt like a bad facelift and must have looked just as plastic. "So relieved that we'd like to take a second to say a prayer of thanks. Can you tell Popsie we'll be out in a second?"

Grammie's no fool. She knew there was something off-kilter about our reactions, and even if she hadn't she definitely would have been alerted by my request for a moment of quiet communion with our Maker. I saw the questions in her eyes and didn't know how I was going to answer them, but just as she opened her mouth to put them into words Tash saved our bacon.

"Oh, Lord, we most humbly thank Thee for what Thou has wrought," she intoned, sinking to her knees in a cloud of yellow and closing her eyes. Kat and I hastily followed suit as she went on. "I mean with Todd and Dean and Lance. We were all like, omigod, maybe they've been in an accident, but then You were like, don't worry, Natashya, your fiancé and those of your sisters, verily they hast—"

The door clicked softly closed behind Grammie. The three of us scrambled to our feet, Tash finishing off her impromptu prayer as she did. "Verily they hast been staked, right?" She looked from Kat to me. "Vamps can't come back after you dust them, can they? And what about the whole daylight thing? Although I guess there isn't much out there today," she added with a worried glance through the window.

"Ask Grandfather Darkheart when we see him tonight," I said shortly. "Correction: if we're alive to see him tonight. But since we don't have our resident expert here to answer those questions, we have to assume the worst. Help me find something to arm ourselves with—maybe a broomstick or—"

Kat pointed to the table beside the sofa. "Will that do?"

"It'll have to," I answered, moving to it and sweeping my bouquet to the floor. "Take a leg and pull, like at Thanksgiving with the wishbone."

Thirty seconds later the three of us stepped into the vestibule of St. Barnabas, where a red-faced Popsie was waiting. Except for the red face, he looked dapper in a dove-gray morning suit, and when he saw us his expression softened.

"I'd like to horsewhip that young man of yours for not getting to his own wedding on time," he said gruffly, crooking his right arm for me to grasp as Kat and Tash took their places. "Lucky for him your sisters' fiancés slipped him in the side entrance without running into me. But I promised your grandmother I wouldn't spoil your big day, so I'll say no more about it. Are we ready?"

As if St. Barnabas's organist had heard and taken Popsie's query for a cue, the huge Hammond at the front of the church began booming out the opening bars of "The Wedding March." I exchanged grim looks with Kat and Tash as two ushers opened the double oak doors leading from the vestibule into the church and Popsie began escorting me down the aisle.

Every female with an ounce of romance in her soul dreams of her wedding day. Even the most tomboyish little girl occasionally takes time out from picking scabs from her knees and beating up little boys to envision what she'll wear and the kind of flowers she'll carry. Now, as I solemnly step-paused, step-paused with Popsie down the velvety red carpet leading to the altar, I realized I was living the fantasy.

Sort of. Then again, sort of not.

Through the lace of my veil I could see packed pews on either side of me and Popsie. The fragrance of the gardenias festooning them was so heady it was like running the spritzer gauntlet in Macy's perfume section. The florist had woven tiny crystals through the dark green leaves, and more crystals dripped in strands to brush the floor. Tash, Grammie's pearls around her throat, the skirt of her yellow satin bridesmaid's dress swinging like a bell and its short train falling from a flat bow positioned at the back of her waist, looked like a fairytale princess. Kat looked like a movie star, with her silver-blond hair worn down and the fishtail hem of her strapless silk organza swishing sexily behind her. I didn't look like a movie star or a princess. In the Monique Lhuillier ball-gown-styled wedding dress I'd fallen in love with the moment I'd first set eyes on it, I looked exactly as I'd always dreamed of looking on my wedding day…elegant and beautiful.

That was the *sort of* part of living the fantasy. The *sort of not* part was the big hunk of broken table leg strapped to my leg by a frilly blue garter—totally Freudian, now that I think of it—plus the fact that as I slowly proceeded toward the three men standing with their backs to us at the front of the church, I felt like turning tail and running like hell.

Or do all brides feel like that?

Whether they do or not, most of them don't bail on their own weddings and I wasn't going to, either. Tash and Kat, as nervous as they were, would see this out for the same reason I intended to. Somehow Todd and Lance and Dean had risen after being staked. I wasn't going to leave an unsuspecting Grammie and Popsie to face them, although right now, *facing them* wasn't the operative phrase.

"This is so humiliating I could *die*," Tash whispered across Popsie, whose hearing isn't the sharpest. "They've still got their backs to us and everyone's beginning to look really uncomfortable. I mean, even if they're vamps, you'd think they could show some manners, right?"

"Sure, sweetie," Kat said under her breath. "Just like the old-world courtesy they displayed last night when they were trying to sink their teeth into our necks."

"They're fudging with our minds, as Grammie would say," I said tersely. "Or as *I* would say, fucking with our minds. They're obviously using some sort of mojo to look normal to everyone here but they'll show their real faces to us just before they—"

A couple of things happened all at once. Well, not all at once, but really close together. The first thing was that "The Wedding March" suddenly trailed off on a discordant note. The second was that Grammie, about fifteen feet away in the first row of pews, stood up and began to make flapping motions at us with her hands, as if she were shooing chickens. The third was that Lance and Todd and Dean turned around.

I stared at Dean in horror. Flames burned in his eye sockets, his canines were impossibly long, his face was dead-white…and no one in the church was screaming.

I didn't bother wasting time wondering about that part. I began fumbling under my crinoline for my stake, determined to get to our undead grooms before they had a chance to take a step closer to Grammie, but even as I did I froze. My stake fell from my hand, bounced once on the red carpet, and clattered to the floor beside the nearest pew.

The three men standing at the front of the church and looking at us weren't Lance and Todd and Dean at all. They didn't have fiery eyes or vamp teeth or white faces—in fact, they looked absolutely ordinary. Two of them were in the familiar blue uniform of the Maplesburg Police and the third wore jeans, an unbuttoned sports jacket and a gold detective's badge clipped to his belt. He narrowed his eyes at Tashya and Kat and me, but when he spoke he raised his voice so everyone could hear.

"Sorry, folks, the wedding's been postponed. The groom and his buddies appear to have gone missing, as everyone here but the bridal party seems to have noticed." In the hubbub that arose from the guests he lowered his tone, this time directing his words only to us. "I'm treating their disappearances as possible murders, ladies. Not that you're suspects, but can the three of you fill me in on where you were and what you were doing last night?" His gaze went to my fallen stake and he went on smoothly, "And can you also explain why you're carrying a concealed weapon at your own wedding, Ms. Crosse?"

Chapter 5

I prefer to forget the few hours that followed. Tash and Kat say they wish they could forget them, too. But though we eventually unloaded our dresses on eBay (note to *brrridegrrl* out in Idaho: thrilled as I am that you looked so beautiful in my Monique Lhuillier when you and Ryan the feed salesman walked down the aisle, if you send me one more picture of you wearing my dress I'm going to post it to the creepiest bride-sex forum I can find on the Internet), and even though we threw away our bouquets and in Tash's case, never wore Grammie's pearls again, it was no use. The whole episode was seared into our memories, although we each had different versions of what we thought we'd seen.

All of us swore we saw three men in tuxedos standing at the altar with their backs to us. Kat said that as soon as the men turned around, she realized they weren't wearing tuxes, but for a moment she still thought they were Lance and Todd and Dean. Tash insisted the tux illusion disappeared for her even before she saw their faces, and that she never saw burning eye sockets or any of the other special effects I was unlucky enough to experience. Our explanations for our differing mirages didn't agree, either. Kat leaned toward the theory that our guilty consciences combined with Grammie's misinformation that our escorts had arrived made us see what we did. Tash was convinced we were still experiencing a residue of the vamp *glamyr* we'd been subjected to the previous night. And I didn't know what to think.

Not then, at least.

So I don't have to dwell on it, here's the Cliff Notes version of what happened next. As soon as Van Ryder—that was the detective's name, and have I mentioned yet that he was a total babe? Melty brown eyes with thick lashes, a full bottom lip just made for a girl to nibble on, and under his jeans his butt looked…sorry, where was I? Oh, right—as soon as he posed his question, Kat went into full-blown sex-bomb mode, revealing a glimpse of her thigh as she withdrew her own stake from her garter.

"Something old, Detective," she purred, fondling the length of wood. "Meg had the borrowed and new and blue, but we *completely* forgot to equip her with something old, and once we'd dismantled a table, well, it seemed sensible to take two more legs for Tash's and my upcoming weddings. I know it was terribly naughty of us to expropriate the furniture, but we didn't want bad luck. Of course, we had no idea then that her groom and our fiancés were missing. I can't think of anything more unlucky to happen to a bride and her bridesmaids."

"Tough on Lance and Todd and Dean, too," Tash said insincerely. She gazed at Van Ryder with wide eyes. "Why are you asking us where we were last night? Do you think *we* had anything to do with their disappearances?"

At that point Popsie jumped in, as full of angry indignation as only a retired lawyer whose granddaughters had just been asked for alibis could be, with Grammie interjecting supportive comments during his rant when she wasn't breaking off to thank the departing guests for coming.

I should digress here for a moment to explain why this rather awkward social task fell solely on poor Grammie's shoulders. As you've probably gathered from Grammie's cheese-steak comment, Dean's father and mother both came from blue-blooded Philadelphia Main Line stock, and not only didn't they bother to disguise their disappointment that Dean hadn't chosen a fiancée from their immediate circle, but they seemed to consider upper New York state an uncouth wilderness totally unsuitable as a setting for their son's wedding. Except for being from Boston and San Francisco, respectively, the Whitmores and Zellwegers held the same snobbish views. It was unfortunate but understandable that their sons had chosen to start their careers in the Big Apple—after all, if a rising young doctor, lawyer and investment banker could make it there, they could make it anywhere. But to choose their *brides* from the Empire State…well, that was simply beyond the pale.

Not that any of this had been said in so many words. Our prospective parents-in-law were far too stuffy to make a scene, but their chilly smiles on the only other occasion we'd met them, which happened to be our three-in-one engagement party, had spoken volumes. So I wasn't surprised to see cold relief flicker over the patrician features of Mr. and Mrs. Hudson as they took in the fact that Dean the Third had apparently come to his senses at the eleventh hour and jilted his eminently unsuitable bride. Kat's opinion is that, given a choice, all three sets of parents-in-law would have preferred knowing their sons and heirs had chosen vamphood over marriage to us, and I think she's probably right.

But, of course, they never did know about Lance's and Todd's and Dean's brief stints as vampires, or how those brief stints had been ended by the Crosse triplets. In fact (spoiler alert here for those of you who care about such things), it's my understanding that they totally bought into the jilting theory I presented to Van Ryder, and still expect their sons to sneak back home one of these days.

But I'm getting ahead of my story. As I was saying, Popsie was ranting, Grammie was fluttering, and the church was emptying fast. To add to the confusion, the organist came to apologise for having launched into "The Wedding March" prematurely, Grammie tartly asked Popsie why he'd continued leading us to the altar when she'd done everything but use a bullhorn to convey to him that he'd jumped the gun—this last cleared up the mystery of her shooing motions—and Popsie broke off his diatribe to growl something about not having his glasses and how was he to know that the three men standing at the end of the red carpet were the local law?

When Popsie finally paused to draw breath, Detective

Van Ryder turned his melted-chocolate eyes back to me. "I'm trying to get a fix on where people were during the relevant time period. We know your fiancés were attending Hudson's stag party at a local watering-hole called the Hot Box until shortly before midnight."

Popsie snorted. "Unless the witnesses who place them there at that exact time had some definite reason to notice the clock I fail to see how you can know when my granddaughters' fiancés left the place, let alone where they went when they did."

Van Ryder pulled a notebook out of the inner pocket of his jacket. "They did have a definite reason to remember. The three men all received lap dances from a stripper named—" he flipped a page "—yeah, a stripper named Zena. She recently bought the place, but I guess she likes keeping in practice once in a while. Even for lap dances, these were pretty steamy. The rest of the party were lined up with their tongues hanging out, waiting for their turns, but when Zena finished with Hudson—" He looked at me. "You're Megan? Hudson's your fiancé, right?"

I nodded. Van Ryder's stare hardened into nonmelted chocolate for a moment. "Hudson got the last hootchie-cootchie dance, as I say, and then this Zena tells everyone to drink up and leave, she's closing the place down at midnight. When the rest of the stag party looked around for Hudson and Whitmore and Zellweger, they'd already left. No one's seen them since."

"So why assume we did?" I injected a teary note into my voice. "I mean, Detective, why even treat this as possible foul play? It's obvious what happened. The boys got a taste of the wild side and spending the rest of their lives with the Crosse sisters suddenly didn't seem all that exciting. They *jilted* us. They're probably halfway to Mexico now and soon everyone in Maplesburg's going to know our fiancés dumped us at the altar!"

My spur-of-the-moment scenario was more true than Van Ryder knew, I thought. Staked or not, Todd and Dean and Lance *had* been standing by the altar minutes ago. Or had they? No one in the audience had seemed to see them, so had the whole thing been my private little hallucination?

"There's a major problem with your theory, Ms. Crosse," Van Ryder said, the regret in his voice as fake as my tears. "After their lap dances with Zena, all three of them came right out and stated they were going to the Crosse mansion. The witnesses who overheard them said your fiancés announced they had one final present to give their future brides." He kept his eyes on me. "So I'll ask again, Ms. Crosse. Can anyone vouch for where the three of you were around midnight last night?"

"*Da, Detektiv,* I can. Granddaughters were at home making overdue aquaintance with their mother's father. This is allowed in America, *nyet?*"

I turned to see Darkheart, his brow creased in a ferocious scowl. But his expression was nothing compared to that of the man behind him.

Mikhail Vostoroff, his golden eyes burning with hatred, was staring at me as if he wanted to rip my throat out.

Okay, that ran a little long for the Cliff Notes version, but living through it seemed to take a lot longer—like several lifetimes. It wasn't until later that night that I was able to sort through my jumbled impressions of what had happened—Darkheart's intervention, which had left Van Ryder without his trio of prime suspects, Grammie's and Popsie's astonishment at the appearance of a man they'd believed dead for decades, Anton's old-world charm as he won them over in three seconds flat, resulting in Grammie inviting him and Mikhail back to the house—since, as she said, we still had to eat even though our meal now wouldn't include champagne toasts and wedding cake.

Over dinner Darkheart filled them in on his Mark Twain-ish "the reports of my demise were exaggerated" situation, explaining that after the car accident that had claimed his daughter and their son, resulting in Popsie's and Grammie's adoption of us, he'd undertaken a research assignment on vanishing folklore for Moscow University. I found out later that this part was true, at least; he's a leading expert in the field of arcane beliefs and legends, which makes sense when you think about it. The part that wasn't true was when he went on to tell my grandparents that during the assignment he'd had an accident in some remote region of the former Soviet republic, had slowly been nursed back to health by the locals, and, when he'd been fit to travel again, had found himself trapped there by one of the many civil wars that kept breaking out in that area.

"Is very isolated region, you understand," he'd told Popsie and Grammie. "Not surprising whole world thinks Anton Dzarchertzyn dead, *da?* But *kollega* Vostoroff—" at this he'd nodded at Mikhail, who looked nothing like any university colleague I'd ever seen "—makes search for me. In end he finds me and I go home. Russia is changed from bad old days, you know. Now is available American newspapers, including *New York Times* Sunday Style

Section, which is big favorite with many. In it I see pictures of my granddaughters saying they are engaged, but newspaper is old, so is no time to waste if I want to see first one take solemn vows of marriage. Is good we come straight to house last night, *nyet?* Police in America must be stupid as to see granddaughters as suspects!"

By the end of the meal, Popsie was insisting that Anton and Mikhail move from the hotel they'd checked into and take up residence in the Crosse mansion guesthouse, Grammie had confided that she and Popsie had planned a cruise to coincide with my honeymoon, which they would now have to cancel, and Darkheart had pounded his fist on the table and growled that he would not hear of such a thing.

"Is *nevynosimyj* that fiancés who run away to Mexico make impossible your plans!" he protested.

Popsie sighed. "If Van Ryder had been on the Maplesburg force a little longer he'd realize how ridiculous he's being. But as he mentioned, his last posting was LA and I suppose he's trying to show the locals how it's done in the big city. I don't trust him not to try to pin these disappearances on the girls if he doesn't get any other leads, and if that happens, I want to be here to get our lawyers on his ass." Popsie can be quite salty when he's aroused.

Grandfather Darkheart folded his arms. "Simple. *I* stay here. If police make trouble, I contact you on cruise ship, *da?*"

I fully expected Popsie to say *nyet*. Instead he flicked a veiled glance at Grammie, who was attempting to make polite small talk with Mikhail. I felt like suggesting she throw a stick if she wanted to get an enthusiastic response from him.

"That's not a bad idea, Anton," Popsie answered. He shot another look at Grammie and leaned in closer to

Darkheart. His confidential attitude raised immediate red flags in me and I felt no compunction about eavesdropping. "Just between you and me, Dottie's been told by her doctor to take things easy for a while. At this point there's no cause for alarm, apparently, but neither one of us is as young as we were, and her heart's been acting up on her a little. As upset as I am for my granddaughters over today's fiasco, I'm more worried about the toll it could take on Dottie."

I went cold inside. Grammie, sick? Maybe in danger of having a heart attack? I darted a quick look at her and saw the paleness under her powder, the effort it seemed to be costing her to keep up her end of the conversation with Mikhail. Fear gripped me as Popsie went on.

"That's why I insisted on this cruise. If I can assure her that we're leaving the girls in your capable hands, Anton, I might be able to persuade her to go. Our boat doesn't leave New York until tomorrow, so let me give you an answer in the morning."

"Tell *Gospozha* Crosse not to worry. I will keep eye on Detective Van Ryder and also try to lift spirits of my grand-daughters," Darkheart declared. "In old country when is sadness, best thing is physical exercise. Perhaps Mikhail teach them some *gimnastika* moves while we stay here. Get broken hearts pumping again, *nyet?*"

His roar of laughter brought an answering chuckle from Popsie and won a weak smile from Grammie. It was the smile that decided me. I knew Darkheart hadn't meant his talk of gymnastics to be taken seriously but all at once I was willing to execute a handspring off a balancing beam if that's what it took to erase the strain from Grammie's expression.

Hours later, however, as I cinched the belt of my shortie

robe and slipped my feet into a pair of pink scuffs, I decided my attempts to convince Grammie that she could leave as planned without feeling she was letting us down could wait until morning. She'd hovered worriedly over us after dinner while Popsie had shown Anton and Mikhail to the guesthouse, not leaving our sides until we'd finally cast meaningful glances at each other, yawned widely, and declared our intention of going to bed. I didn't like deceiving Grammie, but I knew Kat and Tashya were as desperate as I was to talk over the events of the day, and so far we hadn't had a chance to be alone.

Now we did. Quietly I cracked open my bedroom door. The hallway was dark, without the slivers of light I expected to see under Kat's and Tash's doors a few feet away. Moving noiselessly along the hall, I reached Kat's room and tapped lightly before turning the knob.

"Kat?" I began to step across the threshold and then reeled back, overcome with nausea as a powerful stench assailed my nostrils. Gagging, I stumbled backward into the empty hall, only to find it wasn't empty.

Even as my back slammed against a solid chest, I grabbed the stake I'd jammed into my robe's belt before I'd left my room and spun to face the vamp, plunging it straight into his heart.

Or so I believed for about half a second.

"At least you didn't drop it this time, *vampyr*." Mikhail sucked in a hissing breath and yanked out the stake that was sticking into his right biceps. "Now we're going to have to waste time waiting around for this to heal."

He looked at me as if he expected me to know what he was talking about, but even if I had I wouldn't have cared.

I shoved past him into Kat's bedroom, but again the sickening odor repelled me. Fear sharpened my voice as I turned on him. "Where is she? What's that awful smell?"

I didn't wait for him to answer. Instead I ran down the hall to Tash's room and burst through the door. "Tash!" I whispered hoarsely. "Tash, is Kat with—"

This time when the stench hit me I recognized it for what it was. I could feel the hives already starting to rise on my face and chest as I staggered to the doorway, retching. My esophagus narrowed to the diameter of a clogged soda straw and my knees began to buckle as I struggled to pull in a breath.

"You still going to tell me you aren't the triplet who got marked?" Mikhail's voice seemed to fade in and out. I fell to my knees in front of him—not a position I'd ever thought I'd find myself in with Cujo, believe me—and grabbed blindly at him.

"Allergic…" I rasped. "Garlic…bad reaction…"

"Yeah, like the bad reactions you're going to start having to sunlight soon, or holy water." He sounded grimly amused. "You're resourceful, vamp, but if you really were having an allergic reaction you wouldn't just be feeling like shit, your air passages would start to close—"

Painfully I tried to draw breath. A gross rattling noise came from my throat as Mikhail kept talking.

"—your eyes would start to bulge—"

I stared in mute agony at him.

"—and just before you lost consciousness you'd begin vomiting uncontrollably. No, what you're feeling is good old-fashioned vamp revulsion at the wild garlic I hung around your sisters' rooms to protect them from you and—"

In my ears his voice faded into nothingness as I threw up all over his shoes and passed out.

I came to not knowing where I was or how long I'd been out, but all too aware of my humiliating splash-and-crash episode and wishing I could curl up and die. A moment later my eyes adjusted to the darkness and I realized I was in the right place for doing exactly that.

Bulky stone shapes rose out of the ground around me, the nearest decorated with a basket bouquet of gladioli on the fresh-looking sod in front of it. A few feet away, an angel was frozen in the act of praying and farther on I could see a scrolled and curlicued fence, like iron lace.

I was in Maplesburg Cemetery. Correction: I was in Maplesburg Cemetery at night. Double correction: I was in Maplesburg Cemetery at night all alone. I'd been dumped here by Mikhail, either in retaliation for what I'd done to his shoes or because he figured that as a vamp I belonged here.

"The *bastard!*" My heart slamming away in my chest, I sat bolt upright and in the process knocked over the basket of glads. I caught a movement out of the corner of my eye and my heart stopped slamming—or to be more accurate, decided it might be a nifty idea to stop beating altogether. It started up again as I realized that the movement I'd seen belonged to a dog investigating some bushes by the fence. As I watched he cocked a hind leg and annointed them thoroughly.

"Hey, boy!" Normally I don't feel the need to call strange dogs over to slobber on me, just as I don't beckon strange men over at parties to grope me. But being in a cemetery, I discovered, uncovered in me a previously untapped kinship with all living creatures that was almost Zenlike. Besides, if a vamp showed up, maybe it would go for the mutt first.

"C'mon, Rover!" The dog didn't look my way. I could hear it still whizzing on the bushes. "Buster?" I hazarded. "Rags? Spot?" Judging from the sound, the Niagara-sized stream it was arcing onto the greenery seemed to be coming to an end. I tried another tack. "Wanna Snausage, boy?"

I pretended to fumble in the pocket of my robe—lame, I know, but how tricky do you have to be to fool a dog? — and held it in front of me.

"I'll pass, thanks." Mikhail strolled from the direction of the bushes. He gave the fly of his jeans a precautionary tug. "Sorry about that," he said without a trace of sorrow in his voice. "I thought you'd be out longer. Besides, when I'm in wolf form I observe wolf protocol, not human."

He propped himself against a headstone and crossed his arms. Swiftly I stood, feeling anger coming off me like heat. "I could fucking *end* you! You better get me out of this place and back home right this minute or the next time you go into wolf mode I'm collecting a bounty on your mangy pelt! And if that was an example of canine protocol, I'll take cats any day. What you just did on the bushes was totally gross!"

"And the hairball you hacked up on my shoes wasn't?" he asked, his arms still dismissively crossed as he looked at me. "We're not going anywhere. We're staying here until dawn, and even then I wouldn't bet good money on us both walking out of this graveyard alive. This is a demonstration, sweetheart."

"News flash, comrade—I'm not your sweetheart, and since I don't go for fleas and fur, I never will be." I exhaled. "I'm leaving. I'd rather take my chances with any vamps or weirdos I might run into on the way home than stay here with you. And if I get there and find anything's happened to my sisters…" I left my threat unfinished and turned to go.

"Nothing's happened to them." Mikhail's words came from behind me but I didn't stop walking. He continued, "They're attending their first training session with your grandfather."

I whirled to face him. "First training session? First training session for *what?*"

His gaze met mine. "For acquiring the skills they'll need as Daughters of Lilith. Or the skills one of them will need," he amended, "since only one of them is the true inheritor of the title. But learning a few vamp-killing maneuvers might save the non-inheritor's life one day, so until Anton knows for sure whether this present generation's Daughter of Lilith is Kat or Natashya, it won't hurt that they both take instruction."

"What about *me?*" I stared at him in disbelief. "What if *I* run into a vamp? What if Todd and Dean and Lance pop up again like they did this afternoon at the church—do I just expose my neck to them and say, drink up, fellas, this round's on me?"

"They'd probably react the same way I reacted to your Snausage offer," Mikhail informed me laconically. "If you're as far advanced in the change as I think you are, as soon as they got a taste of you it would be thanks but no thanks. *Vampyrs* don't drink from other *vampyrs*. And

Lance and Todd and Dean are dead, anyway. What you and your sisters saw this afternoon was an illusion."

I was so relieved that for the moment I let his Megan-the-Vamp jibe ride. I'd been more terrified than I'd admitted by the possibility that staking might not be a sure thing, I realized, frowning suddenly as the downside occurred to me. "By *illusion* you mean we're crazy."

"No, I mean someone powerful was fucking with your minds," he said impatiently. "Anton thinks that someone was Zena."

"The stripper at the Hot Box who specializes in lap dances?" I didn't bother to hide my scepticism.

"Lap dances that end with her sinking her fangs into her customers." Mikhail shoved himself from his tombstone seat. "Think about it: she gets your fiancés in a lather and next thing you know, they're heading for your house as full-blown vamps. Only an ancient and powerful undead could effect an instant result like that. Add in the interesting tidbits I found out today when I dropped in at the Hot Box and asked a few questions about the owner, like she's never around in the daytime and she's got fiery red hair, and I think it's safe to say Zena the stripper is really the queen vamp who killed your parents." He paused a beat. "And marked you."

"According to your theory," I shot back. "Look, about the garlic thing tonight, I—"

"You're allergic," he interrupted. "Yeah, I finally came to believe that while I was washing off my shoes in the ornamental fountain over there." He jerked his head in the direction of the bushes. For the first time since I'd met him the previous night I sensed an infinitesimal softening in his attitude toward me. "But that doesn't change anything. I don't blame you for not wanting to accept what you are, especially since the change hasn't come over you yet. I couldn't accept the curse I carried, either. Right up until my sixteenth birthday I refused to believe that I wouldn't live a normal life. Of course," he added off-handedly, "the normal life I envisioned included being the starting pitcher for the Brooklyn Dodgers one day."

"Gee, too bad no one tipped you off that they moved to LA back in the sixties," I said acidly, dredging up what little baseball lore I'd absorbed from Popsie. "That might have softened the blow. Besides, Russians become hockey players, not pitchers."

"The Bums left Brooklyn in fifty-seven, not in the sixties." His eyes looked suddenly more golden. "And growing up a trolley-car stop away from Ebbets Field, I never even considered playing hockey."

"Whatever," I said irritably. "But my point is that there's no proof of this mark you insist Zena put on me when I was a baby." I held up a hand to forestall him. "No proof except for your super-duper vamp-sniffing-out talent—which, if you'll forgive me for saying, I find just as unbelievable as the rest of your abilities. Unbelievable and creepy," I muttered.

He looked taken aback. "What's creepy about shape-shifting?"

I inhaled. "Look, this conversation isn't about you, but if you must know, I keep wondering what happens with your bones when you undergo a shift, why your clothes seem to appear and disappear with your human form, how you performed that unpleasant mind thing you did with Tash and Kat and me—and don't think I haven't noticed that your biceps's healed where I stabbed you. All creepy, especially the stretching and compressing bones part. But to get back to me and the possibility that you might stake me—if Darkheart was so frikkin' convinced he had a tiny drooling Dracula on his hands all those years ago, why didn't he do something about it then?"

"Like kill his own grandchild?" Mikhail stiffened.

I sighed. "God, could you people *be* more melodramatic? All these curses and hereditary burdens and flying into darkness—*no*, not kill his own granddaughter! But how about getting her ears pierced or something? I've seen baby pictures of us and I know it wasn't easy to tell us apart, so why didn't he take some precautions?" I scowled in sudden suspicion. "Wait a minute—if one of us *was* bitten as Grandfather seems to believe, there'd be a scar, right?" I planted my hands on my hips. "I don't have one. Neither do Tash or Kat. Guess that means Zena was fucking with Grandfather's mind all those years ago by making him think she'd gotten to one of us before Mom could stop her, no?"

"No." His tone was once again hostile.

"And you're so sure of that, because why, exactly?" I let sarcasm drip into my challenge.

"Because *glamyr*-wrought illusions are just that: illusions. They don't show up on film and they don't translate as reality when someone with my abilities helps a third party relive the scene, as I did with you and your sisters," he said coldly. "Like I said last night, you should have stayed to watch the end. You would have seen the proof with your own eyes—one of Angelica's babies with a pinprick of blood running from the puncture wound in her neck. It didn't have to be large enough to scar, it just had to be enough to infect you. As for why Anton didn't take precautions, my guess is that after what he'd been through he couldn't face the truth, just as you can't now."

For a moment his battering-ram certainty rocked my defences. A hairline crack seemed to run through the very foundation of who I knew I was and what I could trust about myself…and through that crack, a dark fog began to seep.

I say *seep,* but that's not the right word. It *snaked,* as if it were a living thing, a twisting, changing image of despair and destruction and damnation. A horrific series of pictures flashed in front of my mind's eye. A man dressed in rich robes tossed the blood-drained body of a woman off a medieval parapet. A young girl who looked to be little more than a child screamed in rage and flew straight into the stone side of a Gothic-styled church, smashing herself to pieces before she turned to dust. A doctor in a Victorian alleyway slashed the throat of a prostitute, a twenties flapper downed a last slug of bootleg gin before stepping out of a window and impaling herself upon the wooden fence below, a couple at an outdoor rock concert that looked like Woodstock led a teenaged girl with drug-dazed eyes away from the rest of the crowd.

Then I saw myself moving determinedly through an unfamiliar darkened building with murder in my heart…and knew I was hunting for Kat and Tashya.

"No," I whispered. *"No!"*

Chapter 6

Gasping, I severed the connections between my brain and the dark images. Had I experienced another episode of Mikhail's unpleasant mind-control abilities? One look at his suspiciously narrowed expression told me he didn't know what had just happened to me, which meant the pictures in my mind hadn't come from him. Desperately needing to replace the lingering sensation of horror with something—*anything*—else, my mind snatched at fragments that had passed me by earlier.

"Ebbets Field? Trolley cars? *1957?*" I barely cared what I was saying. "How *old* are you?"

"Twenty-eight." His gaze on me was too steady.

"In human years, not dog years!" My nerves, already frayed from the horrors I'd imagined—of *course* I'd imagined them, I told myself—couldn't take much more. "How *old?*"

"Twenty-eight," he repeated. For a second a shadow passed behind the molten gold of his gaze. "I've been twenty-eight for a while. I'll be twenty-nine for a long time, too. It's one of the…gifts that came with the shape-shifting."

"Gifts?" I grimaced. "I could say more, but I think I'll just let my earlier comment on creepiness stand. And you're not Russian?"

"My parents were. I grew up here, but after I turned I went back to the old country to learn how to harness my abilities." Again his gaze looked distant. "When your grandfather told me we had business here I thought I was coming home. I didn't realize how much had changed. The world I knew doesn't exist anymore." Abruptly he shrugged. "But I was telling you how Anton couldn't face the truth when you were marked. He still can't. He hopes that somehow the infection didn't take and you'll make it to twenty-two without changing from human to *vampyr*."

"Besides being able to legally drink in this state, what's the big whoop about being twenty-one?" I demanded, feeling a little more in control of myself than I had a few minutes earlier.

"This is the year you'll turn. Think of it as a long incubation period between being marked and having the infection rage through you. Some discredited legends imply that there've been a few vampire-marked victims who have escaped their fate, but even if the stories had any basis in fact, they don't apply in your case. Like I said last night, as soon as I laid eyes on you my hackles rose. It's just a matter of time before you—"

He stopped and I cut in. "It's just a matter of time before I wonder why the hell you hauled me out here to bore me with the old rising-hackles speech." I gestured toward my shortie robe and the baby-doll pj's beneath it. "I'm not dressed for graveyard-hopping, and even if I were it isn't my favorite pastime—not that any of my past escorts have ever suggested it as a fun date. So if you don't mind, I don't think I'll wait until dawn for your little demonstration, whatever it is."

"You won't have to." While I'd been speaking he'd lifted his head. Now he took a deep inhalation of the night air.

I sighed. "*So* five minutes ago, Mike. You turn into a wolf, do some wolfey stuff, I freak out. Or at least, I would if we hadn't already gone through—"

"They're coming back earlier than I expected. *Arm yourself!*" Without warning, Mikhail strode to the deeper shadows by the row of plantings by the fountain. Even as I stared after him I saw his shape begin to change.

Does that sound as heart-stopping as it was? Probably not. I could spend hours trying to describe what I half saw in the moonlight—the way his broad shoulders began to melt into his body, the way his waist and hips suddenly narrowed, the frightening abruptness with which he fell to all fours and his gait changed from that of a man's stride to an animal's lope. No description could capture the absolute *wrongness* of what I was seeing. I knew he was a shape-shifter. I'd seen him before and after his changes. But actually witnessing Mikhail Vostoroff shifting from human to wolf that first time made me feel as if my insides had been scooped out like a pumpkin's.

He was all wolf now, right down to his midnight-black, silver-tipped tail. Still loping away, he glanced over his shoulder, and his eyes, looking like two suns going super-nova at the same time, met mine.

Arm yourself, Megan, they're coming! His voice resounded through my head as it had done the night before when he'd forced me to watch the replay of my mother's showdown with the *Vampyr* Queen—not like a thought, but as if he had opened those terrible jaws and was speaking out loud. *If you still retain enough humanity that they can't sense you're one of them, they'll tear you to pieces! Arm yourself now!*

Grammie didn't raise any dumb blondes. Okay, she raised Tash, who comes close sometimes. But I didn't need it spelled out as to whom the *they* who were coming might be. Graveyard = Vamp Central. Megan in Graveyard = Not Smart Move. Megan in Graveyard with Shape-shifting Jerk Who Brought Her Here Running Away Like a Rabbit in Wolf's Clothing = Totally Fuckin' Fucked.

I was always good at math. Just so you don't get the wrong impression of me, I'm usually better at swearing, too.

"You *fucker,* Mikhail!" I hissed after him as he disappeared. "What am I supposed to arm myself with—a stalk of gladiolus? Floral wire? There aren't any *stakes* around!"

He'd planned this. He was going to watch from the bushes while I got torn apart by vamps, and when all that was left of me were my pink scuffs and a smear of blood on a gravestone, he was going to trot back home like Lassie and tell Darkheart that Timmy'd had an accident down by the bridge, woof, woof.

Or something like that.

No trees, or at least none with branches low enough to snap off. No handy furniture legs. "By now Kat and Tash

have probably reached the part in their training where they
learn how to McGyver a stake out of a bra strap and some
nail polish," I muttered as I frantically gazed around for
something to use as a weapon. "Not that they need to,
given that they're safe in the House of Garlic. The only
Crosse triplet who might be able to use the handy tips
Darkheart's handing out is the sister who wasn't invited to
their little Daughter of Lilith tea party—the sister who's
about to get killed, dammit!"

And I would be killed, I thought, my brief spurt of anger
draining away. Though he'd made me doubt myself for a
few seconds this evening, I knew Mikhail was wrong about
me being a vamp. I didn't feel like one, any more than I
felt like a hereditary Daughter of Lilith. I just felt terrified.

So I did what any sane person would do in those circumstances: I began running like hell…but on my second step
I tripped over the spilled basket of gladioli and fell sprawling on the newly laid sod of the grave I'd been standing on.

"Oh, my! Theodore, help her—the poor girl's hurt
herself!"

"Back off, bitch! One of my sisters is a Daughter of Lilith,
and if you kill me she'll hunt your vamp ass down and drive
a stake right through your undead—" I'd fallen on my face.
As I fearfully rolled over and scooched backward from the
two figures standing over me, I recognized them and my un-
ladylike greeting came to an abrupt halt.

Mikhail had been wrong about me. He'd been wrong
about incoming vamps, too. Because the two frail people
who stood in front of me looking slightly taken aback
were Dr. Maisel, my sisters' and my orthodontist when
we'd been little, and his wife, Hetty, who'd been his

receptionist and who had served on the Maplesburg Beau-
tification Committee with Grammie last year. For the
second time that evening I felt like curling up and dying.

"Megan Crosse, is that you, dear? Gracious, whatever
are you doing here at this time of night?" Hetty Maisel,
with the same mother-hen concern she'd shown when nine-
year-old Kat and Tash and I had filed miserably from her
husband's office sporting new braces, drew a breath as Dr.
Maisel helped me to my feet. "Land's sakes, child, your
knees! They're positively *bloody*."

"So stupid of me," I babbled, looking down at my scraped
legs and wondering what in Goshen—okay, what in hell, but
when I'm with Grammie's friends I feel like I should keep
even my thoughts Sunday-school clean—I could say that
would keep them from insisting on escorting me home and
delivering me straight to Grammie and Popsie. "I know it
must seem strange, me being here in the cemetery at night,
but there's a perfectly good explanation," I began, dabbing
at my stinging knees with a tissue I'd found in my robe
pocket. "I was supposed to be married today, but you
probably knew that, since I'm sure Grammie sent you an
invitation, and I guess you probably also know that I was jilted
at the altar. And tonight I was at home, feeling as if my heart
had actually *died*, and I thought, well, if that's how you feel,
Megan, then give it a symbolic burial and get on with your
life. So I came here." I looked up with a bright smile. "And
you know, it worked! So now I'm going to go home again
and I'd appreciate it if you didn't mention any of this to—"

"Why a symbolic burial, dear?" Hetty Maisel's face
creased in confusion. I didn't blame her.

"I know, ridiculous," I agreed swiftly. "Which is why I'd
rather Grammie and Popsie never know how silly I've—"

"I did a tip-top job with those teeth, Mother, wouldn't you say?" Dr. Maisel broke in. He peered at me. "Straight and white and even, thanks to orthodontics."

A thought suddenly came to me. "If you don't mind me asking, what are you two doing here?" I asked as he studied me with professional intensity. Obligingly I flashed him a full-frontal smile. "Do you have a loved one, uh, resting nearby?"

"Remind me to take them afterward, will you, Mother?" Dr. Maisel interrupted again. I remembered he'd always been a little hard of hearing.

"Take what?" I asked, raising my voice so he could hear.

"Oh, Theo, you'd forget your own head if I wasn't around to remind you." Hetty twinkled at me. "I tell him that's why he turned me—because he couldn't get along without me after all these years, but he says it was because he missed the hot sex. Men! Aren't they a caution sometimes?"

For the second time that evening my mind reeled as an image assaulted it, this time a picture of Hetty and Theo going kinkily at it in the dental chair, Dr. Maisel wearing his white lab coat and nothing else, an orthodontic probe in Hetty's liver-spotted hand. I shoved the image away in horror.

And then I froze. "Turned you? As in made you a *vamp?*"

Mrs. Maisel was still twinkling at me. "Don't step on my grave, dear," she admonished, her voice suddenly thicker. "You young folks today! So careless!"

"Yes, we are," I said quickly. "We young folks are darned careless. I mean, I haven't even had the courtesy to inquire as to how Dr. Maisel became a vampire." As I spoke I glanced surreptitiously down at the headstone, noting the fresh carving on it. Beloved Wife of Theodore, She Swiftly Followed Him From This Vale of Tears—blah,

blah, blah. I let my gaze move past the writing to the basket lying on its side by the stone. I'd dismissed it before, but now I saw that its handle appeared to be made of one curved branch bound with slimmer ones.

"My part-time practice," Dr. Maisel said. His voice was thicker, too. "I officially retired months ago, but I couldn't give up my work completely. I began offering evening walk-in consultations on Wednesdays and Thursdays, and one of my first patients presented me with an interesting orthodontic problem."

"Let me guess," I said. My best bet would be to smash the basket against the Maisel's gravestone, I decided tensely. "Occluded fangs?"

"Exactly!" Dr. Maisel's eyes glowed a dull red. "Misaligned canines are one thing, but when they lengthen into fangs they can create major problems. Pierced lips, painful bite action, an inability to close the jaw. Fascinating!"

"Only to you, Theo," Mrs. Maisel said indulgently. "Megan's more interested in wondering if I'm going to tear her heart out while it's still beating or kill her first, aren't you, dear?"

"Not really," I said, my mouth feeling as though I'd just eaten a whole box of dry crackers. "I've pretty much resigned myself to the fact that my plan of burying it symbolically and then getting on with my life isn't in the picture anymore. Once a girl passes that point it's kind of futile to worry about what part of me you're going to rip off first." I gathered myself for action. "It's way more productive to figure out which of you two undead oldsters to stake first—and I've decided to go for *you!*"

As I hurled my last words at her I grabbed the basket

and swung it against the headstone. It hit with a satisfying crunch, but as I looked at it I saw that all I'd accomplished was to smash in one of the sides. The handle was still holding firm.

Which kind of took care of plan A. As Hetty Maisel lunged for me, I realized I'd neglected to formulate a plan B.

"First I'm going to tear you limb from limb," she snarled as her outstretched hands grabbed the lapels of my robe. Her voice still sounded motherly, but think Satan's mother. "Then I'm going to reach into your chest and—"

One of my scuffs got tangled up with one of her Easy Spirit Comfort Walkers. I felt myself going down, and without thinking I let my arms slide from the sleeves of my robe. I hit the ground, not with the thump I was expecting but with a similar crunching sound to the one the basket had made when I'd tried to smash it. As I rolled sideways and saw its remains flattened on the patch of grass where I'd fallen, I understood why.

"Oh, no, you don't, Miss Smartypants!"

Even as I frantically wrenched the handle from the now-demolished basket, out of the corner of my eye I saw the waffle sole of Hetty's walking shoe blurring toward me. I tried to jerk my face out of the way, but it was too late. My chin snapped up and I went flying backward against the headstone.

That's when I got mad.

I'm not saying I stopped being scared, because I didn't. Old or not, the Maisels were vamps, and if Hetty's iron grip on my arms or her Bruce Lee-like kick to my face were any indications, along with the dubious privilege of being senior citizens for eternity, they'd also received the gift of super strength in return for their immortal souls. They could easily kill me. They probably would. But that thought wasn't uppermost in my mind anymore.

I'd been kicked in the chops by a woman wearing a powder-blue polyester pant suit. I'd been put in this situation by an Alpo-eating son of a bitch who'd deserted me at the first hint of danger. My sisters had joined a club that wouldn't take me, my maternal grandfather was teaching them all kinds of secret signs and handshakes that I would never know, and I was totally *pissed*.

I spat out the flakes of sod Hetty's waffle sole had deposited into my mouth and grabbed my fallen basket handle. "Miss *Smartypants?*" I gave a short laugh and dodged sideways as her foot came toward me again. With my free hand I grabbed her ankle—*ewww,* she was wearing support knee-highs—and shoved upward. *"Land sakes?"* Her balance gone, she began to fall backward. Her arms flailed wildly, and as she went over, one of them wind-milled solidly against her husband's nose. I jumped to my feet as his red eyes filled with instant tears. "I've got a lot of problems with the whole vamp concept," I informed her, "but giving you centuries to inflict your *Little House on the Prairie* phrases on the world is right up there in my top ten. Fangs and the little old lady act just don't mix, Hetty."

I raised my basket-handle stake, but before I could drive it through the safari-style breast pocket of her truly horrendous pant suit into her heart, Dr. Maisel made his move.

"You snot-nosed little brat!" He grabbed my arm. White spots of pain danced in front of my vision as he bent it behind my back. "You young people, with your damn rollerblades and your fast driving and your Mariah Carey music blaring from your hi-fis think you're so superior to us old fogeys!"

Even in my pain I felt the need to set the record straight. "Hey—I only have *Charmbracelet* because Grammie bought it for my seventeenth birthday. It's not like I *asked* for it or anything."

With the hand that wasn't tearing my arm off he reached around from behind me and twisted my chin around so I was forced to face him. "The tables are turned now, missy. You might be young, but we're immortals. We've got superstrength and superspeed. Best of all, we get to kill anyone we—"

"Wh-what about the shape-shifting into a wolf part?" My words came out in a gasp as he started to give my neck a final painful twist. His fangs poised to tear into my throat, Maisel hesitated.

"What are you talking about?" he snarled.

I blinked in feigned confusion. "All vamps receive the power to—" I stopped, as if suddenly reconsidering. "My mistake," I said quickly. "Go ahead and finish that ripping-off-my-head thing, Doc."

"You old *fool!*" Hetty was on her feet again. With a backhanded blow that Anna Kournikova would have envied, she knocked her husband's hand from me. She shoved me aside and confronted him, punctuating her every sentence with a poke in his chest. "When you told me this vampire deal was too good to be true, I should have remembered the other times you tried to handle business by yourself—like the land down in Florida that turned out to be in the middle of a swamp, or that surefire gold-mine investment that almost lost us our shirts in the seventies!" *Poke, poke.* "Why didn't you *bargain* with her?" She drove her finger into his chest again, fury suffusing her plump face. "But then, you always had a weakness for redheads! Anytime you see one, your brain shuts down and little Theo stands up and salutes—"

She was so intent on reaming out her husband and he was so intent on trying to avoid her finger that for a moment they took their attention from me. Swiftly I stepped behind Hetty and grabbed up the stake. Even as she broke off with a scream of rage, I plunged it into her back.

For a second the two of us remained locked together as if we'd stopped in the middle of an intricate tango step: me behind her, her looking over her shoulder at me, our faces inches apart. The breath went out of her in a chilling hiss and her crinkly old-lady top lip lifted to reveal the full length of her fangs. Dismay clouded her rheumy red eyes, but then she smiled slowly.

"You know what's wrong with young people today?" Her tone was harshly malevolent. "They don't follow through with anything they start. You didn't push it in far enough to reach my heart, dear, and now you're going to die regretting your mistak—"

My grip was still on the stake. As Hetty Maisel's eyes glittered in triumph, I gave it an extra shove.

The scream that ripped from her throat was made up of equal parts fury and terror. Her fingers clawed at the air, her fangs sliced impotently inches from me, and then she disintegrated into dust.

"Thanks for the timely tip," I said shakily, glancing down at what little remained of her. I looked up in time to see Dr. Maisel rushing toward me and I pivoted to face him. He feinted sideways with such frightening speed that I barely changed position in time, and when I slashed at him with my stake he avoided it easily. Panicking, I slashed again in his direction.

His heavily veined old-man's hand darted out and effortlessly batted the stake from my grip. In numb disbelief I watched it arc through the air, bounce off a headstone and land a couple of graves away. I took a deep breath and turned my gaze to my former orthodontist.

"Okay, I didn't want to tell you before, but now I guess I have to," I said, trying to keep the quaver from my voice. "I'm a vampire, too. I know, the fangs haven't come in yet, I don't flash-fry in the sunlight, but those are details." I gave him what I hoped looked like a just-between-us-vamps smile. "I got marked by a queen vamp when I was a baby. You might even know her—red-hair, runs a strip club, goes by the name of—"

Maisel rushed at me, his fangs fully extended. The next moment a stake came flying out of the darkness to bury itself in his chest.

Chapter 7

Whoever had thrown the stake had unerring aim. Maisel turned to dust so suddenly that it seemed as if he'd exploded. I had just enough time to register the thought that tonight apparently wasn't my night to die before a second stake came whizzing through the air straight at my left eye.

"Megan, *duck!*"

Kat's cry came out of the shadows as my hand wrapped around the lethally sharpened piece of wood. I blinked and felt the lashes of my left eye brush against the point of the stake I'd caught in midair. Slowly I lowered the stake to my side.

Then I followed Dr. Maisel's example and exploded. "What the *hell,* Kat!" As she ran over to me I realized she hadn't seen my impossible catch and I found myself feeling glad she hadn't. The whole night had been creepy, but for some reason my fortunate reaction to a stake coming at me unsettled me more than anything else that had happened in the past hour. Putting my unease aside, I glared at my sister.

She was wearing a pair of dark form-fitting pants I hadn't known she owned and a dark racer-back tank top. Instead of sexily skimming her shoulders as it usually did, her hair was pulled into a ponytail. Contrasted with her, in my grass-and-blood-stained Nick & Nora baby-doll short set, I felt like one of those girls with the black bars across their eyes in *Glamour* magazine's monthly Fashion Do's and Don'ts feature.

"I see that the back-in-black look's the latest thing for those after-hours cemetery jaunts," I said sarcastically, "but dressing the part doesn't make you a Daughter of Lilith, Kat. Maybe you should practice with a dartboard." I saw Darkheart and Tashya hastening toward us. "Or ask Darkheart to give you some extra lessons before you blind someone. Judging by his aim a moment ago, he's obviously no slouch at—"

"Omigod, Meg, are you okay?" Tash ran up, a red-gold riot of curls obscuring her vision until she tossed back her head. Her outfit was similar to Kat's, except her pants were even more formfitting and her top more low-cut. "I totally wasn't aiming for you. I got so excited when Kat let fly, I kind of hoped she'd miss and I'd get him. Oh, good, I didn't want to have to search for this in the grass." Relieving me of her stake, she looked down at the pile of dust by our feet. "I didn't get a really good look before he disintegrated, but wasn't that Dr. Maisel?" she asked.

I counted silently to ten. "You didn't get a good look, but you threw a pointy stick anyway," I said tightly. "Yes, that was Dr. Maisel, and his wife's ashes are over there, if anyone's interested." I switched my gaze back to Kat, taking her silence for pissed-offness. "Sorry for flying off the handle like that at you, Kat. I owe you big-time, sis." When she didn't respond I went on in a mollifying tone, "Just how far away were you when you threw your stake, anyway?"

"Thirty-one strides." The answer came from Darkheart, but although he was speaking to me, it was Kat his attention was focused on. He was wearing the homespun cloak he'd worn the previous night and as he drew nearer he undid the silver clasp at his neck. Reaching her side, he shrugged off the garment and deftly flung it around her shoulders. "Was very good kill," he said, his eyes intent on her, "but now you are feeling the reaction, *da?* Not unusual, granddaughter. Breathe deep in and deep out, as earlier tonight I taught you."

A shaft of moonlight lit Kat's features and I suddenly realized that her silence hadn't been caused by annoyance at me. Her face was chalky white and her eyes were closed. She opened them and looked at Darkheart. "He was a vamp. He had to be killed," she said faintly. "I know that, so why do I feel like I just committed murder?"

"You do?" Tash's tone was bright. "Well, with that attitude I can't see how you could possibly be a Daughter of Lilith. And if *you* didn't inherit Mom's title, that means *I'm*—"

"Regret is not bad thing," Darkheart said sharply. "Means merely that chosen one understands burden laid upon her. All *vampyrs*—" as usual, he pronounced the *V* like a *W*, so it came out *wamp-eers* "—were once human, *nyet?* Being Daughter of Lilith does not mean you forget this."

I might as well be honest here and confess that I've

considered skipping over the next part, since it doesn't show yours truly in the best light. It might not even be too much of a stretch to say that I come off pretty much as a jealous bitch.

Which was exactly the way I felt right at that moment.

It was obvious Kat was the Daughter of Lilith in this generation of Crosse females. She looked like one, she staked like one, she even, according to Grandfather, felt the way a true D of L should feel. Maybe the official votes weren't in yet, but unofficially it was crystal clear that Tash and I had been relegated to the status of chopped liver. But at least Tashya had been in the running, however briefly. I hadn't even been given the opportunity to compete for the title.

"Wicked cool throw, Kat. This must be a custom-made jobbie, huh? Silver-bound grip, precisely weighted." I picked up her stake from where it lay in Maisel's ashes, hefting it in my hand as I walked over to where my pitiful basket handle had landed. "When I sent Hetty Maisel's vamp butt to hell, I had to make do with this piece of crap. I guess that's what separates the chosen ones like you from schmucks like me, though. You're given all the training and the equipment and the kudos, and then you get to go all Hallmark-moment afterward."

Even as the words left my mouth, I realized how immature I was being. Kat had just saved my life. I was acting like an asshole. And in my heart I knew it had absolutely nothing to do with any Daughter-of-Lilith issue.

I hadn't seen Tashya's stake come flying out of the dark until it was right in front of my face. It had been humanly impossible to react as I had, and yet the same

Megan Crosse who'd barely managed to kill her vamp fiancé by accident, who'd fallen over her own feet while trying to fight off two oldster vamps tonight and come disastrously close to miscalculating Hetty's staking—that same klutz at killing vamps had reacted with vamplike speed to prevent a stake from entering *her*. The images I'd envisioned earlier this evening came back to me as Darkheart spoke.

"Is big difference between making kill in defence of your own life and defeating *vampyr* to save another, grand-daughter," he said, his eyes more hooded than usual as he looked at me. "Your sister acted as Daughters have done since the beginning of—"

"Damn right I killed in defence of my own life!" I broke in, hardly caring what I was saying as long as I kept the images at bay. "I didn't have an option, seeing as how your shape-shifting sidekick dumped me here tonight and then ran off when the waskelly wampeers showed up—and just as an aside, the word is *vampire*, okay? *Vamp*- with a *V*, *-ire* with an—"

"I didn't run off and leave you. I was watching all the time." Mikhail stepped from the shadows, and in my agitation I felt as if his narrowed gaze could see everything I was trying to keep hidden. I went on the offensive immediately.

"Watching for *what?* To see if my head or one of my arms got ripped off first? I almost got *killed* while you were watching!" I turned back to Darkheart. "And if I had, my blood would have been just as much on your hands. When you forced me to witness my mom's last minutes, I heard you make a solemn vow to her that you'd keep her daughters safe—not just the two you thought might take her place, but all three of Angelica's triplets. Last time I checked that included me, but at one sniff from Mikey-baby, you decide I'm a wannabe vamp who doesn't rate even the most basic instructions in how to keep herself alive!" I felt my precarious control eroding. "All your talk about honor and duty is total *crap,* Darkheart, just like the deathbed promise you gave your daughter! Tashya and Kat can do what they want, but after what happened tonight I wouldn't attend one of your stupid training sessions if you begged me. And don't you ever *dare* call yourself my grandfather again!"

About to turn away, I realized I was still holding two stakes. I held out the silver-bound one to Kat. "You'll need this," I said, already regretting that I'd taken out my fears on her. "From that throw you made, I'd say it's clear you inherited Mom's role as a Daughter of Lilith. Congratulations, Kat."

Instead of taking the stake, she grasped my outstretched hand with both of hers. "Believe me, sweetie—Tash and I didn't know Mikhail brought you here. Grandfather Darkheart didn't, either." She shot a look at Mikhail, who gave us a cold stare in return. "That shape-shifting liar told us you refused to take part in the training. I assumed you were still in denial about all this."

"Me, too," Tash said. "We decided we'd let you sulk until after our lesson and then show you the stuff we'd learned, like how to do a backflip and twist around in the air so you land facing the other way. But by then you wouldn't have been impressed by much, I guess, seeing as how you'd have been dead." She tipped her head to one side. "You can apologize anytime for acting so snotty about my stake-throwing, Meg. I'm the one who saved your ass by finding out you weren't in your room."

"Only because she wanted to borrow your Ro & Me lotus clasp to clip her hair back," Kat elaborated. "And it was Grandfather Darkheart who realized what Mikhail must have done."

"But not soon enough," the Russian said harshly. "You are right, granddaughter—if you had died here tonight my hands would have borne your blood. I would have avenged you by the only means possible to me, but that would not have brought you back. I give thanks that what I do now is not done as vengeance for your death, but as an insurance that never again will you be placed in danger by one I trusted. Mikhail!"

"Someone's in the doghouse," Tash said in a loud whisper to Kat and me as Mikhail walked slowly toward Darkheart.

"He deserves it," Kat said. I darted a glance at her set profile as she watched Mikhail come to a halt in front of Darkheart. Her whole attitude seemed different—stronger, without any of her languid mannerisms. She was already growing into the role, I realized disconcertedly. Whether she accepted yet that she was a Daughter, already a distance seemed to exist between her and the woman she'd been twenty-four hours ago…and between her and Tash and me. For the first time it struck me just how lonely the life of a Daughter could be, and I wondered if Kat had already gotten an inkling of that loneliness. Was that why she'd been so shaken by the kill she'd made tonight?

It seemed to be my night for illogical reactions. I was suddenly angry at Darkheart, not for what Mikhail had done, which I had to accept he'd had no part of, but for his very appearance in our lives. I felt a childish longing to turn the clock back to before he'd told us about our mother and ourselves, but as I saw Kat's gaze harden I knew how futile my longing was.

I'd expected Darkheart to talk to Mikhail in Russian, but he spoke in English. Since that could only have been for our benefit, I presumed he wanted to reassure us that he wasn't going to cut Mikhail any slack just because they were friends. "According to ancient contract between *oborotni* and *vladelcy,* you have right to plead your case, Mikhail Sergeievich Vostoroff," he said, his tone distant. "Do you deny you brought granddaughter of mine here with hope that harm would befall her?"

"Yes, *vladelec,* I do deny," Mikhail said, his words coldly formal. I was about to jump in and ruin the formality by accusing him of lying through his teeth when he went on, "I brought her here to truly understand what she will become. I thought if she did, there was a chance she would make the decision I myself would make if I ever were infected by a—"

"You do not *know!*" the older man roared, his hooded eyes flashing with anger. "I have told you, is in some old books written about possibility that one mark is not enough to lay *vampyr* curse."

"I know you want to believe that," Mikhail shot back, heat replacing his former coolness. "The Queen forced you to kill your daughter and you'd do anything to convince yourself she hasn't made it necessary for you to do the same to one of your granddaughters. That fear is clouding your mind to your most important responsibility—to keep this generation's Daughter of Lilith safe until she comes fully into her powers!" He exhaled tensely. "I couldn't allow your conflict to sway me from my prime responsibility. You yourself speak of the contract that exists between a shape-shifter and the one he is bound to. Have you forgotten that my reason for being what I am is to act as a sword and a shield for the one I serve?"

"Your reason for being is to follow my command," Darkheart said with chilling softness. "I forbade you to act on your instincts about the eldest of my daughter's daughters. You disobeyed. You know the penalty, wolf."

I was close enough to see a muscle jump at the side of Mikhail's hard jaw. He could have been right up there on my man-candy scale, I thought, with those linebacker shoulders and long muscular legs and ripped-looking biceps. The midnight-black silver-tipped hair didn't hurt, either, and neither did those amazing eyes. But as gorgeous as he was, he had one drawback that made him non-babe material in my eyes: he wanted me dead. Maybe not tonight—for some reason, I believed what he'd told Darkheart—but he certainly wasn't willing to wait too long.

Which, since he was convinced I was a vamp, was understandable, I suppose. It was also understandable that I hoped whatever penalty Darkheart had in mind was going to be really, *really* extreme—like being sent back to Mother Russia with his tail between his legs, so to speak.

"I know the penalty," Mikhail assented. "I accept it, as all those who violate the ancient contract must." His eyes held Darkheart's a moment longer, like a wolf staring down an eagle, and then he bowed his head.

"Oh. My. God." Beside me Tash sucked her breath in. "Mr. Tall Dark and Wolfey is *stripping*." Her gaze was fixed on Mikhail. "Totally terrible about him setting you up as a vamp target, sis, but you've got to admit the man *is* yummy-looking."

Since I'd just been thinking the same thing, I really wasn't in any position to snap at her. I did, anyway. "He isn't dropping his laundry for your benefit, birdbrain." He'd finished unbuttoning his shirt and now he pulled it free of his belt. Moonlight gleamed on the skin of his bare stomach and delineated every single one of his six-pack abs. I swallowed dryly. "He's taking off his shirt for a perfectly obvious reason," I continued, trying to keep my voice even as I watched his broad shoulders lift slightly and then fall while his shirt dropped to the ground behind him. "Darkheart's going to banish him back to Russia or something."

Kat glanced my way. "So why's he getting naked?" she asked. "Or half-naked. The jeans are staying on, it seems." Her hard expression of a moment ago had been replaced by a frown. "*Merde,* don't tell me the penalty is a whipping."

My stomach had been fluttering in an anticipatory way. The fluttering stopped with a lurch. "Oh, *no,*" I said, sickened by the possibility. "That would be just too feudal, wouldn't it?"

"Two Russkies talking about ancient contracts, disobeying commands, accepting punishment?" Tash pointed out. "Seems to me feudal would be right up their alley. I don't think I'll stick around to watch the perform—"

"Bare your neck, Misha." As Darkheart's unsteady order cut across Tash's nervous words I jerked my gaze to the two men standing a few feet away. Or at least, Darkheart was standing, a terrible sadness etched on his face. Mikhail was on his knees, his arms hanging loosely at his sides. His head was still bowed, but at the older man's command he slowly raised it and just for a second those golden eyes met and held my disbelieving gaze.

Then Mikhail's head lifted higher. He looked straight up at the moon in the night sky and closed his eyes. I saw a vein throb at the side of his neck, saw his hands clench at his sides, saw him give an almost imperceptible nod.

"Carry out your duty as it is written, *vladelec*," he said in a low voice. "Thrust the knife in deep and release my soul."

"What the—" Kat exclaimed beside me as Darkheart, his features stony, raised his arm high. In his hand I saw the ugly gleam of a curved blade. I heard Tash give a horrified gasp but I didn't wait to hear more.

"Are you people *crazy?*" I yelled as I ran straight at Darkheart. I half turned as we connected, and felt my hip smash into him as the knife began to come down in a glittering arc. He fought to keep his balance, but against a hundred and nineteen pounds of running female—okay, a hundred and twenty-two if we're being picky about it—his efforts were futile. The two of us went down, I gave a yelp as my banged-up knee cracked hard against Hetty and Theo Maisel's headstone, and the side of my face skidded through something greasy before coming to a stop on the grass where I'd fallen. A curved and shining blade *thunked* into the sod an inch from my face.

I'd thought finding myself in a graveyard with a shape-shifter had been the final straw. Then I'd thought Mikhail deserting me had been. I'd changed my mind when I'd realized I was facing two vamps, and I'd changed my mind once more when Tash's stake had nearly taken my eye out. But now I knew for sure that I'd reached my personal limit.

I wrenched Darkheart's handy-dandy throat-slitter from where it was lodged in the ground and jumped to my feet.

"I've had it!" I bellowed. Knife in hand, I pivoted to face Mikhail, who had started to rise from his knees. "Don't *move!*" I ordered. I swung back to see Darkheart attempting to stand. "You stay where you are, too!"

"To interfere is total violation of all laws which govern bond between *oborotni* and *vladelcy,*" he said, "between shape-shifter and master. You know nothing of what you are…" He scowled at Mikhail. "How in English is *nee da dyeloni?*"

"You don't understand what you're fucking up here," Mikhail translated for me. He looked at Darkheart. "I get the feeling she doesn't really care."

"Oh, I care, all right," I retorted grimly. "I care that you two think you can bring your old-world shit here and drop it on me and my sisters. I care that my mother's father is giving a pretty good impression of a homicidal maniac. I care that you—" I nailed Mikhail with a glare "—took it upon yourself to set me up just to make a point, but as jerky as you are, I won't see you get your throat cut over it. Send him back to Russia," I told Darkheart. "As long as he's not around to pull any more stunts like tonight, I'm satisfied. And as for you, you're not getting this knife back until I'm convinced you won't use it on the next person who breaks one of your stupid rules."

"You go, girl," Tash peered at me. "Yuck, did you know you have vamp-goo on your face?"

"Vamp what?" I began, and then revulsion flooded through me. "Somebody get this stuff off me *now!*" I said rapidly, thinking back to my slide through Maisel's greasy ashes and trying to remember whether my mouth had been open at the time. Producing a tissue, Kat stepped up and briskly wiped my face clean.

"Don't look now," she informed me in a mutter, "but I'm not sure your lecture convinced Grandfather and Mikhail. I think they're about to go at it again."

I turned. She was right. Darkheart and Mikhail were both on their feet and talking in agitated Russian, but I didn't need a translator to see from Darkheart's stubborn expression and Mikhail's furious disbelief that they were arguing. As I was about to step in again, Darkheart drew himself up to his full height—which at about six feet was impressive, but still left him looking up at Mikhail. He made a gesture with his hands that seemed to encompass me and his voice rose in volume.

Whatever he was saying, I was pretty sure he wasn't speaking Russian anymore. It didn't sound like any language I'd ever heard, and from the goosebumps that suddenly pebbled my skin, I was thankful I hadn't. The words seemed to creak rustily as they left his mouth, as if they hadn't been spoken for centuries.

Darkheart's voice rose to a crescendo. Mikhail's face went deathly pale. The older man brought his upraised arms down and pointed at me with one hand and Mikhail with the other.

"Hey, wait a minute," I began, but just then Darkheart stopped speaking and clapped his palms sharply together. I jumped, feeling as if I'd just stuck a fork into a toaster. I saw a similar shudder pass through Mikhail. Darkheart nodded.

"Is good," he declared. "Now we go home, get sleep, *da?* Tomorrow is much to do—more training, this time with granddaughter Megan, brief studying of history and legends, further persuasion of Crosse grandparents to go on cruise so they are out of danger from—"

"What just happened?" I demanded. "And don't tell me *nothing,* because I know something did. What did you say in that weird language? Why did you point at me and Mikhail, and what about him going back to Russia? That's still the plan, right?"

"Is not necessary now." Darkheart's tone was almost airy, for him. "I will let Mikhail explain to you. Other granddaughters and I must discuss tonight's training."

He turned to Tash and immediately began telling her why her throw had gone so wild. Kat lifted her eyebrows at me questioningly. "Go ahead with the play-by-play," I told her. "I'll handle this." I turned to Mikhail. "Well?" I demanded.

He was putting his shirt back on. At my one-word query, he looked up. "Well, what?" he said curtly.

Frustration overwhelmed me. I took two strides toward him—not as much of a power move as it sounds, since I was still wearing my fluffy pink scuffs—and confronted him. "Look," I snapped, pointing the knife for emphasis, "you owe me. A few minutes ago I saved your sorry ass from a really messy death. Even a jerk like you has to be grateful for that, so help me out here. What the hell was that incantation-sounding thing Darkheart was spouting?"

"An incantation." Mikhail finished tucking in his shirt and made a move as if to follow Darkheart and my sisters toward the graveyard gates. He took two steps and then stopped, as if he found it physically impossible to take another.

I pressed my lips together. "Smart move. Because if

you'd walked away from me, you'd have felt this knife slipping between your shoulder blades."

He shook his head. "That's not why I stopped. You can put the knife down. I can't take off on you, and I can't harm you. Your grandfather took care of that."

"Darkheart," I corrected him. "I've decided I'm perfectly content with having Popsie as my only grandfather. What do you mean, he took care of it?"

"He bound me to you," Mikhail said in a leaden voice. "I'm your creature now, not his. I go where you go, take my orders from you, lay down my life for you if necessary."

I stared at him. "You're joking, right?" I took in the set expression on his face. "You're not joking. Well, we'll just have to make him reverse the incantation!"

Mikhail gave me a sour smile. "It doesn't work that way. Even if I was at his throat trying to kill him because you'd ordered me to, he couldn't undo the transfer. I'm your *oboroten,* your werewolf. You're my mistress. Until one of us dies, we're stuck in this relationship."

"But that's worse than *marriage!*" I saw a straw and grasped at it. "If Darkheart broke the bond, why can't I?"

Relief passed over his face. "Of course, I didn't even think of that solution. All you have to do is say the Aramaic incantation out loud and we're free of each other. Okay, shoot."

My heart sank further. "I don't know the Aramaic incantation. And Darkheart's not going to write it down for me, is he? Are you telling me we're totally screwed?"

Mikhail met my bleak gaze with a bleaker one of his own. "Screwed, blued and tattooed. In other words," he said bitterly, "the two of us are fucked."

Chapter 8

"Watch your back, Meg!"

At Kat's shouted warning I whirled around. The vamp flew through the air toward me, her fangs dripping blood and her clawlike fingers outstretched. I began to raise my stake, realized I was holding it too far down the shaft and propelled myself into a backwards flip that would take me out of harm's way.

I'd forgotten the wall three feet behind me. I remembered it when I was looking at it upside-down halfway through my flip. "Shit," I said just before I smashed into it.

"Vamps four, Meg zero," Tash said in a bored voice from the sidelines as she reeled in the cardboard cutout of a vampire strung on one of the wires crisscrossing the living room. "And I'm not counting the one you staked in the butt, sis."

"Is getting better," Darkheart said as he helped me up. "No, truly," he insisted at my incredulous look. "Did not knock yourself out this time, *da?* So in three days is big progress."

"In three days is big joke," I said, wincing as I picked up my fallen stake. "Kat, are you sure Detective Van Ryder meant it when he told you on the phone yesterday that we weren't prime suspects anymore? 'Cause right now I wouldn't mind taking a nice relaxing vacation in a cell."

"That's what the man said," she replied, sinking into a forward lunge to warm up her leg muscles. "Now that Lance and Todd and Dean aren't the only men who've gone missing in Maplesburg, we're in the clear. His call was only a formality, anyway. Van Ryder admitted the same thing to Popsie the day after your nonwedding, when that men's choir bus was found abandoned on the outskirts of town." She held the lunge. "Since that was the clincher that persuaded Popsie it would be all right for him and Grammie to go on their cruise as long as Darkheart was here to watch over us, I'm afraid I'm not with you on that vacation-in-a-cell idea, sweetie."

"You should be glad your grandparents are out of harm's way," Mikhail said. He was standing a few feet away, his arms folded across his chest and his eyes shooting daggers at me, but since he'd been wearing the same expression for the past three days, the menace factor was wearing off, although the irritation factor was growing by leaps and bounds. I'd asked, threatened and even begged Darkheart to teach me the words that would sever the bond that kept Mikhail by my side all day and outside my bedroom door at night, but he'd refused. This morning I'd finally come up with a plan to win my life back and I intended to put it into practice this afternoon.

For now all I could do was try to ignore Mikhail as he went on, "But all that matters to you is you, right? It wouldn't occur to you that if your grandparents had stayed, Zena could kill the two of them just as easily as anyone else would run down a couple of rabbits and rip them to—" The flush that appeared on his cheekbones robbed his dark and brooding pose of some of its *Wuthering Heights* quality. "As easily as anyone else would swat a fly," he finished unconvincingly.

I gave him a withering look. "Please. You're salivating over running down bunnies and you've got the nerve to criticize me? For your information, I was completely down with the plan to get Grammie and Popsie out of Maplesburg while Zena's gunning for us, although I have to say I'm not too impressed with her efforts. If she wants us so badly, why not come after us herself instead of sending our fiancés to do her dirty work for her?"

Darkheart nodded. "Is understandable you wonder this," he said, slapping his palm on the balance beam beside him. I spared a thought for Grammie's reaction if she could see the living room at this moment—all her precious antiques shoved into corners and shrouded with sheets to make room for the gymnastic equipment that had been delivered the day after she and Popsie had departed. Tash hoisted herself up onto the balance beam and went into a cautious handstand. Slowly she began to walk on her hands along the beam as Darkheart continued talking. "Would have been more simple to carry out attack herself. Instead she buys Warm Package—"

"Hot Box," I corrected.

"Hot Box," he went on, unperturbed, "sets herself up in town of Maplesburg, USA, and then arranges for foolish young men who are to marry granddaughters to come to her."

"That part's pretty far-fetched," I disagreed. "Having Dean's stag at the Hot Box was only a coincidence."

"One thing you better learn fast is not to use *coincidence* and *Zena* in the same sentence," Mikhail growled. "Trust me, somehow Zena arranged for your fiancés to be there that night."

I flicked a glance at him. "Trust you? If I trusted you, I might wonder why my *oboroten* let me slam into a wall a moment ago instead of saving my ass like he's supposed to."

"I'm only compelled to save you from death or serious injury," he answered. "Even that rule ceases to apply if—"

"Misha is right, is part of plan that fiancés meet Zena," Darkheart broke in. "Now turn around to face starting place again," he said to Tashya, who'd reached the end of the beam and had been about to resume an upright position. She wobbled slightly and her upside-down face looked briefly mutinous, but she began her turn. He kept his eyes on her as he spoke. "But your question is why does Zena make big plan at all? Why not arrive in America from old country, go straight to granddaughters and kill them, and then return home with deed done?"

"I wasn't dwelling on the kill-granddaughters part, but that's the gist of it, yes," I admitted.

"Talismans I send for you to wear around necks—talismans you discard," he emphasized with heavy disapproval, "had power to keep her away for—*nyet*, Natashya! If must fall, throw weight forward as I have taught you!"

It was Tash's turn to lie in a crumpled heap on the floor, I saw with sisterly callousness. She'd landed on the protective pads that had been strewn around for just such a contingency, so all that had been damaged was her ego.

I waited for her to flounce off in a huff, but to my surprise she got to her feet.

"I'm okay." She scrambled onto the beam again. "I can't believe I blew it! I'm *so* going to whip this puppy this time."

Kat had changed. Tash obviously had, too. I suddenly felt as if I were on the *Titanic* watching the last lifeboats pull away with everyone I cared about on them waving goodbye to me as I stood on the sinking deck.

"The brat's determined, I'll give her that." Kat gave me a sideways glance as Tashya began hand-walking along the beam once more. "Remember when she was on the cheer-leading squad and vowed she'd be better than the rest of the girls? And when she threw herself into salsa dancing a few years ago? Our little sister's found a new obsession in this vamp-staking thing, no?"

I kept my eyes on Tash's maneuvers and Darkheart's approving expression as she made the tricky reverse. "I know what you're trying to do, Kat," I said evenly. "Quit it. I know I'm the odd woman out here, so don't try to pretend nothing's different between the three of us."

"Feeling sorry for ourself, are we, sweetie?" she said in the honeyed drawl she hadn't used for a few days. My angry gaze jerked toward her, but before I could speak she continued, her tone losing its sweetness and taking on a peppery sharpness. "Since you're so hot on hearing the truth, here it is. You're a klutz at this and I seriously doubt you could stake a tent-peg, let alone a vampire. But what really worries me is that one day soon we're going to need your particular strength, and you'll be so sunk in self-pity that you won't be there for us."

"My particular strength?" I gave a short laugh. "And what's that?"

"Doing what you've always done—being the glue that holds the three of us together," she replied. "Think about it, Megan. Who never lets the squabbling get too far out of hand? Who cuts Tash down to size when she's being particularly Tash-ish, and who else would toss a perfectly good mickey of vodka out the window because she knew another drink was the last thing I needed? You've been holding us together for so long that I can't remember a time I didn't count on you for that. Without you we'd just be triplets—with you we're *sisters*."

She didn't let my feigned inattention deter her. "We need to be sisters now more than ever, Meg," she said with low vehemence. "Remember what I said that first night about the circle being closed? I still don't know where those words came from, but I know we don't have a chance in hell to get out of this situation alive if the three of us aren't united. You asked why Zena didn't just kill us herself. I asked Grandfather Darkheart that same question the day you drove Grammie and Popsie into the city to board their cruise ship, and you know what he told me?"

It was the first time in days that she and I had really talked. Emotion filled me, but perversely I kept it out of my voice. "Apparently I'm about to."

Kat looked like she wanted to shake me. "The bitch is afraid of us," she said flatly.

I was jolted out of my pose of indifference. "Oh, please! She's the big evil and until a few days ago, all we'd ever gotten lethal with was a credit card. Why would Zena be afraid of *us*?"

"Because we're Darkhearts. And Grandfather says Darkhearts have fought against her and her kind for centuries," she said simply. "Some of us have been Daughters of Lilith, some have been trainers and keepers of knowledge, like he is, but we've always been the enemy." Her expression shadowed. "Zena thought she'd won when she infected Angelica—she'd turned a Darkheart away from the light and made her one of hers. She never thought Grandfather would be able to kill his own daughter."

"But he did," I said slowly. "If I were an evil bitch like Zena, I think I might just take that as a personal defeat."

"Believe it, sweetie." Kat's smile was more of a grimace. "In the normal course of things, once we'd been spirited out of the old country she would have left us alone. We were an ocean away, after all, and as babies we weren't any threat. But Grandfather learned through his network of contacts that she'd sworn to wipe out every last Darkheart and put an end to us once and for all. That's when he went into hiding...but the last thing he did before he let the world think he was dead was to have those necklaces made and sent to us."

I couldn't help thinking that Darkheart had certainly been a busy little hive of information with one of his granddaughters, at least. I raised my eyebrows. "Megan-denial-mode here, but how could some silver crosses on chains keep us safe for all those years? Who made them, Merlin?"

"They were made by a silversmith Grandfather knew," she answered, her eyes on mine. "But their power came from what they were made of, according to Grandfather. You're the brain, Meg. Don't tell me you've never read about the Lost Grail."

"The chalice used at the Last Supper," I said impatiently. "It's what the knights of the Round Table were supposed to be searching for, the silver cup that had been used by—" I stopped. "Shut *up*," I said in weak defiance. "That's where the silver in our crosses is supposed to have come from?"

"The man whose son Grandfather saved from vampires years ago swore that's what it was when he gave him part of a broken silver handle that had been in his family for generations." Kat raised her shoulders in a helpless gesture. "I honestly don't know what to believe, but it's no more far-fetched than having our fiancés turn into vampires, right?"

I was too stunned to respond for a minute. "So for over twenty years we were safe from Zena. Then the crosses' power began to wane."

"More like ours began to stir." Again she shrugged. "Maybe you'll understand Grandfather's explanation better than Tash and I did. All I know is Zena no longer found it impossible to come after us, but she had no way of knowing whether she was up against three normal American girls who still knew nothing about their heritage, or—"

"Or two normal girls and one vamp-killing Daughter of Lilith. So she sent Lance and Todd and Dean, just in case." I looked at her. "You know you're the one, don't you, Kat? You're the Daughter in this generation."

She shook her head. "I think it's Tash. I said she had determination, but more importantly, she's got heart."

I followed her glance. Both Mikhail and Darkheart were spotting Tash, but it was obvious she didn't need them. During the minutes we'd been talking, she'd not only mastered the move she'd been practising but had added a few individual flourishes of her own. I winced in anticipation as she ran along the beam on her hands and propelled herself upwards. With the insouciance of a top-gun fighter pilot throwing his jet into a daredevil maneuver, she tucked her head to her chest and clasped her knees to her body as she spun through the air. As she started to descend, she snapped out of her curled-up position and landed on her feet in a crouch, facing the way she'd come.

"She's got heart," I agreed as Tash took a quick breath and immediately began the move all over again. "But my money's still on you." The phrase was an unpleasant echo of Mikhail's earlier words to me, and from the flash of anger in my sister's eyes, I knew she recognized where I'd unconsciously borrowed it from.

"*Merde,* sweetie, I hope you're not still hung up on what our unfriendly local shape-shifter predicted." Mikhail's back was toward us but as if his senses had alerted him, he swung his gaze suddenly around to meet ours. Kat smiled sweetly at him, raised the middle finger of her right hand, and turned back to me. "Think he got the message?" she said with a wicked smile.

"Five by five." My amusement faded. "But you watched the flashback right to the end, so you saw what I missed— the part where one of Angelica's babies got bitten. I'm finding it hard not to get hung up on that detail, especially when said unfriendly local shape-shifter seems so certain I was that baby."

She looked exasperated. "As Grandfather's explained, the old stories say that one mark isn't enough to infect. Anyway, for all we know, Tash or I was the one who got bitten. What you and Grandfather *haven't* figured out is that Mikhail's reaction to you hasn't got a thing to do with his anti-vamp radar, it's got to do with him having the hots for my big sister." Without looking away from me she added, "This is a private conversation, Cujo, so turn off your canine hearing."

Startled, I glanced at Mikhail. He was still in position by the balance beam, but his seething glance at Kat and me was a dead giveaway—he *had* heard everything we'd said. For about the seventieth time in as many hours I mentally cursed Darkheart for his misguided efforts to protect me. "Don't even go there," I told Kat shortly. "He hates me because he thinks I could turn vamp any day now. I hate him because he's an asshole. Our relationship may be totally dysfunctional, but at least we both know where we stand."

She gave me the exact look she'd given me fifteen years ago when I'd told her how much I despised Alan Arksey for putting a frog in my book bag, but she didn't argue. "Whatever you say, Meg, so long as you accept the rest of our heart-to-heart."

"That I'm your and Tashie's own personal bottle of Elmer's," I said, "keeping you stuck together? I guess I can live with that, although you could have chosen a more flattering image."

"How about this image, then?" All lingering humor left her expression. "You're the far-seeing gaze of the eagle. I'm beginning to think that whatever I was tuned into the night this all started, I got some valuable clues, including those cryptic references to our individual destinies. One of us will be the striking talons, and since *striking talons* can only mean Daughter of Lilith, I think that refers to Tash and you think it'll be me. One will fly us into darkness.

Again, maybe Tash…more likely me." The turquoise of her gaze deepened. "I mean, sweetie, I'm the Crosse sister who can tie a cherry-stem with her tongue, as I believe I might have unwisely mentioned to Lance just before he tried to give me the undead version of a hickey. Even you don't know all my naughty secrets, but believe me, I've flirted with the darkness more than once. However, we're talking about you right now." A thoughtful crease appeared between her eyebrows. "You're the only one of the three of us who's occasionally turned down a shopping orgy or a party to finish a book that had you hooked, and you never once had to hide your report card from Grammie like Tash and I did. One Darkheart or another has always been a keeper of the knowledge—the person who studies the ancient books and keeps everyone else on track. If that's not you, then I don't know who else it could—"

"Do I totally rock or what!" Tashya ran up to us, her face red but glowing. "I completely kicked ass on that balance beam and my stake-work's getting better, too. I think Grandfather's beginning to wonder if I'm the Daughter, not you, sis," she informed Kat with satisfaction.

"Nothing could make me happier," Kat answered. She saw Tash's immediately suspicious expression. "Honestly, sweetie—the job's yours if you want it. I liked my life just fine before working up a sweat became part of my daily routine. Besides, being in training means I've had to cut my cocktail consumption way back," she said as she headed toward the balance beam.

"I've got two words for her." Tashya turned to me. "*Bitch* and *goddess*. Did you hear what she just said? The job's mine, like it's last year's skirt and she's *giving* it to me!"

"Take a pill, brat. She didn't mean it like that," I said, but she wasn't listening.

"Kat's so used to always getting whatever she wants that the only way she can handle losing out to me is by pretending she doesn't want this, when really she can't *stand* that I might actually be the Daughter instead of her!" Her gaze narrowed on Kat, who, oblivious to the resentment she'd churned up, was executing a flawless backflip before throwing her stake through a cardboard vamp's outlined heart.

"How do you think I feel? I haven't even graduated to the balance beam yet," I pointed out. "Besides, it's not a contest."

"Oh, it's a contest," she said fiercely, "and just because you've already lost doesn't mean I intend to come in second. I bet if I ran into Zena today I could stake her, no problem. I guess everyone would know *then* who's the Daughter and who's not."

For someone whom Kat saw as the glue who kept the three of us together, my reaction to Tashya's outburst was a) insensitive and b) not too smart. "And how are you planning to pull this off—by swaggering into the Hot Box like a Wild West gunslinger?" I said with a roll of my eyes. "If you do, just remember, the sharp end's supposed to go into a vamp's heart, not its eye." I gave her braid a careless tug. "You're too wired over this, Tashie. I'm thinking of playing hookey from the rest of today's training. How about you and I spend the afternoon at the mall looking at shoes and clothes? I need to swing by Starbucks, so we could finish up with lattes." I shrugged. "It might not be a bad idea to start showing our faces around town again to prove we've put the infamous wedding fiasco behind us."

For a moment I thought my last comment had persuaded her. She knew as well as I did that not everyone in Maplesburg—for *not everyone,* read Mandy Broyhill, the BI who'd thrown my lame bachelorette party, and her crowd—bought into the notion that I'd been left groomless at the altar and my sisters' fiancés had disappeared because of presumed foul play. As Kat had wryly noted, after years of being occasional bitches ourselves, it was payback time for the Crosse triplets.

Tash's set expression wavered. Then her scowl returned. "Is that what you and Kat were discussing while I was on the balance beam—how to distract me from my training so I don't have a chance to beat her? Sorry, it's not going to work. Grandfather Darkheart's taking one of us out on a trial run tonight, and I'm going to make sure *I'm* the one he picks." With that she stalked off.

I didn't bother going after her. And for *that* little mistake I got a major karma smack down later that night…when I nearly lost my soul.

Chapter 9

You know how in horror movies there's always a female who goes upstairs to investigate a noise? Never mind that half the movie's cast have been slashed to death by some creepy killer, Little Miss Ditz sashays upstairs, usually in see-through night attire, to meet her doom. You know why? It's simple, really. She does that because she's Too Dumb to Live. I just *hate* those heroines…or I used to before I became one of them.

But I've left out a bunch of stuff, and while the missing pieces don't excuse my TDTL actions, they might make them easier to understand.

After slipping out of the training session— Okay, not *slipping,* precisely: How it went was I walked up to Darkheart and said, "I blow at this. I'm going shopping," and he nodded and said, "*Da,* is probably not bad idea. Pick

me up some black bread if near grocery store, please."
After leaving Kat and Tash to their stake-hurling and
balance-beam-leaping, I escaped to the bathroom to have
a long, hot shower. Steam rose around me, my abused
muscles began to relax, and the scent of rosemary-mint
body wash filled the air. By the time I stepped out of the
shower all thoughts of vamps, dire predictions and burden-
some legacies had temporarily faded, to be replaced with
the burning question of what to wear.

Which isn't as shallow as it sounds. After all, it was the
first time I'd ventured out in public since my wedding had
come to a crashing halt with the non-appearance of my
groom and the appearance of a homicide detective. I
needed to look good, but not so good that I gave the
impression of seeing my fiancé's disappearance as an
opportunity to haul out my most to-die-for outfit and cold-
bloodedly start hunting for his replacement. Then again, I
didn't want to look like a jilted bride whose self-esteem had
sunk so low she didn't care what she wore and had
probably started eating ice cream from the carton. Last but
not least, whatever I chose had to look as if it was the first
thing that had come to hand when I'd opened my closet,
and I hadn't spent any time angsting about my appearance
at all. And that, ladies, is why God invented Juicy Couture
French-terry track suits.

"The pink ones are too girly-girl," I mused out loud as I
padded down the hall in a towel. "The white set's too 'Hey,
I'm still in bride-mode, folks!' and the black set might give
the impression I've started putting on misery weight and I'm
trying to hide it." I opened my bedroom door. "The lilac set?
With a lime-green push-up bra showing at my half-unzipped

cleavage? Sexy yet casual, appropriate for a shopping expedition, and if I run into Mandy and her posse it's obvious that although I've gone through an unfortunate ordeal, I'm getting on with my life."

As relieved as a Japanese poet who'd hit upon the perfect last syllable to complete a haiku, I opened the mirrored doors of my walk-in closet, letting my towel drop to the floor. The swinging doors caught the reflection of the man behind me.

"Let's get a few things straight," Mikhail said. "I don't have the hots for you, I still say you got marked by Zena, and since you know I have to stay close to you, don't blame me for the fact that you're naked in front of me. You going with the lilac, or do I have ten more choices to suffer through?"

I had a couple of options open to me: scream at him to get out while I grabbed my towel, which would have been humiliating, or act like I didn't give a damn that I was standing in my birthday suit in full view of a man who'd been pissing me off since the moment we'd met. Since I'd had my fill of humiliation in the past few days—splinters in my butt, getting clocked by a senior citizen and hurling myself into walls are some examples that come readily to mind—I decided to hang on to my dignity for once.

"The lilac," I said. "And I don't blame you. Since we're agreed that the two of us don't ring each other's bells, I didn't think it would matter about the nude-in-front-of-you thing."

I pulled open a lingerie drawer and selected my lime push-up and matching thong, leaving the bra draped over the drawer and stepping into the thong. From one of my closet's shoe shelves I chose a pair of chartreuse Sergio

Rossi stiletto sandals with straps that wrapped around my ankles. They normally wouldn't have been my first choice for a day of shopping—I think I've mentioned that as much as I adore the way three-and-a-half-inch heels make a girl's legs look like they go on forever, after a few hours of wearing them my feet are crying for mercy—but I was going for the big guns here.

"I've realized we have to come to an understanding," I went on, presenting him with a view of my thong-bisected posterior as I bent over to criss-cross the soft leather straps around my ankles. "At first all I could think of was that you'd been foisted on me 24/7 and that it was a life sentence. Then I realized something," I looked past my bare calf at him. From my position he was just a pair of jeans-clad legs, but I thought I could detect tension in those legs.

"What did you realize?"

Bingo. He *was* tense, I could hear it. I finished winding the straps around my ankles, determined not to let him miss out on any of the kinky bondage symbolism. With both shoes on, I was well aware that my legs had achieved the desired going-on-forever look and my elevated tush was as taut as an apple.

"It isn't a life sentence," I straightened up and reached for my bra. "Excuse me, I need the mirror." Lime-green lace dangling from my finger, I brushed past him in my *Playboy*-worthy outfit of thong and heels. "I turn twenty-two in October."

"I don't get your point." His voice had been reduced to a gravelly mutter. I notched the heat higher by slipping my arms through the bra's straps and adjusting its cups to my breasts before fastening the back clasp and bending forward at the waist to get my girls safely settled.

"When I haven't turned vamp by then, you'll have to give up your hate-on for me, Darkheart won't have to worry anymore, and he'll teach me the words to say so that I can bind you to him again," I said from my bent-over position as damp hair tumbled around my face. "Of course, October's four months away, and at the present you *do* have a hate-on for me." My breasts securely embraced by their lace demi-cups, I turned to Mikhail. "I'm right, no?" I asked. "You've got one major…*hate-on* for me right now, don't you, Mikey-baby?"

I let my gaze stray south of his belt and saw what I'd hoped to see. He took a breath. "Something like that," he said, his tone more even than I'd guessed it would be. "What kind of understanding do you propose we come to?"

I smiled sweetly at him. "What you should know first is that this was just a test, Mike. Instead of a shower, I could have taken a bubble bath, and instead of wrapping a towel around myself, I might have trusted to a few little bubbles here and there. I imagine the condition you're in right now can't be very comfortable as a permanent state." I sighed sympathetically. "But I don't want this to turn nasty, so here's what I propose: you stop glaring at me all day long, stop growling under your breath at me, stop acting like you expect me to go all fang-girl at any minute. And my bedroom's off-limits unless hell freezes over and I invite you in. In other words, play nice with me and I'll play nice with you, because if you don't I'll vamp you every chance I get, Mikey-baby—and I don't mean undead-vamp, I mean living, breathing female vamping. Deal?"

He started to growl, thought better of it, and nodded tightly. "Deal. But there's one thing you should know, too."

I'd won. I could afford to let him have the last word if that's what he needed to keep his male ego from feeling completely annihilated. "What's that?" I asked, reaching into my closet for my lilac French-terry hoodie and pants.

"The moment you turn vampire, all bets are off," he said softly. "*Oborotni* are bound to humans…but when you're no longer one, the contract between us is broken. And even though I react just like any other man to a sexy woman, vamp *glamyr* doesn't work on me at all." He turned to the door. "I'll be waiting in the hall. And just for the record, sweetheart? Sweetest ass I've ever seen, bar none."

As he walked out I found myself wishing I hadn't let him get in the last word, after all.

For all those of you who hate shopping with a man—that would be about 99.9% of the female segment of the population—here's something to make you feel better: shopping with a shape-shifting wolf is twenty times worse. From the minute we hit the Maplesburg Mall, Mikhail was in agony, his super-senses nearly suffering a meltdown from overload. I guess I'd be in agony too if I could hear a couple of hundred snatches of conversation going on all at once while at the same time smelling KFC chicken, Taco Bell burritos and Orange Julius smoothies from the food court, mixed with a passing parade of Dior's Poison, JLo's Glow and Versace's Blue Jeans. Despite our confrontation in the bedroom, I felt sorry for him, so after six hours I cut my shopping expedition short, stopping only at Starbucks to get what I needed before heading home.

On the drive back he had his window rolled down. At one point he stuck his head out into the slipstream, looking happier than I'd ever seen him, but at my narrowed glance he immediately pulled it in and sat normally for the rest of the way. Since we'd made a deal not to say anything nasty to one another it was a silent drive, but I used the time to refine the plan I intended to try out as soon as we got home.

It wasn't enough that there was an uneasy truce between us. Not feeling golden eyes continuously glowering at me was a relief, but I needed my space, and this afternoon had been a perfect example. At the Nordstroms' Urban Decay display, I happily could have spent an hour trying out lip-stain shades on the back of my hand, but I'd caught Mikhail's baffled expression as I pondered the merits of Bitten versus Spank and suddenly I'd felt totally shallow. The only upside to his presence were the Whoa!-check-*him*-out looks on the faces of other females, but even that didn't make up for my lack of privacy.

I felt like Audrey Hepburn in that old movie where she's a princess dying to break loose for a while. While I didn't have a Gregory Peck to aid in my temporary escape, I had something better. I'm a pack rat when it comes to useless scraps of information. Somewhere along the way I'd come across the interesting but irrelevant fact that smugglers pack coffee around shipments of cocaine to baffle drug-sniffing dogs. In my current situation that snippet of knowledge was suddenly *very* relevant.

Or so I hoped. I sped into the house, dumping all but one of my parcels in the foyer and barely taking time to punch in the code that turned off the security alarm—Kat and Tash and Darkheart were out, it appeared. Halfway up the stairs I realized my breakneck speed might seem suspicious to Mikhail, who was right behind me as usual.

"My feet are killing me," I explained over my shoulder. "All I want to do is get these shoes off, completely cover my poor crushed toes in lavender and peppermint foot cream and then lie back on some pillows and pig out on the chocolate-covered espresso beans I got at Starbucks. You want some?"

"No, thanks," he said stiffly. He still hadn't quite gotten the hang of casual conversation with me, but that didn't bother me now. I smiled at him as I entered my bedroom.

"When I'm pampering myself, I don't like to rush things. Why not go downstairs and make yourself something to eat?"

"I'll wait here." He folded his arms and leaned against the hall wall. "Take all the time you want."

A comment which, if I *had* been looking forward to some personal sloth-time, was guaranteed to have killed my anticipation stone-dead, I reflected as I closed the door. Since I hadn't been lying about needing to rescue my feet, I took a moment to change into sneakers but as soon as I had, I lost no time in dumping the contents of the Starbucks bag onto my bed.

The chocolate-covered espresso beans were on top. I snatched them up, ripped open the flavor-seal package, and tossed one in my mouth. As soon as I bit into it my mouth was flooded with the heavenly taste of dark chocolate and rich coffee. I tossed another bean back, chewing on it the way Grammie had always taught us not to—with my mouth open.

"Mmmm," I groaned out loud. "*So* delish. I could eat a *million* of these things."

In theater parlance, I believe my little maneuver would

be called "setting the stage." Mikhail's wolfey sense of smell would now be getting a massive hit of coffee aroma. In a second the coffee smell would start getting way stronger, but he'd simply put it down to my chocolate espresso beans. If I hadn't prepared him, he might have begun wondering why all he could suddenly smell from my room was an obliterating scent of coffee.

I ripped open the first bag of Italian roast. Sneaking to the door, I poured it in a thick line along the rug. The second vacuum-packed bag was Sumatra blend. It joined the Italian roast by the crack under my bedroom door, and was topped up with a bag of French mocha. I backed away, gave a moan that I hoped suggested estatic chocolate-satiation, and crept to my window.

I'd left it open earlier. Now it was a simple matter to unlatch the screen, set it aside, and sling my leg over the sill. I paused, waiting for some reaction from the hall, but there was none. Mikey-baby's hearing was good, as he'd inadvertently revealed to Kat and me today, but he relied on his canine sense of smell to tell him where I was at any given moment, and I'd just seriously screwed up his Megan-radar with my coffee ploy.

Five minutes later, after clambering down the oak tree by my bedroom window and letting my Mini roll noiselessly down the drive to the road, I was speeding along the road that led out of Maplesburg, with Fergie of the Black Eyed Peas singing "Fly Away" on the CD player, which I thought made a perfect soundtrack for my getaway. My plan was to drive around for half an hour, return home and sneak back into my room the same way I'd sneaked out. If Mikhail hadn't noticed my absence, I'd clean up the coffee and use it again tomorrow to buy myself a longer period of AWOL.

Like I say, that was the plan. I still think it was a good one. Things just didn't work out as I'd anticipated.

I was heading back into Maplesburg when my cell rang. I pulled it out of my pocket and flipped it open, pulling the Mini over to the side of the deserted road while I took the call.

"Sweetie, you'll never guess where we are." Kat's voice sounded hollow and echoey. It also sounded depressed.

"With Darkheart?" I guessed without taxing my brain too much. "Oh, shit, tell him I forgot to pick up his black bread."

She ignored my added comment. "In a mausoleum," she informed me with a marked lack of enthusiasm. "We're waiting here until sunset to see if any of the crypts start opening up and disgorging vamps. Grandfather says I can stake them before they know we're here," she sighed heavily. "Tell Tash from me that missing out on this wasn't worth her getting into such a snit. I've got water dripping down the back of my neck, this place smells really bad and—" static replaced the sound of her voice but then she came back again "—out patrolling till dawn so I guess I'll see you and Tashie tomorrow morning. Try and talk some sense into her, Meg. Grandfather said she'd get her turn tomorrow night, but she seemed so—" Again the static intruded on her words, and this time I did, too.

"She's not with you?" I heard sharp worry in my question, but I couldn't help it. I *was* worried. "How bad of a snit? Did she say anything about going to the Hot Box? Kat?" The phone went dead. Hastily I called her back and heard the recorded tones of an operator telling me that the customer I was dialling was unavailable.

"So tell me something I *don't* know," I said through gritted teeth as I tossed my cell phone on the passenger seat beside me and stared irresolutely at the setting sun, "like, would Tash really be stupid enough to try and take down Zena herself? Could she be at the Hot Box right now waiting for her to appear?"

But I already knew the answers to those questions. I remembered the excited glint in Tashie's blue eyes when she'd talked about staking Zena and the stubborn thrust of her chin when she'd vowed to prove that she was Daughter of Lilith material. Tash *was* stupid enough—or if not stupid, at least blinded by her feelings of competition with Kat. She was at the Hot Box. I knew it in my suddenly tight chest, my suddenly clenched stomach and my suddenly sinking heart.

The sun was already straddling the horizon. I started the Mini and put it in gear. Swinging it onto the road, I made a U-turn and ended up facing the way I'd just come…away from Maplesburg and toward the turnoff to the Hot Box.

I didn't know it at the time, but I'd just performed the vehicular equivalent of walking upstairs in a see-through negligee to meet my doom. I'd just become Too Dumb to Live.

The Hot Box was a low, unprepossessing building out in the middle of nowhere, built of concrete block and distinguished only by the candy-striped awning that stretched along its length. The pink-and-white stripes were repeated in the flashing neon of the sign that not only pro-claimed its name, but also the fact that inside there were Girls, Girls, Girls! Classy.

But besides noting that the neon's pulsating message was becoming increasingly more visible in the gathering dusk, I was too preoccupied to take much in. "Get Tash, get the hell out. Get Tash, get the hell out. Get Tash—" I mantrad under my breath as I parked my car near the entrance and ran across the gravel to the awning-protected door. My gut feelings had been right: as I'd sped across the expanse of parking lot, I'd seen the tell-tale white Mini, identical to mine, parked among the other cars at the side of the building.

"She didn't even leave it where she could get to it in a hurry," I muttered, breaking off my mantra. "What was she *thinking?*" Stupid question. I knew damn well what had gone on under the riot of red-gold curls that Tash had probably tossed as she'd marched from her car—a vision of herself uttering a few cool quips during a brief battle with Zena that quickly ended in the queen vamp's death-by-staking.

My fantasy differed in a few key details…key details like who would be killed and who would walk away in any confrontation between my sister and a vamp who had gone up against hundreds of over-confident opponents in her blood-soaked career.

The double doors at the entrance to the club had oversized gold-toned handles. As I drew closer I saw they each depicted a female thrusting forward perkily uptilted breasts. I grabbed a gold-toned boob, pulled open one of the doors and went in.

And immediately winced. Being inside the Hot Box was unnervingly like being inside a giant…no, I can't go there. Let's just say that whoever the interior designer had been, he'd taken the tacky name of the club as a theme and run with it. Everything was an almost *throbbing* pink, from the flocked wallpaper to the worn carpeting to the grubby upholstered doors a few feet ahead of me, from behind which came the muffled sound of music. Since I doubted Tash was watching the show, I glanced around the foyer, hoping to see a door marked Private or some other subtle indication as to where the non-public areas of the club were. My gaze fell instead on the six-foot-tall figure swiftly approaching me.

"Don't tell me—Cherry's sick again and you're filling in for her. I'm getting a little pissed with our resident Lady Godiva being a no-show and sending eleventh-hour replacements, but what the hell. Dressing room's down the hall, make a left. Where's your stuff?"

The above speech was accompanied by a long stream of cigarette smoke blown my way. I waved it aside and saw that the speaker couldn't be Zena, for a couple of reasons. One, there was still daylight outside; and two, Zena, as far as I knew, actually *was* a female, so she didn't have to impersonate one.

Which wasn't to say that the statuesque babe in the red evening gown towering over me couldn't bring a construction site to a wolf-whistling halt. At least, he could—sorry, *she* could—if she replaced the platinum Marilyn Monroe wig she'd just taken off her skull-capped head. As if she realized the brown buzz-cut hair sticking through the tight nylon cap ruined her image, she turned to the foyer mirror and began to put on the wig.

I could see her reflection in the mirror, another indicator she wasn't a vamp, I thought as I shook my head. "Sorry, I'm just here looking for my sister—strawberry curls, blue eyes, about my size. Did you see her come in?"

"A sister act? The campers go crazy over sisters." Pseudo-Marilyn caught my frown as she patted her wig. "Campers, the creeps in the audience with tent-poles, get it?" she elaborated. "You never heard that expression in any of the other clubs you strip at?"

"I'm not a strip—" I stopped, my thoughts racing. Then I took a breath. "I prefer to think of myself as an exotic dancer," I said firmly. "But Cherry only called me on my cell ten minutes ago to ask me to fill in for her, so I didn't have a chance to go home and get my costume." A vision of Grammie's and Popsie's appalled faces suddenly rose up in my mind as I went on, "Can I borrow some pasties, girlfriend?"

Chapter 10

Arguing with Marilyn over what I was doing here would have used up minutes I didn't have, I thought as I sauntered away from her. I turned into the corridor and my saunter became a sprint.

"Get Tash and get the hell *out* of here!" My mantra now had an extra edge of fear. The sun had surely set by now, and I wasn't basing this solely on the fact that it had been slipping below the horizon as I'd entered. It *felt* as though night had fallen. All of my senses had gone to Def-Con One and I felt as nakedly vulnerable as some prehistoric cave-dweller wondering if the sounds outside in the dark were coming from a sabre-toothed tiger or something even worse.

I halted at a partially open door. Letting the light from the hall illuminate the room, I stuck my head inside and saw it was some kind of storage area. I looked over my shoulder, but the hall behind me was empty. "Tash! Tash, you in here?"

There was no answer. I let the door swing shut and resumed sprinting down the corridor, thankful I was wearing sneakers instead of the killer heels I'd had on earlier. Ahead of me was one more door before the corridor branched left and right. Marilyn had said that the left branch led to the dressing room, and since it wasn't likely that the strippers paraded through the foyer to get to and from their sets, taking a right turn would probably lead me straight onto the club's stage, staring like a deer caught in the headlights at a roomful of expectant and horny men. Running into Zena was almost preferable, I thought with a shudder as I came to a stop outside the closed door.

Cautiously I opened it a crack, my heart-rate tripling as I saw a glow of light. But mere illumination wasn't the only difference between this room and the last. This was someone's office—a decadently luxurious office with red silk covering the walls and faux-zebra and panther skins layered on the floor by an elaborate desk. The lamp on the desk had an unusual globe shade made of some kind of intricately carved material. Its dim light, escaping only through the piercings in the carving, was barely enough to reveal a fur-draped sofa and the shadowed outline of a closet door beyond the desk.

I took all this in at a glance, my blood congealing in my veins. Office. *Sumptuous* office. Office that could only belong to Zena, aka Queen Vamp, aka sworn enemy of all things Darkheart, including me. It was too exposed to be her daytime lair, but it would be the first place she would come when she arose every night. And if I'd reached that conclusion, Tash would have, too.

I wanted so badly to turn and run from that room. In fact, my feet had already started retreating back into the hall before I made them stop, forcing myself to ignore the "get the hell out of here" part of my mantra and focus on the "get Tash" part.

Quickly I stepped into the room. Before the door had closed behind me I was flying past the desk, almost wiping out as one of the faux-panther rugs—no, real panther, I realized as my sneaker sank into silky fur—slid sideways under my foot. "Tash, if you're in here you'd better come out now, or when we get home I'm going to *kill* you!" I hissed as I sped to the closet and wrenched open the door. "Zena could show up at any—"

Take it from me, there's nothing, and I mean *nada*, that can cut off a ranting female in midsentence as fast as having the nearly nude dead body of a woman fall on her. There's nothing that can turn her skin to the texture of a plucked chicken so instantly, either. As Closet-Girl tumbled onto me, the ropes that had been binding her fell free and tangled around my neck.

"Shit oh shit oh shit oh shit…" I had a new mantra, not quite as catchy as the previous one but even more heartfelt. I tore at the ropes and stumbled backwards from the dead woman so fast that I crashed into the desk behind me. Out of the corner of my eye I saw the lamp begin to fall and realized with panic that if it did I wouldn't just be in a room with a corpse, I'd be in a dark room with a corpse. I grabbed at the globe shade and immediately felt sick

horror. Or, since I was already feeling sick horror, I suppose I should say *new* sick horror.

The body at my feet was terrible enough. Realizing I was holding a human skull that had been carved and pierced and fitted to a lamp as a shade was almost worse. I let go of the thing so abruptly that it nearly tipped over again, at the same time ripping the last strand of rope from around my throat.

Except it wasn't rope, I realized. It was hair, jet-black and long enough for an enterprising stripper to use it as a prop in a Lady Godiva act. I'd just found the missing Cherry…and she was a whole lot sicker than Marilyn had suspected.

But I still hadn't found Tashya. A heartbeat later, I realized why.

The sudden sound of my cell phone ringing should have startled me into the screaming meemies, but as I grabbed my Nokia from the pocket of my hoodie and glanced at the caller display I found myself clutching it as if it were a tiny, Swarovski-studded lifebuoy. Mikhail had found my cell number on the house phone's speed dial. He'd realized I'd tricked him and was calling to find out where I was. Yes, he'd go all wolfey and pissy and start doing his glowering-at-me thing again, but that was a small price to pay for him getting his tight-bunned ass over here to save mine and Tashya's.

He'd be able to track her scent, I thought hollowly. It would have been helpful if I'd thought of that before I'd marched into the Hot Box all by myself.

"I know you're furious and I've probably violated some arcane rule of behavior between *oborotni* and *vladelcy*, but—"

"Earth to Aunt Bea," Tashya's irritated voice said. "God,

Meg, it's like you're some flustery old lady who doesn't know how to read a call display. Where *is* everybody?"

The air shot out of my lungs. I dragged some back in and produced a whispered shout. "What the hell do you mean, where's everybody? Where have *you* been? Kat thought you were with me, I thought you were with her and Darkheart—"

"And I would have been if my stupid car hadn't started making a bunch of weird sounds," Tash snapped. "I mean, how totally unfair was it, Grandfather choosing Kat to go on the first hunt instead of me? I decided to follow them anyway, but the guy at this ratty garage I pulled into said I was lucky I hadn't blown the engine. As it was, he told me it would be an overnight job and I had to get a taxi home. Did you know about that orange light and how you're supposed to change your oil or top it up or whatever when it goes on?"

"Of course I knew," I said tightly. "I also know better than to leave my car with some crook of a mechanic for him to go joyriding in and end up at the Hot Box. Put Mikhail on the line. I need to talk to him."

"That's why I called—I'm here all alone. Isn't he supposed to stick by your side night and—" I heard her make a sound a lot like the one I'd made a moment earlier when the air had rushed out of my lungs. "Meg?" She said my name in a breathy squeak. "Please tell me you're not at the Hot Box."

"I'm at the Hot Box," I said flatly. "You're probably not going to have much luck reaching Kat, but if you do, tell her and Darkheart the situation. If Mikhail returns, tell him, too. And Tash?" I heard a quaver in my voice.

"Yes?" There was a quaver in hers, as well.

"If I show up on the doorstep later tonight looking better than I ever looked in my life, shove a crucifix at me. If I'm still me, fine and dandy, but if I'm not…" I swallowed. "If I'm not, stake me, Tashie. No matter what I say or how I plead with you, stake me before I kill anyone I love, okay?"

I didn't wait for her reply. Snapping my cell phone shut, I started for the door, but then I turned back.

The woman on the floor was no one to me, but Zena had targeted her and that gave us something in common. If she was dead, there was nothing I could do for her. If she was undead, however… My gaze lit upon an ivory and leather letter opener on the desk. I snatched it up and turned back to Cherry, steeling myself for what I needed to do next.

I'd never seen a dead person, much less touched one. As I pushed aside the silky curtain of hair that provided more cover for her near-nudity than the pale blue G-string and scrap of bra she was wearing, I thought I could feel warmth beneath my fingertips. It also seemed to me that her flesh didn't have the marble hardness I imagined a corpse's should have.

"But what do I know?" I spoke under my breath. "The whole rigor mortis thing's a big mystery to me. I don't have the faintest idea when Zena killed you, aside from the fact that it must have been sometime before dawn this…" My words trailed off as I saw the unmistakable double fang-marks I'd hoped I wouldn't find. My grip tightened around the letter opener—there seemed to be an unwritten rule that yours truly wasn't allowed to go up against a vamp with an honest-to-God stake, I thought—and I flicked an apprehensive glance at Cherry's face.

She'd been a beautiful woman, with features that still looked vaguely childlike. Her lashes lay like fans against the pink of her cheeks and her lips, as red as her namesake, were slightly pouted in exhalation. I wondered what kind of person she'd been, and whether I'd have liked her if I'd known her.

"It's too bad we never met," I told her slowly. "We could have gone shopping together, maybe gone to a bar to check out guys. Can you imagine how they'd have hit on us—a brunette and a blonde, both of us young and totally hot-looking? And if I got my sisters to go with us, there'd be a sudden epidemic of whiplash in the male population of Maplesburg."

"I know, right?" Cherry agreed, opening her eyes and curving her red lips into a smile. "Like, no other girls would stand a chance against the four of us. We could get a place together, throw parties, kill everyone we don't like." She looked thoughtful. "My trailer's kind of small but it's close to Rodney Park so it's too convenient to move from there. I know—we'll take over the trailer next to mine! It's way bigger and the couple who live there had a hot tub put in last fall!"

"I'm already packed." I smiled back at her. Her eyes were a delicious purple shade, and they sparkled at me as if we'd been best friends forever. "But if there's a couple living there already, how do we get them to move out?"

"Uh, by ripping them into bloody pieces?" Cherry giggled.

"Works for me," I said solemnly, before I cracked up and began giggling helplessly with her.

"Girlfriend, we're going to have a *ton* of fun together," she said through her laughter. "Hand me that letter opener."

"What letter opener?" I glanced at my hand and saw the

slim leather and ivory dagger I was holding. "Oh, *this* letter opener." I went off into another bout of laughter.

"Yeah, that one," Cherry said, her tone abrupt. She softened her demand with a smile from her red lips. "Unless you were planning to open some letters with it?"

I shook my head, still laughing helplessly. "God, no, I was planning to stake a vamp with it, girlfriend."

Instantly cutting off my laughter, with one swift move I raised the letter opener and plunged its blade into her chest. A gout of crimson immediately spewed upwards from the entry point, dying the filmy blue of her skimpy bra a dark red. Her violet gaze widened in shock and then a dull film shadowed her eyes.

"It might have been fun, right?" she rasped. "Us being girlfriends, I mean. We could have gone shopping, maybe done each other's hair. I kind of missed out on that stuff, being a working girl and all." She moved suddenly and I tensed, but her grasp on my wrist was weak. "My name was Lorraine Deagan. I came from a little place in Iowa called Greenvale. Tell my folks there hasn't been a day since I ran away that I didn't wish—"

Her hand on my wrist went first, allowing me to turn away from the sight of the rest of her dissolving to dust. I stood up, closed the closet and tried to get myself under control.

I didn't feel sick about staking Cherry, the way Kat had felt about staking Maisel. I just felt an incredible sadness for the crappy deal life had handed her and for a mother and father who hoped every time the phone rang that it was their runaway daughter. A cold spark of anger flickered beneath my sadness—flickered, and then steadied into an icy flame.

Zena was a total fucking bitch. I'd been seeing her as

the big evil, which was how Darkheart saw her, and how Kat and Tash and presumably Mikhail saw her. They were right—she *was* evil. But thinking of her like that was a way of giving her a measure of respect, and I didn't want to give her that. She was like every crisis-creating, clique-leading, esteem-destroying mean girl I'd ever known in my life. I wanted to see her brought down, if for no other reason than for turning a messed-up young woman into a vampire I'd been forced to kill.

"If I ever meet her, I hope I live long enough to tell her how I feel about her to her face," I said under my breath as I let myself out of her office. "Of course, if I don't get out of Club Sleaze right now, I might find myself doing just that."

I set off down the hall at a brisk trot, passing the storage room I'd first investigated and heading toward the curve that opened out onto the entrance area. I heard voices approaching from the direction of the foyer and came to a skidding halt.

"…can tell Bambi to do a second set. The campers are so drunk they won't even realize she was on half an hour ago."

It was Marilyn. I turned back toward the storage room, intending to slip in there until she and whoever she was speaking to had passed, but at the sound of the second speaker I froze.

"Is no problem. Cherry's friend is probably in bathroom getting sick with nerves. You have to lend her extra pair of pasties from costume supplies because she says she doesn't have own? She is definite first-timer. I tell her get her ass on stage or her friend Cherry gets fired."

Before another night passes she will be hunting with me, not against me… The last time I'd heard that voice had been in the vision in which I'd seen my mother die. Zena was here. In a moment she would turn the corner and see me.

I raced toward the storage room, but as I neared it I changed my mind and kept running. How smart was it to take refuge in a small room with only one escape route? At the end of the main hall I made a second snap decision and took the right-hand corridor that I assumed led to the stage.

It was my only option. Left would have taken me to the dressing room, where Zena and Marilyn were apparently heading. From the stage in the main room of the club, I could a make a beeline for the foyer and then to my Mini waiting outside.

The first hitch occurred as I yanked open the door at the end of the short corridor. I burst through and the next moment I felt myself barreling into something solid. The something-solid was no match for my momentum and we both went sprawling.

If I'd learned anything over the past few days, it was how to take a fall. I braced myself, prayed I wouldn't land on any part of my body that was already decorated with large saffron-and-indigo bruises and anticipated the jarring impact I knew would run through me. But this time none of that happened, because instead of slamming down onto a hard surface, I found my fall broken by a soft pillow. Two soft pillows, in fact.

An outraged yell exploded by my ears. "Get the fuck off my goddamn boobs! Be *careful!*"

Careful wasn't in my repertoire at that moment. I jumped to my feet, nearly stepping on the G-string-clad woman lying in front of me. Her breasts were more than impressive, they were awesome—perfect globes that must have needed at least a triple-D cup to rein them in.

"These sisters cost me five thousand bucks," the woman snarled, checking them over—for leaks, I supposed. "And since the friggin' IRS didn't agree they were a business investment, that's five thousand without any tax write-off." She glared up at me, but as she took in my attire her glare morphed into an incredulous stare. "You're going on dressed like *that?*"

I glanced down at my half-unzipped Juicy hoodie and my suddenly meager-looking 32B lime-green bra. I could see what she meant. Beside her, I looked like a Mennonite.

"Not if I can help it," I said quickly. "Look, I'm sorry about crashing into you. Is there a way into the audience area that bypasses the stage?"

"Up those three stairs and past the curtain," she said, after giving me a calculating look. "You better hustle. The new owner's some Russian bitch, and if she finds you hanging around backstage you'll be in major shit."

"Thanks for the advice," I said, starting for the small set of stairs she'd indicated. "And again, sorry about the falling-into-your-boobs thing," I added politely over my shoulder as I sprinted up the stairs and pushed past the curtain.

If you're wondering, the Hot Box's stage isn't really a stage, *per se*. It's more like a model's runway, but instead of black-clad fashionistas eyeing the new fall line like crows spying something bright and shiny, the Hot Box's runway was surrounded by men. I know this from first-hand experience.

I was moving so fast as I burst past the curtain that my

impetus didn't slow until I was halfway down the runway. By then I knew I'd been screwed by Balloon Lady. I spared an instant to hope fervently that one or both of her five-thousand-dollar investments were deflating at that very moment, and blinked over the bright footlights that lined the stage.

I like men. I really do. I think they're funny and sexy and adorable and sexy and endearing and sexy. On the other hand, a small percentage of them are charter members of Slimeballs Anonymous, which—coincidentally, I'm sure—appeared to be holding its weekly meeting at the Hot Box that night. Around me was a sea of slack jaws and bleary eyes. Behind the alcohol-induced bleariness, however, most of the gazes fixed on me held something that made me rethink my assessment of them as mere slimeballs, and escalate it to potentially dangerous assholes.

That something was a mixture of fear and hatred and hunger. Right now, the hunger was uppermost, but I could see it changing to unsettled wariness as they took in the fact that I was fully clothed and apparently planning to stay that way.

"You gonna show us something, sweetcheeks, or you just gonna stand there?" My heckler was a veritable Adonis, if Adonis had been about forty-five, had a beer gut straining over his belt, and hairy forearms like slabs of pork with the bristles still attached. He was sitting at a table near the front with a couple of equally to-die-for cronies.

I squinted through the lights. "Sorry to disappoint, but no. I'm with the local electrical board. We received a complaint that some of these lights were shorting out, but they seem fine to me, so I'll just get out of here and let you boys watch the rest of the show." As I spoke I walked down the runway, ignoring the charming comment of, "We came here to see a show, bitch!" that one of his compadres growled at me.

Maybe in recounting this I'm giving the impression that I was cool and collected and in command of myself. But my brave front was just that, a front. Though the men in the room weren't vamps, I had the impression they could sense fear as well as any undead predators. They hadn't come here because they liked women. They were here because the opposite was true.

Brazening it out was my best strategy. I got to the end of the runway, dodging two chrome-plated poles of the kind you see strippers rubbing up against in movies, and shielded my eyes. "Sir, can you move your chair out of the way so I can get down?" I said with electrical-employee courtesy to the lone man at the table in front of me. I couldn't see his face, but he was obviously younger than the hecklers. In fact, from what I could see he wasn't bad-looking, and I wondered briefly why he was at the Hot Box instead of out on a real date.

Then he looked at me and my question was answered.

He was a vamp. His smile was feral, the tips of his canines just showing under his lifted top lip. He got to his feet and I saw with no surprise that he was hovering an inch or so off the floor. "I'll even help you down," he said, extending a hand.

I took a hasty step backward. "On second thought, it might be easier over here," I said, moving to the side of the runway. There was a table of men staring up at me, all near-clones of Pork-Arms and his cronies, except for one. The hairs on the back of my neck rose as I saw he was a vampire, too.

By now my eyes had adjusted to the bright line of lights ringing the stage. My heart thudding crazily in my chest, I scanned the packed room and began to pick out a vamp here, a vamp there, all watching me the way vultures watch a wounded animal. The rest of the audience began to get abusive.

"Take it off, girlie!"

"Tits and ass, babe!"

"Wrap those skinny legs around a pole!"

"Megan! Over here!"

Startled, I squinted into the crowd to see who'd called my name, and in a corner near the exit I glimpsed a familiar face.

Detective Van Ryder's melted-chocolate eyes held an expression of disbelief and anger. I saw him shoulder aside two men as he began to make his way to the stage and then disappear from view as three burly bouncers stepped in front of him. More bouncers spread through the room, but the combination of alcohol and my non-performance seemed to have ignited a fuse in the crowd and the volume of the insults and obscenities rose.

"Silence!"

The one-word command was thunderous. My back was against one of the chrome poles, and I felt it vibrate like a tuning fork at the voice behind me. Slowly I turned.

In the vision Mikhail had forced my sisters and me to witness, Zena had worn a medieval-looking red velvet robe. Her wardrobe had been updated since then. Her white breasts gleamed like pearls against the black satin of her bustier, her legs were clad in leather boots that rose nearly to her thighs, and her outfit was completed by studded leather wristbands and a choker.

Oh, and a whip. I almost forgot the whip.

She kept her gaze on the crowd as she spoke, her voice a purr now. "Impatience is understandable. You come to Zena's club to see most beautiful girls in world reveal charms, *nyet?* So you shall, my friends." Her smile was sexily catlike, and her green eyes glowed like emeralds in ice.

A voice from the crowd broke in. "Can the talk, Russkie, and get down to business! If blondie's so fuckin' shy, why don't you start grinding that fine ass of yours? Or do you do something with that big mother of a whip you're holding?"

It was Pork-Arms who'd called out to Zena. He made a pumping motion with his hands and grinned as his buddies guffawed at his suggestion. I felt a thin rush of air pass by me, and the next moment my stomach lurched with nausea.

Pork-Arm's grin had widened from ear to ear. Zena's whip had widened it for him. Instead of a mouth, he now had a slash bisecting his face, the wound severing the tendons of his jaw so that the lower portion of it dangled down. His eyes bulged and the muscles of his neck stood out as he tried to scream, but all that came from his ruined mouth was a high whistle of agony. A pair of bruisers came up on either side of him, grabbed him by the elbows and escorted him out.

And no one in the room, not even the men who had been laughing with him, seemed to notice that anything had happened.

I couldn't see Van Ryder anywhere, but I couldn't worry about him right now. Seeing that the vamp directly in front of the runway was directing his gaze toward Zena, I made a sudden dash, intending to leap into the crowd and try to make my way to the door before he or his undead companions could catch me.

I reached the end of the stage, began my jump, and felt myself being jerked back. Barely keeping my balance, I looked down at the thick leather whip coiled around my waist. It jerked again, and I found myself whirling around to face Zena, her red hair spilling like living fire around her creamy shoulders.

"I promise you most beautiful girl will reveal charms, gentlemen, and Zena keeps promises. But she needs some persuasion, *da?* Not with whip, but persuasion of more erotic type." She raised her voice over the growing roar of approval from the room. "Watch and you will see how I seduce her into doing my will. Will be killer of show, gentlemen!"

As if the crowd held no more interest for her, abruptly she turned her back to it, her emerald gaze fixing for the first time on me. I returned her stare, forcing my eyes not to waver.

"I keep my promises, too," I said, wishing my voice didn't sound so thin. "I promised myself that if I ever met you face to face, I'd tell you what I thought of you."

"Da?" She gave me the catlike smile she'd used on the crowd. "And what do you think of me?"

"That you're a total bitch," I said, knowing I was about to die.

Zena's smile grew intimate, as if she and I shared a delicious joke that no one else in the world could ever appreciate. She took a step closer to me; her perfume, a heady mixture of jasmine and spices and something I couldn't identify, wrapping around me along with her body heat.

"So what's so bad about being total bitch, my beautiful darling?" she laughed softly, her upcurved lips almost brushing mine.

And right then and there, I felt myself falling in love.

Chapter 11

I know what you're thinking. Whoa, Meg-baby, a little bit of a one-eighty without any warning, no? One minute you're all "Mikhail's tight butt" and "Van Ryder's bedroom eyes" and the next minute you're in let-me-count-the-ways mode with a female. What's up with the no-foreshadowing, girlfriend, and are you bi or gay or what?

Okay, point taken, and to answer your questions in order: sorry, sorry again, I can see how it would seem that way, and excuse me all to hell for not foreshadowing, but my reaction to Zena wasn't foreshadowed to me, either.

And as for your bi/gay/straight question? I'm boringly straight. All right, when I was fifteen I had a dream one time about Christina Aguilera, but that was it, and in my dream we decided to be just friends.

So when Zena looked deep into my eyes and called me

her beautiful darling, there was no way my heart should have gone pitty-pat, given that she was a vampire as well as being female. I knew that. I knew I was in the danger-ous presence of a *glamyr* a hundred times more powerful than any Dean or Cherry had been able to conjure up, and that Zena's *glamyr* had to be what was fogging my synapses into making me think I was falling for her. But all I could see was her white skin and her teasing red lips and her incredible emerald eyes.

"I…I guess there's nothing so wrong with being a total bitch," I said as she gave the handle of the whip another tug. I spun around, the lash uncoiling from my body, and when I came to a stop I grabbed the chrome pole in front of me to keep from falling to the stage. I shook my head to clear it. "No, wait a minute," I said more strongly. "There's a *lot* wrong. For one thing, you killed Cherry, and for another, you killed my mother!"

We were no longer face to face, but a few feet apart. As my hand moved toward the letter opener I'd dropped into my pocket after staking Cherry, I heard three sharp cracks and instantly felt three hot bee stings: one on either arm and a third on my stomach. Just as I was wondering in distracted anger where the bee had come from and where the little sucker had gone, I heard a roar of approval from beyond the glaring footlights.

"Is partial revealing of charms, my friends." Zena gave a mocking bow to the room. "More to come, I promise."

As she spoke I glimpsed Van Ryder again. No longer hampered by bouncers, his struggle to reach the stage was still being impeded by the press of the crowd. Our gazes locked, and just for a second I forgot Zena, the drunks and everything else that should have been occupying my attention right then. The sudden flare of heat in his dark brown eyes seemed to indicate that he was having an identical lapse of memory.

Then his expression hardened and he resumed his attempts to make his way through the crowd. Recalled to my own situation, I reached for the stake in my hoodie pocket. My hand clutched at thin air, and in confusion I looked down at myself. For a moment I didn't believe what I was seeing.

From the waist up I was naked, except for the lime-green bra. My lilac hoodie lay in scraps at my feet. As my arms crossed instinctively over my breasts, I saw thin red lines running from my shoulders to my wrists, and a similar red line running down my stomach. They no longer felt like bee stings, they felt as if burning wires had been placed against my skin. But even as I watched I saw the thin red lines blur and thicken, and in shock I realized what they were.

I'd been sliced by Zena's whip—not as deeply as Pork-Arms had been, but with razor-blade precision. My hoodie had been sliced, too—once down each arm and once down the front, so that it fell away in three pieces. It was an exhibition designed not only to stir up the creeps in the audience, but to let me know she could have killed me…and hadn't.

I raised my eyes and saw she was watching me, the lash of her whip twitching on the floor beside her like the tail of a big cat. I let my arms drop to my sides. This was a game to her, and by covering myself against the leers directed my way, I was playing the role she'd constructed for me. I didn't want to play Zena's game. What I didn't understand until later was that I'd been playing it all along.

"Why?" My tone was flat as I posed the question. She didn't pretend not to know what I was talking about.

"Why I don't kill you, but merely disrobe you?" Her wrist moved slightly and the whip jumped in her hand, its lash curling around my ankles like a caress. Her voice was equally caressing as she moved toward me. "Is because you are my darling. You do not feel same way to me, even a little?"

"I've already told you what I think of you," I answered, trying not to look directly into her eyes. "If I had any doubts, which I don't, they would have vanished an hour ago when Cherry's body fell out of your closet onto me."

"But I do not kill stripper," she protested, uncoiling the whip from my ankles and flicking it so that it wound around the top half of my body, trussing me to the chrome pole I was backed up against. "I give gift of being always young and beautiful. *You* take Zena's gift away and kill girl, just as grandfather once killed mother."

I tensed as she drew nearer. "Darkheart killed Angelica for the same reason I killed Cherry—because you turned them into vamps." Zena was so close now that her breath played upon the skin of my neck as she exhaled. As she placed one hand under my chin I tried to jerk away, but the lash held me tight. Without warning she dipped her head. The next moment I convulsed in shock as I felt a velvety warmth trail upwards along my exposed stomach. Slowly Zena raised her gaze to mine, her bottom lip made redder with the single drop of my blood that clung to it.

The Hot Box exploded with whistles and raucous yells and I forced myself to ignore the tiny *frissons* that seemed to be running up and down my abdomen. "The next time you taste my blood you'd better make sure you either turn me or kill me, because if you don't, you're dust, *vampyr!*"

Seemingly unperturbed by my outburst, Zena walked around me and stopped at one side of the chrome pole. Constrained as I was, I could only see her out of the corner of my eye, but I felt her fingertips, as light and cool as snowflakes, brush my shoulderblades and then sink into my hair as she went on in a murmur. "I had hopes you would come tonight, my beautiful one. I needed to make sure you delayed your departure long enough so that we would meet. Finding Cherry was good delay, *da?*"

She moved around in front of me, her hand still in my hair, and dipped her head a second time. "I don't believe you," I said tightly. "You had no way of knowing I was coming here—I didn't know, until just before sunset. You may be a vamp, but you can't read minds and unless everything I've learned from Darkheart is way off base, you can't foretell the future, either."

"But I can make guesses." There was more of my blood on her lips now, individual drops that gleamed like tiny rubies. "I guess that old man will take only one sister on hunt, the other sisters will be too angry to stay away—will seek vengeance. In end is completely turning out the way I guess, *da?* You and I meet as I have hoped, my darling." She flicked a dismissive glance at the room. "Unfortunate is necessary to have first interlude together in public, but do not be afraid. Pleasure will be exquisite. Is always so when is grand passion, you agree?"

I knew what her intention was even before I saw the tips of her canines begin to lengthen past her bottom lip. Fear sluiced through me. "You expect me to believe any of that?

How did you know Darkheart wouldn't choose me to take on the first hunt? Because if he had, our little date here would have been kind of rained out, wouldn't you say?"

"I knew was impossible. Old man takes future Daughter of Lilith on hunt, *da?* This could not be you. I feel such bond between us, I know you must be mine from many years ago."

"What are you saying, that I'm the triplet you marked?" Her lips brushed my shoulder but I no longer had the strength to pull away. Even my earlier hopes of Van Ryder's help now seemed irrelevant. My reality had narrowed to Zena and myself and the cold stone of despair that had lodged in my heart.

She kissed my temple. "Is what I believe, da," she breathed against my mouth. "Is what I feel, my beautiful love."

From somewhere deep inside me I dredged up a final burst of anger. "I need to hear what you *know!*" I exploded, trying not to tremble as I felt her touch on my neck. "You put your mark on one of Angelica's babies, damn you— you must know which one!"

From the floor it probably looked as if I was making a titallating last-ditch effort to stave off Zena's advances. The noise in the room swelled, but it didn't drown out her reply.

"I am not one who knows this truth. You are," she said, bringing her face to mine. "You came to me. You feel the pull. You tell yourself to fight against it, but in your heart you want to stop fighting, *nyet?*" The color of her eyes intensified, deepened, until they seemed not to be merely emerald but the essence of emerald, holding within them a blend of everything green in the world…an unblooming field of clover, a deserted lawn at midnight, a green-flowing river with the drowned bodies of suicides turning in an underwater ballet beneath its surface.

"You're right, there's no use in fighting anymore…" As I let myself fall deeper into her gaze, I wasn't sure if I'd said the words out loud or whether words were no longer necessary between us. "I came to you…"

I bared my neck to her and the pinprick of red I saw behind her irises seemed more beautiful to me than the green it obliterated. Closing my eyes, I waited for her fangs to pierce my neck, slice my jugular, spill my blood. The whip fell away from me as the tips of her fangs touched the pulse in my neck, and from deep in my throat came a low, menacing growl. I felt Zena freeze. I opened my eyes as another hate-filled growl trickled from my throat.

All of a sudden I realized what had been about to happen to me—what I'd been about to *let* happen.

I guess if I'd been the queen of the tumblers, like Tash, I might have done a triple back-flip with a twist, run on my hands in a circle around Zena, and cunningly attacked her from behind. Or if I'd possessed Kat's Dead-Eye-Dick skills with a stake, I could have whipped the underwire out of my bra and speared her with it, although that probably wouldn't have done much good, bras not being made of wood. But I was the Crosse triplet who sucked at ye olde art of *vampyr*-killing, as taught by Darkheart, so I just punched Zena in the face as hard as I could.

"Keep your hands and teeth *off* me, vamp!" I shouted as she rocked backward from my blow. One of her boot's stiletto heels caught on the whip's coils and the next moment she landed on the stage floor, her legs sprawled out in front of her. I bent down to the remnants of my Juicy hoodie and grabbed the letter opener from its pocket. "You want a girlfriend to cuddle up with on those long lonely days in the coffin, take out an ad in the *Times* personal column," I said tightly, "under 'Single Chalk-White Undead Female Seeks Same.' But don't you *ever* put the moves on me again!" I moved toward her. "Why am I telling you this, though? In a second you're going to be a big old grease spot."

Okay, here's a tip for if you ever get the drop on a vamp—don't piss it away by taking the time to deliver a few lines of snappy dialogue à la Bruce Willis in those old *Die Hard* movies. For one thing, the rest of us aren't Bruce and we're not in a movie, and for another, in a situation like that there's a good chance that the words coming out of your mouth probably aren't snappy dialogue, but nervous babbling.

I raised the letter opener and brought it down in an arc toward her. "Say your prayers, vamp, because you're about to—"

Something grabbed at one of my ankles. I crashed sideways, hitting my head hard on the chrome pole. Zena was on her feet in front of me, the whip in her hand.

"The old man bonded *oboroten* to you," she hissed. "Was bad mistake. For that he will live long enough to know you came to me not easily, as I planned, but in most unbearable agony."

She snapped her wrist and I felt the lash uncoil from my ankle. The tip of the lash darted toward her as she raised the stock, and I realized she intended to bind me to the pole again.

Tossing aside my stake, I threw myself into a desperate leap, closing the few feet between us and catching the whip as it began whistling into the air. It sliced like a hot blade through my palms and I forced myself to tighten my grip. I felt a sharp jerk and heard Zena snarl as she threw the lash down.

"No fucking problem, darling. I simply rip your arms off before drinking blood, *da?*" Her version of snappy dialogue, I suppose, and it just goes to show that even vampires shouldn't grandstand while they're going in for the kill. She took a step toward me and all hell broke loose.

I realized later that all hell must have been breaking loose for a few minutes. I'd been vaguely aware of a scuffle at one of the tables while I'd been doing my ill-advised Bruce Willis imitation, and the fight had apparently spread throughout the room. My attention only became riveted on the situation, however, when a gun went off at the side of the stage.

"Police! Don't take another step, lady, or my next one won't be a warning shot!" Detective Van Ryder held his weapon on Zena, obviously ready to carry out his threat. The problem was, he didn't know it was a hollow threat, since he was addressing a vampire who could take a lead-jacketed licking and keep on ticking, so to speak. Dropping the whip from my lacerated palms, I opened my mouth to warn him but it wasn't necessary.

Zena smiled her catlike smile at me, her gaze glittering. She still had a drop of my blood on her lip and as I watched she brought her finger to her mouth, caught the drop on the tip of it and licked her finger clean, her eyes never leaving mine. "I will wait for you to come to me again. I think wait will not be long," she purred. "*Do svidaniya,* my darling."

"I said stay where you—" Van Ryder's words ended in an oath as Zena, in the act of leaping off the stage and into the crowd, grabbed her whip and gave it one final flick in his direction. His gun flew from his hand and skittered across the stage.

I snatched up my stake and began sprinting down the runway after Zena, who was now slashing her way through the fighting crowd, but as I raced by Van Ryder he stiff-armed me, knocking the wind from my lungs and causing me to double over in an attempt to get my respiratory system back online again.

"Wha…the *hell?*" I wheezed furiously, glaring at him from my hunched-over and stomach-clutching position. "She's getting away!"

"She won't go far—this is her place of business," he said. "That's why I dropped by tonight in the first place, to question her about what happened here the night of your fiancé's stag party. I'll have her picked up tomorrow if I have to. Right now, my main concern isn't Zena or asking you what the hell you're doing on stage at a strip club, it's getting you out of here alive, and there's a good chance that won't happen if you wade into that crowd. Where's security?" he added tensely. "I know this dump has bouncers, dammit, a bunch of them already tried to stop me."

My breath had returned. I squinted past the footlights to the smoky and inadequately lit room, my anger at Van Ryder dissipating into stunned disbelief as I took in the scene.

It wasn't just a bar fight anymore. Even as I watched in shock I saw a man crash backward into a table, his throat streaming blood. Another patron a few feet away had fallen in the crush of brawlers, and I heard a high scream of pain come from him as a heavily-booted foot came down on his ankle. The next boot came down on his face and his scream abruptly cut off. Sickened, I glanced away and saw one of the burly bouncers who'd impeded Van Ryder clamp a hand on the shoulder of a man who was attacking another patron. Relieved, I began to turn to Van Ryder. Then I stopped, my blood turning to ice in my veins.

The bouncer probably died before he knew what was happening. The man he'd grabbed launched himself at the security man like a jaguar taking down a bull. I saw the flash of fully extended fangs as his canines impaled themselves into the bouncer's thick neck, and then the vamp gave a powerful sideways shake of his head. His fangs were so deeply embedded that the motion almost tore the bouncer's head off. The vamp stayed with him as he fell, drinking the blood that pumped upwards in weakening jets.

Now that my eyes had adjusted to the dimness beyond the bright stage, I realized similar scenes were taking place throughout the room. The handful of vamps I'd seen when I'd tried to escape from the stage earlier hadn't left with their mistress as I'd assumed they would; they'd stayed, and there were a lot more of them than I'd realized.

The Hot Box had turned into a slaughterhouse. That was terrible enough. But there was something that made it even worse, I realized with slow horror as I watched the carnage.

I wanted to join in.

"This place is a war zone." Van Ryder's strong fingers bit into my arm. "We've got to get out of here while we still can!"

"Have you called for backup?" I resisted his pull on my arm, my gaze on the unequal vamps-against-humans battle. Van Ryder hadn't seen how the bouncer had died, I decided, or maybe he had and his brain refused to process it. He was a homicide detective. Vampires weren't exactly part of his mind-set. His next words bore my supposition out.

"My cell phone's showing no reception in here so I'll have to call from the car, but the Maplesburg force isn't equipped to handle a full-scale PCP-fueled riot, anyway. We're going to have to call in the state troopers, maybe get the fire department over here with high-powered water hoses to use on these crazies." He jerked me toward him. "Every second counts, Megan. Move!"

He jerked my arm a second time and something inside me seemed to explode. "No, *you* move, Detective!" I thrust off his grip and, so swiftly that I barely realized what I was doing, I brought my stake up under his chin. The ivory tip pressed into his throat above his Adam's apple, and a minute bead of crimson welled up to stain the blade. Ignoring the agitated voice inside my head that was saying, *Uh, Megan, please let's take the stake out of the nice policeman's throat and go with him quietly, okay?* I went on hoarsely, "Back away from me very carefully, Van Ryder. Then get that gorgeous butt of yours in gear and get to your car as fast as you can. Drive like hell away from here, and whatever you do, don't change your mind and come back to try and save me," my hand clenched with the effort to keep myself from pushing the stake deeper, "because instead of thanking you, Detective, I think I might kill you."

"Zena Uzhasnoye drugged you somehow, didn't she?" he asked tightly, not moving away from me. "She did a Jonestown, put something in the drinks served here tonight that turned everyone wacko. Listen to me, Megan—I need to get you to a hospital where they can find out what's in your system and—"

I could feel my precarious control slipping completely away, and knew I couldn't hold on any longer. In one swift movement I stepped backward so that the stake was safely away from Van Ryder's throat and I was standing at the edge of the stage. Flexing my knees, I flung myself into one of the back flips that I'd had so little success with during my lessons with Darkheart.

But this time my form and execution were perfect. I landed lightly on my feet and looked up at Van Ryder on the stage. "I don't need to go to the hospital to know what's in my system, Detective. It's not spiked fruit punch and the poison didn't just enter me tonight. But as long as there's a trace of the real Megan Crosse left in me, I'm going to go down fighting, and if the infection that's working in me gives me the ability to take some of Zena's followers with me, so much the better." I hesitated before turning into the crowd. "When you call for backup, tell your people to bring stakes, not guns."

The first person I saw was Marilyn. The tall transvestite was holding her own against two vamps, but they were slowly backing her into a corner from which she wouldn't be able to escape. Blond wig askew, she raised a size-twelve stilettoed shoe and spiked it into the nearest vamp's kneecap before turning her attention to his undead pal. One large-knuckled hand crashed into the vampire's chin, while the red-painted acrylic nails of her other hand raked at his eyes. As her first opponent rushed at her again, I decided to even up the odds.

I took three fast steps toward the vamp, and then broke

stride. Acting under a compulsion I couldn't explain, I pressed the leather and ivory hilt of my stake to my lips and kissed it. "Be with me," I said under my breath. I didn't know where the words had come from, but as soon as I uttered them, an icy calm seemed to descend upon me. I reversed the stake in my hand and took two more strides toward the vampire.

His back was to me and he had seized Marilyn. As he went in for the kill, I thrust the polished ivory blade between his back ribs. Remembering Hetty Maisel's mocking advice, I gave the hilt the extra shove that would propel the stake's pointed tip deep into his unbeating heart. He dusted so quickly he didn't have time to turn his head to see who'd sent him to hell.

"So these mothers really *are* vampires?" Marilyn grunted. Her deep voice seemed less disconcerting than before, since the platinum wig was pushed back on her head like a casually-worn ball cap, exposing the buzz-cut brown hair. The tattoo revealed by the pushed-up satin sleeve on her muscled right forearm was a tip-off as to her gender, too. "I've been trying to tell myself they're some goth gang taking their wannabe fantasies a little too far, but that scenario isn't working for me anymore."

My side vision caught a blur of movement as the vamp she'd raked with her nails leapt at me, and I reacted without thinking, pivoting sharply to meet him side-on and back-handing my stake directly into his heart. Impaled in midair, he gave a fury-filled scream that broke off abruptly as he disintegrated.

I turned back to a disconcerted-looking Marilyn, the strangely icy calm that filled me not affected in the least by what I'd just done. "Not wannabes, the real thing," I confirmed, my gaze roaming the room to find my next target. "My advice to you is to find a place to hide and—"

"Bull-*crappies*, girlfriend!" Marilyn's arched and plucked eyebrows drew into a ferocious scowl. "This leatherneck's never run from a fight yet. Pantyhose or no pantyhose, I don't intend to start now!"

My concentration was temporarily broken. I glanced at the tattoo on her arm and saw the inked depiction of an eagle, a globe and an anchor. "You were in the marines?" I asked, trying to keep the surprise from my tone.

"*Semper* fuckin' *fi*, and proud of it, girlfriend," Marilyn growled. "So what do I do, find a hunk of wood and start aiming for the hearts of these unfriendlies?" Even as she spoke she grabbed a nearby chair, smashed it against a table and selected a length of chair-leg from the wreckage.

"That's basically it. Although you seemed to be doing pretty well with those nails. Revlon Red?" I couldn't help asking as I began to turn away.

"Cherries in the Snow," Marilyn corrected me. "And these acrylic wraps are way too expensive to risk breaking one, girlfriend. Before you go, tell me—with moves like that, who are you? Some kind of hereditary vamp killer like the chick in that old TV show?"

I was unable to keep the bitterness from my tone. "No, I think I'm what they call a vamp, girlfriend. Like you, I've got the moves and the accessories—" I gestured to my stake "—but I'm just an impersonator. Good hunting, marine."

Marilyn's gaze narrowed, as if she were sizing me up as a future enemy. "Good hunting, vamp," she said slowly, before moving into the crowd and becoming lost to my view.

I saw sights that night I'll never completely get out of my mind and if it's all the same to you, I'd rather not dwell on them in gory detail. There must have been a couple of dozen of Zena's boys there—all the *vampyrs* at the Hot Box were male; I assume because they'd been better able to blend in with the rest of the campers earlier—and by the time I joined the fray they'd already killed or savaged too many to count. I stepped over bodies, stepped on bodies, saw bodies piled up like cordwood; and through it all, I moved like an automaton, searching out my prey and staking them as expeditiously as I could. About twenty-five minutes into my self-appointed mission, it became obvious that the vamps had begun to realize that someone in the room was an opponent who knew how to kill them and my encounters with them became increasingly hard-fought. But I kept staking, the *vampyrs* attacking me kept turning to dust in front of my eyes, and my icy certainty of what I was kept increasing.

My strength was vamplike, my agility was vamplike and my bloodlust was vamplike. I hadn't completely turned yet, but I was definitely the triplet who'd been marked by Zena.

Which meant I couldn't ever go home again.

Chapter 12

The way I almost got killed was stupid, but in my own defence, I was running on empty by then. Worse, I didn't know it. I'd killed thirteen vampires in ninety minutes, which works out to a right arm so sore that I'd switched the stake to my left and a numbness I attributed to determination, but which was probably post-traumatic stress. My decision to find another place to live so I wouldn't have entrance privileges to the Crosse mansion was part of that stress, but my reserves drained completely when I saw Marilyn among the dead. During my search-and-destroy exercise, I'd glimpsed her using her chair-leg stake like a bayonet and grinning ferociously everytime she nailed an unfriendly. But her luck had run out.

Ignoring those Hot Box patrons who were wandering around like shell-shocked soldiers—who could blame them; one minute they'd been drunkenly revved up to watch nekked wimmen, and the next they'd seen the gates of hell open—I was glancing around the room to see if there were any vampires left to kill, when my gaze fell on a scrap of red beneath an overturned table. I knew it was Marilyn even before I lifted the table and saw the marine tattoo on the outflung arm. Her wig was missing, and suddenly it seemed important to me to find it and replace it on her head.

"Looking for something?" I turned to see the vamp I'd noticed from the stage when I'd been trying to escape. He spun the platinum wig on his finger before tossing it aside. "Let's rock and roll, blondie. You wiped the floor with those other undead wimps, but let's see how you do against a real man."

"*He* was a real man," I said, glancing again at Marilyn. "You're just dust in the making." I turned as if to walk away. At the moment I gauged his rush at me had brought him within striking distance, I whirled, my arm straight and the stake reversed in my hand so the point was directed backward from my fist. Feeling the momentum of my spin drive it deep into his chest, I yanked the stake out and began heading for the door, exhaustion rolling over me like a wave.

I heard a sharp grunt behind me and turned to find myself face to face with the vampire I thought I'd killed. My stake still reversed in my grasp for a backhand strike, I wasted a precious nano-second getting it into position, knowing even as I began my thrust that I'd left it too late.

Since I was expecting to have my throat ripped open, it was kind of anticlimactic to feel something sharp jabbing into my palm. I said, "Ouch!" before I could help myself, wished in chagrin that my last words before I died hadn't made me sound like Vamp-Killing Barbie and then watched in astonishment as the vamp I hadn't restaked dusted.

When he did, I saw the man who'd been behind him. Detective Van Ryder's skin was gray and his eyes held the same staring-into-hell-too-long expression I suspected mine did. He looked exhausted and strained and hotter than Brad Pitt. I debated whether to thank him for saving my life or dispense with the small talk and ask him if he wanted to have meaningless sex with me all night long. In the end I just gritted my teeth at him.

"Uh, my hand?" The business end of the chunk of wood he was holding was still inserted into my palm. He followed my gaze.

"Shit!" Gripping my left wrist to steady it, he carefully withdrew the stake. The point hadn't gone all the way through, but it had done enough damage so that as it was extracted the blood welled up like a miniature oil well. Van Ryder exhaled. "This should be cleaned and stitched and those whip-slashes need to be disinfected. I'll take you to the hosp—"

I cut him off. "No hospitals, no doctors. I don't want to run the risk of some E.R. physician giving me a shot of something that could dull my reflexes while I still need them." I hesitated, remembering my own initial denial and wondering how I was going to convince him not to dismiss what he'd seen tonight. I was still groping for words when he spoke, his tone wry.

"God, and to think I asked to be transfered from L.A. to get away from all this craziness for a while. Nice little upstate New York town, I thought, probably spend most of my time investigating missing library books. Two weeks after I arrive, I find out I've landed in vamp central."

I blinked at him. "You know...I mean, you believe in..."

"Vampires? Yeah," Van Ryder's smile faded. "Ever since Carmel Lopez, my former partner, went up against one and was killed. Or maybe it's more accurate to say that I began to believe in them the night after I attended Carmel's funeral, when I found my newly undead partner waiting for me in an alley. That was also the night I realized the movies and books were right, and staking them through the heart was how you killed them," he shrugged. "But this was a murder spree. I'd bet my badge none of these victims is going to rise again."

"I don't think so, either." I looked at him. "What now, Detective? Do you call the police station and see if they buy the PCP-riot story you tried to sell me earlier?"

He shook his head and met my eyes. "Now we leave before someone else calls the cops and we have to try and explain what happened here. You hungry?"

"God, no," I began reflexively. Then I stopped. "Actually, I am," I said, surprised. "Ravenous, in fact."

Van Ryder's smile widened. "There's a big pot of spaghetti Bolognese sauce on my stove at home. I'll let you eat as much as you want in return for telling me how a nice girl like you got so good at vamp-killing." He looked thoughtful. "And also whether you really meant it when you told me I had a gorgeous butt."

So that was how I ended up having my first date with Detective Bedroom Eyes, aka Van Ryder, whose last name wasn't Van Ryder, but simply Ryder. His first name was

Donovan, short form Van, which meant that I'd been constantly calling him by his full name up until then, like some bodice-ripper heroine. You know—as Althea felt herself falling into Rock's eyes, she breathed, "Rockwell Wilder, I believe I'm falling in love with you." And don't think that very sentence didn't run through my mind a couple of hundred times that night, without the Rockwell Wilder part, of course. Van was funny and sexy and easy to talk to, and as a major plus, his spaghetti Bolognese was to die for.

"So you or one of your sisters inherited this Lilith title from your mother?" Van picked up the bottle of California red we'd been depleting. I held out my wineglass.

"Daughter of Lilith," I clarified. "That's how it works if you come from one of the ancient families with slayer blood, apparently. You're the chosen one, *bam*, that's your destiny whether you had other plans for your life or not. Tash would be perfectly okay if it turned out she was this generation's Daughter of the Darkheart line, but Kat's non-thrilled about the prospect."

"After watching you in action tonight, I don't think either of them has to worry." He reached for my plate. "More spaghetti? More salad? I promised you could pig out, remember?"

"I already have." I let my glance linger on his rear view as he rinsed our plates in the sink but when he turned to open the dishwasher I hastily pretended to be gazing around his apartment. That took about half a second, since the decor in Van's walk-up bachelor over an appliance-repair business seemed to consist more of unpacked boxes than anything else. I reflected without enthusiasm that tomorrow I'd be looking for an apartment myself. I didn't trust myself to be in the same house as my sisters in case I turned, and although I hadn't told Tashya that when I'd phoned her an hour ago to let her know what had happened, tomorrow I intended to warn both her and Kat. I wondered if Van's apartment was typical of what was available in Maplesburg, and tried to counter my sudden depression with another gulp of wine. But the *in vino, veritas* thing kicked in just then and the glow that the wine had spread through me fizzled away, leaving me to face the truth.

I had no right to be sitting here at Van's kitchen table wearing one of his shirts, eating his spaghetti and checking out his butt. He seemed to think I'd fought at the Hot Box like a Daughter of Lilith, but I knew better. I'd slaughtered like a vamp, coldly and mercilessly. And I couldn't wait to do it again.

But I had even more compelling proof that I bore the mark of evil: the sick desire I'd felt when Zena had been seducing me. Some of that desire had been a mirage created by her *glamyr,* but not all of it. She'd seduced me too easily. That had to mean that part of me hadn't needed to be seduced. And although I'd found the strength to reject her tonight, I couldn't count on having that same strength the next time the darkness rose up in me. That next time could be a week from now, a month from now…or a minute from now.

I shoved my chair back from the table so abruptly that my wineglass almost tipped over. "I've got to go," I said to Van's back as he finished filling the coffeemaker on the counter and flicked its switch. "Thanks for the spaghetti and the wine and the Bactine on my hand," I babbled.

"And for saving my life back there at the club, of course. But when I phoned Tash I told her I'd be home soon." I reached the door. "I'll have your shirt laundered tomorrow, okay? Uh, thanks for the meal—"

"And the wine and for stabbing you in the hand while saving you from a vamp you probably could have killed yourself. I think we've already established the thanks part, Megan." Van crossed the nine feet that separated his so-called kitchen from his so-called living room in two long strides and put his hand on the edge of the door. I switched tactics.

"Well, I am grateful and I wanted you to know it. But like you just said, you also shoved a giant splinter into my palm and although I totally don't want you to feel bad about that, I guess I'd better go to the emergency room and have it looked at by a doctor. So that's what I'll do." I looked expectantly at him and then at his hand, still gripping the door. "Now," I added, just in case I hadn't made myself clear.

"To the same hospital you didn't want to go to an hour ago?" He shook his head. "My keenly honed detective intuition's telling me you're feeding me a line of bullshit," he stepped away from the door, "which is okay, if that's what you feel you have to do. I just want you to know I recognize crap when it's being shoveled at me, even when I don't know what I did to merit it. I'll walk you down to your car."

I felt like what he'd just accused me of shoveling at him. I nudged the door with my foot, swinging it closed again, and walked back to the table. Lifting my wineglass, I drained it. Then I picked up the almost-empty bottle, tipped it to my lips, and drained it, too, which sounds more dramatic than it was because there were barely a couple of drops of wine left in it. But even if I'd knocked back a half-dozen shots of Jack Daniel's they wouldn't have made what I had to say any easier.

"It's not you, it's me," I told Van by way of preamble.

"Save it, Megan," he replied, looking irritated. "I thought I felt something good starting between us. You didn't. The speech isn't necessary."

"It kind of is," I insisted, "because in this case the speech goes, 'It's not you, it's me. I'm a vamp.'" I glanced at the wooden salad bowl, still on the table, and the wooden servers resting inside it. I extracted the fork server and thrust it at him. "You should arm yourself."

Van took the server from me, flicked a stray piece of lettuce from its tines and tossed it onto the table. Gently he pushed me back into my seat and pulled his own chair beside me, taking my hands loosely in his. "I've seen enough cops go through what you're feeling right now that I should have recognized the signs. Guilt comes with the territory of any job that forces violence upon you. You think there must have been some way you could have handled the situation better, maybe saved a few more lives. From there it's a short step to believing you're just as responsible for the carnage as the bad guys—"

I pulled my hands from his. "There's one part of the Darkheart legacy I didn't tell you. Zena put her mark on one of Angelica's babies during their final battle. That baby was me."

Slowly, Van sat back. "And now the Vamp Queen's calling in her marker, so to speak?" he asked carefully. "That's what that little performance on the Hot Box stage was all about?"

I chose my words with equal care. "More like her marker's calling itself in. I told myself I had a good reason tonight for ending up at the one place where I'd be almost sure to run into Zena, but when I looked into her eyes, I realized the truth."

"Which was?" he prompted with professional detachment.

I looked down at my hands. "That I'd been drawn to her," I said, my whisper unsteady. "That from the start some part of me had known she was my destiny."

With those words I felt as if a floodgate had opened inside me. I let everything pour out on Van—the violent need to join in the blood battle taking place on the Hot Box floor that had swept through me, my vamp cruelty and coldness during the fight. I told him how inept I'd been during Darkheart's training, and how starkly that ineptness contrasted with the dark power that had settled over me when I'd bleakly accepted what I was. I even related the vision I'd had of myself stalking Kat and Tashya.

"That part *won't* come true," I said with sharp emphasis. "I'll make sure that Kat gets a locksmith out to the mansion to change the locks and security codes. It won't be my home anymore, so when the final change comes I won't be able to enter. But by that time I'll have done what I have to do, anyway."

"You intend to stake yourself." The warm brown of Van's eyes took on a chill.

"I don't know if I could," I said. "So I've come up with another plan. Tomorrow I'll buy a length of heavy chain and a padlock at the hardware store. As soon as I start feeling that the vamp part of me is taking over the Megan part, I intend to go to my car and chain myself to one of its axles. Then I'll throw the key to the padlock away and wait for the sun to come up."

"Dammit, Megan, you're talking about killing yourself!" he expostulated.

"I'm talking about killing the monster I'll become," I corrected him. I held his gaze. "I felt something good between us tonight, too, Van, and if things were different I'd have liked to take things further with you. But I don't have much of a future and you do. Starting something with me would be the stupidest mistake you ever made."

For the second time that evening I rose from his kitchen table. He rose with me, his posture tense. "Stupider than jumping off a garage roof with a bedsheet parachute when I was seven? Stupider than going white-water rafting on the Colorado River when I didn't have the first clue about what I was doing, just to impress a girl I had a crush on at the time?"

I shook my head, wishing he weren't making this harder. "It's not the same thing," I said, turning to leave.

"Okay, how about stupider than falling like a ton of bricks for a woman who was wearing a wedding dress the first time I laid eyes on her?" he demanded, his hand on on my shoulder. He turned me to face him. "And the whole time I was attempting to question her about her missing groom, barely being able to think past the way she looked, the perfume she was wearing, how beautiful her eyes were? If we're talking about stupid mistakes, that one's got to be in the top ten, wouldn't you say?"

"My point exactly." I tried to shrug off his hand but he tightened his grip.

"And mine is that I'm a risk-taker from way back. I still remember how it felt to fly off that garage roof, dammit—

like just for a second, I was an angel. Yeah, I busted my leg, but it was worth it. Same with the rafting. I didn't get the girl, but I'll never forget the thrill of staring death in the face and knowing I'd beaten it." His voice was a rasp. "What I'm trying to say is that if there's a risk here I'm willing to take it, because I think there's a chance it could be worth it—for both of us. You don't know for sure whether or not you'll turn, just as I don't know whether I'll get shot on the job tomorrow," he smiled with sudden wryness. "Of course, after a few days of getting to know each other, you might end up bored to tears and I might decide you're too high-maintenance, but at least we won't spend the rest of our lives wondering what might have been."

Regretfully but firmly, I told him that I intended to do the responsible thing and walk out of his life. I looked into his eyes, part of my mind wondering if I'd describe their color more as bittersweet chocolate or milk chocolate. I noticed a tiny scar by his mouth, and knew I'd never have the chance to ask him if he'd fallen off his bike when he'd been a kid or whether it was a legacy of his roof-jumping days. I let myself appreciate the broadness of his shoulders, the sexy fullness of his lower lip, the muscled length of his legs, and virtuously turned him down because I'm a friggin' saint, right?

Wrong.

"You have to promise me one thing," I said, bringing my hand to his mouth and brushing a fingertip against the tiny half-moon scar by his lip. "No, two things."

"I promise." His response was immediate.

"Hear me out first. If I start going fang-girl, you've got to stake me."

He nodded. "I promise, Megan. But I'd do it for the same reason Darkheart staked your mother—to save you, not myself."

"I know," I said softly, moving the tip of my finger from the corner of his mouth. "I never paid you for the meal," I murmured, slipping my fingertip past his bottom lip and feeling his teeth gently catch hold of it. "You know, telling you whether I meant it when I said you had a gorgeous butt?"

He released my finger long enough to speak. "That was just a ploy to get you here. I knew you meant it. You kept checking me out, the same way I kept checking you out. What's the second thing I have to promise?" He caught my finger again. His tongue flicked against it, and I felt like I was about to miniorgasm right then and there.

"Second promise?" I asked weakly. "Oh, right, your second promise. It involves police-issue handcuffs."

"The unsanctioned use of?" Van said against my finger. "On you or me?"

"Me," I decided. "For tonight, anyway. After dawn we can try them on you."

"I'm a police detective," he reminded me. "Do you really think I'm going to let a woman who was recently a prime suspect strip me, cuff me to my bed and do whatever she wants to me while I'm helpless to stop her?"

"Yes, I do, Detective," I breathed, moving my fingertips from his mouth and rising slightly on my toes so that my lips were against his. "In fact, all the evidence seems to indicate that you're getting hot just imagining how it's going to be."

"Hot? Try on fire," he muttered, bringing his mouth harder against mine in the beginning of a kiss.

I say the beginning of a kiss because just as my tongue and his touched, something thudded so resoundingly against the apartment's one small window that for a moment I thought it must have broken. Locked in our embrace, Van and I stared at the window for a split second.

"Zena," I said.

"Or one of her undead posse," he agreed shortly.

We flew apart, me grabbing my stake from the waistband of my Juicys and Van reaching for the wooden salad fork on the table. We both reached the window at the same time, and he unlatched it while I raised it. As the warped frame screeched reluctantly upwards, an even more spine-tingling sound assaulted my ears. Van frowned. "Vamps don't howl. That's a damn dog."

"Guess again." Anger gave me the strength to shove the window fully open. I stuck my head out and looked past the metal fire escape to the Dumpster below. From atop its reeking contents, golden eyes glared up at me and black-tipped hackles rose as the silver muzzle rose again in a howl. I ducked back inside and slammed the window shut.

"It's not a damned dog, it's my damned *oboroten*," I said wrathfully.

Chapter 13

"Oh. My. God," Tash exclaimed in the doorway of unit seven, Park Vista Motel. "Could you have *chosen* more of a dump?"

"On the plus side, it's right across the road from Take-a-Nip Liquor," Kat said dubiously. "Handy for when you want to serve your guests something a step up from rubbing alcohol."

It was the morning after my non-roll in the sheets with Van and I was in no mood for my sisters' comments. The Park Vista *was* a dump, but at least it had a bed. I'd awoken this morning in the backseat of the Mini, and my temper hadn't been improved when I'd glanced into the front of the car. During the night Mikhail had shape-shifted again, this time from the human form in which he'd confronted me after we'd driven away from Van's apartment, back to a wolf again. He was curled up cozily, his canine form a better choice for car-sleeping.

"I can't *believe* you were spying on me," I'd raged at him after making a hasty apology to Van, promising to see him the following night and racing out of his apartment to the Dumpster. My speed caught Mikhail by surprise, giving me the opportunity to haul him out of the Dumpster by his ruff before he could begin shape-shifting from wolf to man. I'd kept my grip on him while we'd made our way to the car, coming out of the alley to the sidewalk just as a late-night dog-walker and his pooch went by.

The man had smiled sympathetically at my furious face. "Someone won't hurry up with his tinkles? I swear, some evenings Fritzi drags me around the block a dozen times before he goes."

I hadn't replied, but had grimly opened the door of the Mini for Mikhail. By the time I'd gone around to the driver's side he was six-foot-four of gorgeous male again— not that I cared.

"You violated the contract between *oborotni* and—" he began ominously, but I cut him off.

"*Screw* the contract! You violated my privacy!" Out of the corner of my eye I saw him stiffen. Then he leaned over and sniffed me. I jerked away from him, almost running the Mini onto the deserted sidewalk. "Stop that!" I said, taken aback. "God, talk about rude! *Oboroten* or no *oboroten,* you just can't go around sniffing—" I stopped, hearing a growl trickle from deep in his throat. I braked for a red light and turned to him. "What?" I snapped, my patience at an end. "Stop inhaling me and tell me what your problem is."

"You stink of *vampyr,*" Mikhail said coldly. "I can't tell if it's you or the bitch who tried to turn you tonight. Go, it's green," he added.

I'd stared at him, flabbergasted—a word I've always wanted to use, by the way. Then I collected myself and started driving again. "Okay, so you know about the Hot Box and Zena. You want to tell me how you found out?" I said in a terse, no-more-fucking-with-me voice. "Oh, and also? How about filling me in as to why you didn't try to *save my ass!*"

"Because you made sure I couldn't by using a childish trick to get away from me!" he shouted back. "I arrived at the club in time to see you and Van Ryder peeling out of the parking lot in separate cars and I had to start tracking your fucking vehicle again! It's not like following a human scent, sweetheart!"

I was momentarily distracted. "You followed the scent of my *tires* to the Hot Box?"

"How else?" he demanded. "But before I began tracking you and your detective to his place, I took the time to trace your movements inside the club." His voice descended to a low, flat tone. "You were in her office. You killed a *vampyr* there, but not Zena—the scent clinging to the ashes wasn't strong enough to have belonged to an ancient. Then you went on stage and that's where she found you. Her undead stench is all over you, but somehow you escaped her and began killing."

"*Vamps,*" I said in the same flat tone as he'd used. "I began killing vamps. That's a good thing, as I understand it."

"Did it feel like a good thing while you were doing it?"

Wrenching the steering wheel over, I pulled the Mini

into a parking lot and turned to him. "What's that supposed to mean?" I demanded. "If you're asking whether I felt a twinge of remorseful kinship every time I dusted one of the creeps who were trying to kill me, the answer's no! I may have killed like a vamp, but none of my targets were human, okay? That should be proof enough even for you that I haven't turned yet!"

"You killed like a vamp?" Mikhail went very still. "That's how it felt to you?"

I took a breath, intending to bluster my way out of my unfortunate slip of the tongue, but then I stopped, knowing it was no use. I let my breath out and met Mikhail's eyes. "That's not just how it felt, that's how it was," I said in defeat. "You were right, Mikey-baby—I'm the one she marked. And tonight I realized that the change in me has already begun."

We spent the next two hours in the car while, for the second time that night, I confessed all…my reaction to Zena, the vision I'd had of stalking Kat and Tash, how I'd felt darkly alive and focused on the club's killing floor. Mikhail didn't say "I told you so," as I'd been expecting him to, and part of me wished he would be his usual abrasive self so I could be a jerk, too. But all he did was listen to the end, agree that going home wasn't a good idea, then tell me that I looked tired and I should get some sleep.

His staggeringly unsatisfactory response totally bore out my theory that if men are from Mars and women are from Venus, shape-shifting wolves are from another solar system altogether and even if intergalactic travel becomes possible in my lifetime, I don't want to go there.

Anyway, as I said, he had a good sleep, I didn't, and now

here I was in the Park Vista Motel listening to my sisters' reactions to my new home away from home.

"I'm not sitting on that bed," Tash declared.

"Suit yourself. Go outside and join Darkheart and Mikhail at the broken picnic table if you want." Totally depressed, I lay back on the grungy-looking coverlet and punched a pillow under my head before reaching under the bed and coming up with the paper-bagged bottle I'd stashed there an hour ago. I peeled off the bag and squinted at the label before twisting off the cap. "I can't offer cocktails, but as you noted, Kat, the Take-a-Nip is mighty handy for those times when nothing but six-week-old Scotch will do. This is one of those times."

Kat grabbed the bottle from me, but not before I'd taken a sip. I sat up on the bed, gagging, and she looked at me without pity. "You're not a drinker, Meg, especially not of rotgut at eleven in the morning. Pull yourself together."

"That's easy for you to say," I choked. "You're not the one who's turning into a fucking vampire." The tears that had welled up from the raw liquor suddenly began gushing for real. Appalled, I tried to hold them back, but it seemed as if a water main had abruptly sprung a leak behind my eyes. "Look at me," I wailed, catching a glimpse of myself in the dresser's cracked mirror. "My hair's a mess, I haven't had a shower this morning and I'm wearing a crumpled man's shirt over a blood-speckled bra. I'm living in the motel from hell and I'm bound by some ancient contract I can't get out of to a shape-shifter who tells me I smell of vamp. And you know what's the worst part?" I caught the roll of toilet paper that Tash, standing in the doorway of the bathroom, tossed my way. Blowing my nose on the trailing end without bothering to tear it off, I looked miserably at my sisters. "This is the friggin' *upside!* Things are only going to go downhill from here!"

"I never thought of it that way, but you're right," Tash said. "Wow, your life really *does* suck, Meg." She looked at Kat. "Are you going to tell her or am I?"

"Tell me what?" I sniffed. A thought struck me and I tried to rise above my self-pity. "Oh, God, Kat—you proved yourself a Daughter of Lilith last night? You cleaned up that vamp hotbed of a mausoleum and Darkheart realized you were the triplet who inherited Mom's title, right?"

"Not right," Tash said before Kat could reply. "She and Grandfather Darkheart waited all night for nothing. There weren't any vamps there."

"Although I did see a couple of really husky-looking rats." Kat shuddered delicately. Her gaze grew serious. "When you phoned this morning and told Grandfather Darkheart what had happened at the Hot Box last night with you and Zena, including the part where you and she almost…" She paused considerately.

"Where she and I almost got it on together?" I finished for her. I waved a listless hand. "Don't bother trying to tiptoe around the subject, Kat. I fell for a female, big deal. Yeah, she's older than dirt, and yeah, she's undead, but hey, all that went through my mind when we were nearly lip-locking was how hot she was and how great it would be to sleep with her in the daytime and hunt with her at night." Fresh tears leaked from my eyes and I reached for the toilet-paper roll again. "I'm going to hell, aren't I? I'm going to turn into a mini-Zena and end up in hell after I'm dusted."

"Not necessarily," Tash said over her shoulder as she peered into the mirror and fluffed her curls. "All we have to do is stake her before you turn vamp. In fact, even if you *do* turn vamp, as long as the mistress who made you is destroyed before you taste blood, you're home free. Good news, huh?"

Slowly I set down the roll of toilet paper. I swung my legs off the bed and planted my sneakered feet on the floor. "And just how long has everyone but me known this choice little nugget of information?" I asked in an ominous voice.

"Only since this morning," Kat said quickly. "Grandfather told us there might be a way we could save you."

"*We've* only known since this morning," Tashya corrected her. "Grandfather Darkheart's known all along, but he didn't want to tell us until we were further in our training, in case we did something rash like try to take on Zena before we were ready."

"Which is kind of ironic, since *I* was the schmuck who went up against Zena with no preparation," I said tightly. "I suppose Mikhail knew all along, too?"

"I don't think so," Kat frowned. "Sweetie, Tash overstated things slightly. Grandfather said there *might* be a way we could save you. Zena's an ancient, and the rules that apply to ordinary vamps don't apply to her. She can take some sunlight without bursting into flames, she's learned to fake a heartbeat and it's possible that her death won't save her victims from turning when their time comes, the way it would if she weren't so powerful. But Grandfather's focused his research on this one point and he's found two old references to a *vampyr* called Alexa, who by all accounts was even more powerful than Zena.

One of the references states that when this Alexa was staked by a Daughter, those of her victims who hadn't yet hunted with her reverted to being human. The other reference insists that didn't happen, and anyone she'd infected stayed infected."

"But Grandfather says the second book's author was a crackpot monk whose work's been discredited," Tash volunteered.

"Let me get this straight," I said, trying to keep the shakiness from my voice. "Despite the fact that it's commonly believed the death of a vamp like Zena won't release her victims, from the start Darkheart's known of at least one documented case where they got a get-out-of-vamphood-free card when the queen was dusted? And he let me go on believing I was *doomed?*

"Not exactly, Meg," Tash rushed hotly to Darkheart's defence. "Don't forget, because you only bore a single mark, not two, he hoped you wouldn't turn at all. Although he did mention he'd gotten that particular theory from the mad monk's writings," she added a little less confidently.

"That's it." I got to my feet, my hands clenched at my sides. "I'm having this out with him right now. No wonder Mom tried to break away from him and live her own life, instead of having him run it for her!"

"Sweetie, wait." As I began to push past Kat, she stopped me. "He's already heard the lecture," she said firmly. "From us. We told him we weren't going to stand for his paternalistic grandfather-knows-best crap anymore. When we said we wouldn't continue training until he promised to change his ways, he agreed, so don't go marching out there and upset all our delicate blackmail-slash-negotiations. Tell him you'll be happy to join our Zena-hunting group tonight and you don't even mind wearing a cross against your skin, so if anything starts happening with you we'll get a heads-up. I didn't think that was necessary but—"

"No, he's right to take some precautions against me, Kat," I interrupted. "You're having the locks changed today, too?"

"I'll call the security company as soon as I get home," she promised. She looked at her watch. "Which will be soon, since we should have started our Sweatin' with the Vampies workout ten minutes ago. Usually Grandfather gets totally antsy if we don't start on time, but our little chat with him this morning must have put the fear of the Crosse triplets into him, no?"

"Uh, more like the fear of Mikey-baby," Tash said in an odd voice as she stared out of the window. "That *is* Mikhail standing over Grandfather, isn't it, Megan?"

My startled glance followed hers. Outside on the handkerchief-sized patch of weeds with which the motel's owners justified their establishment's name, an unsettling tableau was being enacted. Darkheart was lying prone on the ground by the picnic table. Mikhail, in wolf mode and with his silver-tipped ruff making his muscular form look even more intimidating, was baring his gleaming teeth only inches from Darkheart's throat.

"Yes, that's my *oboroten*," I said slowly. "I think he might be a tiny bit pissed off at his old master for keeping me in the dark about how I can save my life. I'd better call him off as soon as I change into the clean clothes you brought me, Kat."

Before I give the wrong impression here, let me just say

that I *did* hurry. No, really, I was out of my grubby Juicy pants and borrowed shirt and into the Paper Denim & Cloth jeans and Custo top Kat had brought in less than five minutes. Okay, ten, because I had a five-minute shower in between outfits, which is a land speed record for me. And brushing my hair only took a few minutes more. Still, there was quite a knot of nervous onlookers surrounding Darkheart and Mikhail when my sisters and I exited unit seven. Ignoring my fellow motel guests, I walked up to Darkheart and looked down at him.

"Mom wanted us raised in a country where we wouldn't be shackled by the past," I said. "I respect you for carrying out her wishes. But you've got to respect us, too. We're not the babies you remember, we've grown into women who can work with you, but not under you. Are we clear on that, Darkheart?"

"*Da*, is clear," he said, meeting my eyes. "Was total fuck-up on my part, granddaughter."

I was startled into a smile and saw an answering glimmer of humor in his gaze. "And from now on you'll keep us in the loop?"

He nodded, the flash of humor I'd seen disappearing from his expression. "I lost daughter through my own fault," he said quietly. "Will not make same mistakes with granddaughters."

There was no mistaking the throb of emotion in his tone. Before the leaky water main behind my eyes could go into action again, this time with an audience of strangers surrounding me, I gave Darkheart a quick nod. "I'll see you just before sunset tonight." I snapped my fingers sharply. "Mikhail, release!" Immediately the huge wolf moved away from Darkheart to my side. "Come on, big guy, we're going for a car ride," I said as I turned toward my parked Mini.

"You know I had no choice about what I did back there," Mikhail said a few minutes later. He'd transformed from canine to human form in the backseat and now he maneuvered his jeans-clad legs into the front of the car before wrestling himself the rest of the way into the passenger seat.

"Even so, it was sweet of you to almost savage an old man in my defense," I retorted. "But I think you did have a choice," I added in an undertone.

He gave a short laugh. "If you're trying to convince yourself I went for Darkheart because I'm beginning to feel something for you, you're wrong. My mandate's simple— someone puts you in harm's way, I go after him. Anton should have told you there might be an escape clause to becoming a vampire, to save you the pain I saw you going through last night."

I took my gaze briefly from the road. "You saw my pain last night," I said disbelievingly. "Yeah, right. You saw my pain so deeply that it was all you could do to stay awake while I poured my heart out. Mike, honey, a word of advice—stick to what you do best, which is glaring and growling. Don't try to pretend you're a sensitive male."

"I'm not," he folded his arms across his chest. "I couldn't be even if I wanted to. In case you haven't realized it, I'm not human the way you are or Anton is, and my responses aren't always human, either. That doesn't mean I'm insensitive, it just means I'm part wolf." He was silent a moment. "Besides, I was getting a lot of sensory input from you last night," he muttered. "I was trying to filter that out while I was listening to what you were saying."

"Sensory input?" I asked curiously. "Like what?"

"Like nothing." He seemed suddenly uncomfortable. "Just a wolf thing, it's not important. Do you have a destination in mind, or are we just driving aimlessly?"

"I have a destination in mind," I said, proving it by slowing for a left turn. "But really, I'm interested. What kind of sensory input were you getting from me?"

He looked out the window beside him. "Scent."

"You mean you could smell Zena on me?" I sighed in exasperation. "Look, enough with the telling me I reek of vamp. I get it. I'm tired of hearing it. I don't need to be reminded of it everytime we talk—"

"Sex." His interruption was barely audible.

"Sex?" I repeated, confused. "What do you mean, se—" Appalled understanding suddenly swept through me. I shot him a furious look, heard a car horn blare, and jerked the Mini's wheel just in time to avoid clipping another car. "I didn't *have* sex with Van last night," I said tightly. "Maybe I wanted to, but just when things started heating up between us, you crashed our party! So there's no way I gave off any kind of scent, okay? And for your information, I shower afterwards, anyway. *God,* I can't believe you!"

"I didn't say I could smell a man on you, I said I could smell sex. *Your* sex—the heat you felt." He took his gaze from the window and directed it at me. I kept my eyes straight forward and felt the burn in my cheeks. "So what's he like, this Van Ryder who got you so hot?"

"He's a human," I snapped. "He's funny and considerate and interesting and like I told you last night, he's up on the whole vamp thing, from his time with the LAPD. And yes, he's totally hot. Can we talk about something else? Start looking for a trailer park, I think there's one around here somewhere."

"You try shape-shifter sex, you never go back," Mikhail observed, looking out the window again. "Why a trailer park?"

"Dream on," I snapped in response to his comment before answering his question. "Cherry, the stripper I had to stake last night, mentioned she lived in a trailer. I want to find an address for her parents so I can let them know she's dead." The bright day seemed to cloud over as I remembered her dying words.

"Okay." Mikhail was silent for a moment, and then he cleared his throat. "That's really considerate of you. You must feel pretty sad about having to stake her, and I imagine that writing to her parents is going to be hard for you. Do you want to talk about it?"

He sounded so much like a bad imitation of Barbara Walters that I couldn't help myself. I laughed, and all of sudden the day was sunny again. Mikhail glared at me, I laughed harder and slowly his glare faded.

"I thought I'd give it a shot, but it's not me, is it?" Smiling wryly, he reached over and tucked a piece of my hair behind my ear. "It's not that I don't feel these things, it's just that I don't think of putting them into words. I get a constant flow of information from you without you saying a thing, and I forget that your senses don't work like mine."

His teeth gleamed white against the tan of his skin. The June breeze coming in through the partially opened windows ruffled the midnight blackness of his hair, while the sunlight glinted off the silver-chunked strands. His one-sided smile created a slash of amusement in his cheek and as his gaze rested on me I could pick out tiny flecks of green mixed in with the hazel and gold. Shape-shifter sex probably involved a lot of ripped clothes, I mused…screams of ecstasy…multiple orgas—

"Trailer park." Mikhail's voice sounded strangled. "Over there. Make your turn."

I felt as though someone had thrown a bucket of ice-water on me. Jerking my attention back to the here and now, I saw a poorly paved drive leading from the road and cranked the Mini's wheel over to make the turn. A peeling sign announced Shamrock Trailer Court, but I barely took it in.

"You sensed what I was imagining, didn't you?" I said between clenched teeth. I braked the car. "It was idle curiosity, okay? People do that—they think of things all the time, like how would it feel to do it in a balloon, is tantric sex really all it's cracked up to be, what would it be like to have a one-night stand with a stranger. Thinking about something doesn't mean you're panting to do it." I took a breath and looked at the group of mobile homes at the end of the paved drive. "This can't be the right trailer court."

"Why not?" Mikhail's tone was as clipped as mine.

"Because Cherry said it was near a park and there's nothing but factories and warehouses around here." I flicked a glance at him. "So was I close?"

"Pretty close," he replied without returning my glance. "And the multiple orgasms part was right on track."

"I see." I tapped my fingers on the steering wheel for a second, but stopped when I realized it was beginning to hurt. "I guess we'd better keep looking for the trailer court near Rodney Park," I said, putting the Mini in gear. "Or Rodnaye Park. However Cherry pronounced it, I've never heard of—"

"Rodnaya?" Mikhail asked slowly.

I looked at him. "That sounds right. Do you know it?"

"It's not a park," he said, his gaze darkening. "*Rodnaya pochva* means native soil…and to a *vampyr,* that literally means earth from the country he or she once called home. We've found Zena's daytime resting place."

Chapter 14

Except we hadn't found Zena's daytime resting place, of course. We'd narrowed our search down to a few square miles, maybe, and if you think that sounds promising, all I can say is you try playing find-the-vamp in an area that size.

Part of our problem was that the trailer park was plunked down in the middle of abandoned farm acreage; now zoned as future light industrial, according to the signs by the side of the road bearing a faded picture of a realtor with the unfortunate name of Steve Butt. So we're talking fields and slogging through waist-high grass everytime Mikhail spied a falling-down barn or an empty farmhouse on the horizon. Old farmsteads, apparently, were prime locations for old wells.

"See, if I were Zena, this is *not* the first place I'd think of when I was looking to settle in with my box of dirt and my toaster-oven," I observed as we climbed yet another rusty barbwire fence. "I mean, a dry well? You can toss around all the silk-covered throw cushions you want, and it's never going to be Home Beautiful."

"Wells are dark," Mikhail answered, transferring the coiled length of nylon rope we'd bought at the beginning of our well expeditions from one shoulder to another.

"I'm just saying we could have checked out some of those warehouses near the trailer park after lunch before resuming our down-on-the-farm routine," I argued.

Abruptly he stopped walking. "Close your eyes."

"Why?" I was in no mood for games.

"Just do it," he said implacably.

Feeling like an idiot, I did. "Okay, they're closed," I said, tapping my foot on a clod of dirt. "Can I open them—"

"Don't talk. Be still for a moment and listen."

I wanted to ask him what I was supposed to be listening for, but I decided that the fastest way to get this over with would be to do what he wanted. Stopping my foot-tapping and keeping my eyes closed, I listened.

To nothing. Well, maybe not nothing; from somewhere in the field the single violin note of a red-wing blackbird pierced the air and I could hear the breeze riffling the grass all around me. The summer sun felt warm on my skin, and as I inhaled I could almost taste it, like sweet butter, on my tongue. Another unidentifiable smell lent a faint cool top note, like a wash of blue over a watercolor.

I opened my eyes and saw a cornflower, the pale saturation of its petals almost hallucinogenic in intensity, swaying in the grass a few feet away from me, as deeper back in the field the blackbird took wing. The flight of the bird and the fragility of the flower seemed suddenly to twist at my heart.

"Isn't this better than being stuck in a warehouse?" Mikhail was saying, but I barely heard him.

"This is what I'll lose," I said in a low tone. "If I turn vamp, I'll never experience the world in the daylight again. Zena will have taken all this from me." I looked at him. "You know why I didn't want to tell Darkheart and my sisters what we learned today, don't you?"

Slowly he nodded. "You want to be the one who stakes her. But if we're still looking tomorrow, we're going to have to ask them to help."

"Because I'm running out of time or because the honor of killing Zena should go to a Daughter of Lilith?" I shrugged. "I know—a little of both. I won't argue with that, but let's cross this last well off our list of places where she isn't before we call it a day."

The silence between us as we resumed walking wasn't uncomfortable, but I needed conversation to take me away from my thoughts. "I'm sure Kat and Tashya got a lesson on the meaning behind the term *Daughter of Lilith,* but I must have been playing hooky that day. Wasn't Lilith supposed to be Adam's first wife, the one before Eve?"

"According to legend. The stories say that the first time God made man and woman, they were both created from dust. Since she'd been made the same way Adam had been, Lilith didn't see why she should be considered inferior to him and when he tried to order her around, she told him to go fuck himself." A corner of Mikhail's mouth tugged upward. "Or words to that effect. Adam went whining to God, Lilith ended up banished from Eden and Adam was given the chance to create a wife to his own personal specifications. Except what he ending up creating was a soulless monster, Bala…or as Anton calls her just before he spits on the ground and crosses himself, the Mother of All *Vampyrs*."

"So vamps are yet another world problem created by the male of the species," I said dryly. "Why do I get the feeling that it fell to a female to clean up Adam's mess? And why do I also get the feeling that the reason for the bad rap Lilith's gotten over the years is because men don't like to admit they had to call on a woman to save their asses?" I frowned. "After she killed Bala, how'd Lilith get pregnant with a daughter to start the whole Daughter of Lilith thing? I mean, there was only one available man—*please* don't tell me she went back to her ex."

We'd reached the farmhouse's yard. Earlier in the day I'd nearly plunged through some rotted boards covering the first well we'd found, so I came to a halt as I waited for his answer.

He stopped, too. "No, Lilith never went back to Adam. Her hunt for Bala took years, and by the time they finally had their showdown, Lilith's daughter was a woman herself. Who her father was isn't exactly clear, but again, according to the stories, Lilith consorted with demons during her banishment."

"A girl's gotta take it where she can find it," I said dubiously. "The woman deserved some R & R, after all, what with having to kill Bala, plus going after all the vamps she created."

He shook his head. "Lilith staked Bala, but the wounds she'd received in their battle were mortal. It was left to her daughter to carry on the fight against Bala's creatures."

"And her daughter's daughter, and so on right up to Kat

today?" My guess confirmed by his nod, I began to walk carefully through the weeds, looking for the broken bricks or splintered wood that would indicate a long-disused well. "Totally unfair that Lilith didn't get made a saint or something."

"Her bones were protected as relics for centuries," Mikhail said, squatting down suddenly and parting the grass. "But they disappeared during some long-ago war and…here it is."

He unslung the coiled nylon rope from his shoulder while I donned leather work gloves, bought at the same time as the rope, and started to clear clumps of grass from the well opening. This one's cover was dangerously rotten, and I made a mental note to contact Steve Butt and threaten to raise hell if his realty company didn't do something about the safety of their properties.

"Ready?" I asked Mikhail as he walked back to me from the gnarled apple tree around which he'd tied one end of the rope.

He threw the other end down the well's exposed mouth. "You want me to leave any spiderwebs for you?"

"No, thanks." I grimaced. "You can have the pleasure of brushing them away."

He put on a pair of gloves similar to the ones I was wearing and grasped a length of the tough yellow nylon. Tugging on it, he backed up a step to the well and then began walking down its walls, his feet and back braced against the stone interior, his gloved hands gripping the rope. I peered over the edge, but after he'd descended a few feet I couldn't see him any longer. I began to descend, too, my thoughts on the man in the darkness below me.

"You try shape-shifter sex, you never go back," I muttered with a snort. "Mikey-baby, you may have your problems, but a shrinking ego's not one of them. To be fair, though, you haven't been as much of a pain in the ass today as you usually are."

In fact, I reflected as the last of the light from the opening above was swallowed up and the beam from the flashlight clipped to my belt became my sole source of illumination, Mikhail hadn't been a pain in the ass at all, which left him with only three drawbacks as far as I was concerned. One: He and I were still bound together. Two: He spent at least a third of his time as a wolf—not his fault, but it shifted him from the totally hot male category to the totally-hot-except-when-he's-got-four-legs category. And three: He didn't have melted-chocolate eyes.

My heels hit the ground and I released my grip from the rope. Surprised that I hadn't bumped into Mikhail, I swung my flashlight around the well's interior. Here at the bottom it was relatively wide, about six feet in diameter, and like the others we'd explored, dry as a bone. A century and a half ago when these early homesteads had been built, Maplesburg had been a tiny village, but over the years it had grown into a large community that had needed to divert and control its water supply. As a result, the water table here had lowered.

But I wasn't exactly in a Mister Science mood at the moment. My hand was already on the stake shoved into a belt loop on my jeans when Mikhail's voice floated eerily out of nowhere to me.

"...opens into a tunnel. You coming?"

The beam of my light darted across the stone walls of

the well and halted at a dark hole. My heart lurched in my chest. "Are you serious?"

"…gets easier…" His voice grew fainter as I mentally took back what I'd said about him not being a pain in the ass.

The next few minutes were as bad as I'd feared. On my knees and acutely aware of the tons of rock above me, I inched along the tunnel with my eyes squeezed shut, fighting the claustrophobia that threatened to turn me into a gibbering, immobile wreck. Even when the space got larger I still couldn't shake off the certainty that at any second the ceiling would give way and crash down on me.

"What took you so long?"

I opened my eyes to see Mikhail standing in front of me, his figure bathed in a pale green-white glow. "Nothing," I lied, getting to my feet. "Where's the weird light coming from?"

He jerked the beam of his flashlight up to the ceiling a foot above his head. "Bioluminescent moss," he said briefly, "but the real show's behind me."

He stepped aside so I could fully see the chamber we were standing in. The dim glow from the moss showed the shadowy bulk of the walls, but as far as I could see, the space was empty.

"Whoa, cool," I said, turning to the tunnel. "Wouldn't have missed this for the world. I'm heading back."

His hand wrapped around my upper arm and he shone his flashlight around the cavern. "Check out the walls."

"Why, what's so special—" My words died in my throat as I aimed my flashlight in the same direction as his. Without being conscious of reaching for it, I realized my stake was in my hand.

The walls were honeycombed with dark openings just

large enough for a prone vamp body. Which was handy, since that was what was in them. "Have you counted how many are here?" My question came out in a whisper.

"Ten." Mikhail's voice was equally low. "She obviously likes keeping her current favorites close by, although two of the openings aren't occupied yet."

I already had goosebumps. Now I felt goosebumps on my goosebumps. "One of them was—by Cherry. But you're right, the twelfth occupant didn't show up last night as planned." My voice hardened. "Since Zena obviously meant for me to round out her cosy little slumber party, I don't feel too bad about crashing it now. How do you want to do this?"

He didn't hesitate. "I drag them out, you stake them as soon as their feet hit the floor. You good with that plan?"

"Totally in bed with it," I said tightly. "What are we waiting for?"

He shot me a frowning look but as I squared my shoulders and stared impatiently at him his expression grew shadowed. Without a word he turned to the occupant of the first rock-hewn shelf, grabbed its shoulders, and pulled it from its resting place.

It wasn't Zena. I felt a sharp stab of disappointment, but then the same vamplike coldness that had settled on me at the Hot Box Club took over and all emotion drained away. The vampire Mikhail was holding upright had been a man in his fifties when he'd turned. He wore an expensively flashy suit and his hair was expertly cut and styled, but those superficialities didn't take away from the lurking brutality hinted at in his shark-thin lips.

His eyes snapped open. "No problem, Tony. There's a

single mother on the jury. We get word to her that either our guy walks or her kid has an accident, and—" He blinked. Comprehension filled his flat black gaze but before he could act I thrust my stake into his chest.

"From a made man to an unmade vamp in one easy step," I said, pushing my face close to his. "I guess your guy's trial is going to have a different outcome now. *Ciao*, creep." But my last words were delivered to dust. A flicker of distaste crossed Mikhail's carved features as he reached for the next vampire.

His attitude sparked defensive anger in me. "If you've got a problem with this, I'll handle it myself," I said coldly. Briefly I met his eyes before looking at the vamp he'd hauled to its feet. This one was a woman, younger than the male I'd just staked; probably with her *glamyr* on full blast she could pass for twenty-three or twenty-four, but if she'd remained human I doubted she would have seen thirty again. Her transition from unconsciousness to total awareness held none of the confusion of the mobster's, but I thought I was ready for her.

I wasn't. Instead of launching herself at me she twisted in Mikhail's grip and went for him, her fangs slashing across his throat before he could wrestle her away. I saw him fall backward as she went in for the kill.

"Hold it right there, vamp!" I said hoarsely. I spun her around to face me. "If you want him you'll have to go through me first!"

"Where have I heard that before?" the blonde sneered. "Oh, yeah—from the old bag who was my rich husband's first wife before I convinced him to trade her in for me. You can't stop me any more than she—" Her boast ended in a gasp as she looked down at the hilt of my stake protruding from her. She raised her eyes to mine. "Shit. You're a Daughter of Lilith," she said hollowly.

"Wrong again, bitch," I said as she disintegrated. Kicking aside the pile of ashy dust she'd become, I knelt beside Mikhail, my heart thudding as I saw the thick ribbon of blood soaking into the collar of his shirt. "Oh, God— hang in there, Mikey-baby. I don't know how I'll do it, but I'm going to get you out of here and to a hospital." I bit my lip. "Or should I take you to Darkheart? Can you hear me, Mikhail? Does Darkheart know some ancient incantation that will help you heal?"

"Hell, how could I have been so *stupid?*" he muttered, opening his eyes. "I told you once before, it takes a lot to kill a shape-shifter." His gaze narrowed on me. "Are you crying?"

"Some vamp-dust in my eye, is all," I said quickly. "I'll take care of the rest of these undead while you heal up, okay? I'm not wearing a watch but I'd say we've been down here almost an hour. The sun's going to start setting soon."

"'If you want him you'll have to go through me,'" he quoted with a crooked smile. "You sounded pretty tough when you said that, Crosse, but the vamp-dust excuse doesn't fool me. I'm glad you felt some emotion when you thought the bitch had killed me. I was afraid you'd moved past that particular human weakness."

"Only when I'm staking," I replied. "I want to take down as many vampires as I can before I turn into one myself, and since Zena's not here to stake, my turning vamp is a distinct possibility." My chest felt tight with despair. "You already knew she wasn't among them, didn't you? If she had been, her scent would have overpowered everything for you and you would have been more on your guard."

I didn't wait for his reply, but turned to the crypt's next occupant. This time I didn't waste time in speculating whom he might have been or how he'd turned. The vamp's snarling jaws had barely dusted before I gave my attention to my next kill.

The coldness that had been momentarily interrupted by my fear for Mikhail enveloped me, and although I knew that each time it returned I took another step closer to becoming one of the creatures I hated, I was glad for the unfeeling resolve it gave me. As a Daughter, Kat would never embrace the darkness the way I could, I reflected grimly as I staked a heavily-tattooed biker before his fangs could sink into my neck. But her destiny would be easier if she could bring herself to let the shadows in enough that her kills didn't tear her apart.

But what did I know, I asked myself when I finally slipped my stake through its belt-loop holster and wiped my suddenly-clammy brow with the back of my hand. Kat was Darkheart's pick to be a Daughter of Lilith. I was a queen *vampyr*'s pick to be her hunting buddy and main squeeze. I was hardly in a position to give destiny-enhancing advice, especially since my plan to find Zena and stake her hadn't panned out. I turned to Mikhail and saw him watching me intently.

"That's right, I forgot you didn't catch my performance at the Hot Box last night," I said coolly. "I've come a long way since my encounter with the Maisels, wouldn't you say?"

"You were still fighting against what you were at that

point," he replied, his gaze flaring gold. "But even then your reactions were well-honed when a stake came flying at you."

I stared at him. "You saw that? Why didn't you tell Darkheart when he was about to kill you?"

He opened his mouth to reply but before he could, a noise came from behind us. We both whirled around, Mikhail with a growl and me with my stake drawn.

"Sorry for startling you, folks!" The red-headed man quickly raising his hands near the entrance to the tunnel looked somehow familiar, but I couldn't immediately place him. He gave a shaky smile. "I heard voices coming from down here and I thought someone had taken a header through the old well." He lowered his hands and a puzzled frown creased his freckled face. "If you don't mind me asking, what the heck *are* you doing here?"

I remembered where I'd seen his face—on the faded For Sale signs posted by the road. "You're Steve Butt?" I asked, stalling for time while I tried to think up some excuse for Mikhail's and my presence in an abandoned well that wouldn't sound totally ridiculous. "The Realtor who's handling this property?"

His frown disappeared and he stuck out his hand. "No 'buts' about it." He grinned, his salesman's instincts overriding his puzzlement. "You folks interested in buying?"

My hand was halfway to his when I yanked it back and grabbed my stake. "Not from a vamp. Gotta watch out for that hovering-above-the-floor thing, Stevarino," I added as I swiftly stepped forward to plunge my weapon into his heart.

Maybe I was tired. Maybe I was overconfident. Or maybe at that moment I was just a klutz, but whatever the reason, at the very second my stake should have been turning Steve Butt into a Mr. Dusty, my foot slipped on a rock and instead of staking him I crashed into him, sending us both tumbling to the ground. I had an instant's glimpse of a shock of red hair and a Huck Finn freckled face contrasting jarringly with the exposed fangs zooming in toward my neck before Mikhail's powerhouse kick connected with Butt's ribs and sent him flying into the wall. I scrambled to my feet, my cool vamp-hunter persona kind of wrecked by the flame of embarrassment I could feel spreading over my cheeks. But my persona was about to suffer an even worse blow.

"Oooh, a big bad Daughter of Lilith," Butt was laughing so hard he could barely get the words out. He dodged out of my way. "Watch out for the Daughters, they told me. Those bitches are hell with stakes, they told me. I can't believe I listened to them!" He went into another round of laughter, rattling me so badly that when I tried to stake him I missed again.

"How'd you miscount the piles of dust, Crosse?" Mikhail said from behind me. "There's only nine here. This jackass must have woken up and come out while our backs were turned."

"There's ten piles," I snapped. Seeing that Butt was still doubled over with laughter, I quickly scanned the floor of the cavern. "See-eight, nine…oh." I focused my gaze on the ashes of the bitchy trophy wife. "I ran through hers. They're spread out a bit, and I guess I counted them as two."

"Stop, I can't take any more!" Butt went into a fresh peal of giggles, covering his fangs with his hand. "You *miscounted?*"

"You were the kind of kid who pulled the wings off flies,

weren't you?" I said. "Keep laughing, creep. In a couple of seconds you'll be laughing in hell."

But Butt wasn't listening. He'd stopped laughing and now he peered at me. "Hey, wait a minute—you're the chick Zena's been trying to turn, right? Hell, this is my lucky day!" He cocked his index fingers at me as if they were six-shooters and gave me a grin. "Gotta go, Peaches, but I'll be back with the boss-lady. You know, this undead gig isn't so different from sales—you see an opportunity to get in good with management and you go for it." Even as he finished his sentence he was diving for the tunnel. I dove after him, but Mikhail shouldered me aside.

"I'm faster," he said tersely as he entered the opening.

"And I'm smarter," I said as I followed him into the claustrophobic confines of the tunnel. He was already yards ahead of me, so I raised my voice. "Butt can't leave until the sun's completely set, remember? As soon as he's halfway up the well he'll realize his mistake and turn back."

"Unless he bursts into flame while he's climbing our rope." Mikhail's reply echoed off the stone walls of the tunnel. "Our plastic, meltable rope! I don't know about you, but I don't want to be stranded here in a vamp hideout with no way of escape."

I froze. Then I began crawling faster, but as I burst out of the tunnel into the slightly lesser blackness of the well I realized Mikhail hadn't caught up with Butt in time. Above me, the yellow beam from the flashlight clipped to his belt betrayed my *oboroten*'s progress after the undead real estate salesman. I pulled on my gloves and began climbing after them.

"Maybe it's later than I think and the sun's already set,"

I muttered as I shinnied upward. "If it has and Mikhail catches the little creep before he can take off, I'm staking him myself. *No*body calls me Peaches and gets away with it!"

In a moment I was grasping clumps of grass and hauling myself out of the well into the near-dusk. I got to my feet running, but then stopped, a slow smile spreading across my face.

The sun was no more than a razor-thin sliver on the horizon and the fields were almost completely in shadow. But what Butt couldn't see, his mocking face turned over his shoulder at Mikhail, was the final weak shaft of sunlight coming through a break in the trees surrounding the property.

He ran straight into it and exploded into fiery oblivion.

"My hero," I said admiringly to Mikhail as I walked up to him. "You totally steered him toward that break in the trees, didn't you? I thought we were in trouble when I saw it was nearly dark, but you must have planned—"

"We *are* in trouble." Mikhail cocked his head to one side, looking way too much like the RCA Victor mutt in those antique advertisements. I frowned at him.

"Okay, what you're hearing has to be one of those silent dog whistles, because it's not reaching my ears. Come on, let's go—"

"Look what's coming out of the farmhouse," he said tersely.

I followed his gaze and felt a chill settle on me. "Tell me those are just ordinary bats, Mikey-baby," I whispered. "Tell me they're just ordinary bats that happen to be heading our way in a great big flock."

"They're vamps," he said flatly. "They've honed in on your human scent. We won't make it to the car before they're upon us." He turned to me, his eyes glowing more golden than I'd ever seen them. "There's only one thing we can do to escape them," he growled.

The next moment Mikhail's arms were around me and his tongue was in my mouth in a deep, toe-curling kiss.

Chapter 15

As any girl knows, there's nothing so explosive as having the submerged hots for someone and then finding yourself participating in a triple-X-rated kiss with him.

Before I go any further I just have to say one thing—*God,* he was good.

In fact, that was my first dazed reaction as Mikhail's mouth covered mine. I felt the tips of my toes brush the ground as he lifted me slightly off my feet—I mean, hand me a fan, somebody, that was a total orgasmic rush right there—and as my lashes drifted down I thought, oh, honey, you are *way* too good at this.

And then I heard the wings. They didn't sound like bird wings, they sounded like great leather windmill sails rustily creaking in the darkening sky over the field. My eyes snapped open and I found myself staring into Mikhail's brilliant gaze. He spoke against my mouth, his voice hoarsely urgent.

"Kiss me back, dammit!"

He knew we were about to die. He wanted to spend his final moment of existence with my arms around him, my taste on his tongue. How sweet, how Romeo-and-Juliet-ish, how flattering...

How freaking *insane* was he? Maybe our chances weren't great, but if we started running for the trees right now we *might* get out of this alive. I struggled in his arms but with my feet dangling like a marionette's I couldn't break his grip on me.

"Let go of me, Vostoroff!" I ground out. "Remember ancient contract thingy? You're supposed to *protect* me, not hand me over to the vamps with a '*bon appetit*, folks'!" I drew back my foot and kicked him hard in the knee.

"Kiss me back, Megan!" I knew he'd spoken the words because I saw his lips move. But somehow he'd also pulled the same stunt he'd pulled the night he and Darkheart had arrived, his words resounding in my head the same way they'd done then. Just as I had that first night, I found myself unable to ignore them.

"We're going to die!" I screamed into his face. Then I laced my fingers behind his head and pulled him to me.

He wanted a kiss? I thought in impotent rage. I'd give him such a mind-numbing kiss that when the vamp-bats struck us down Mikey-baby would go to his shape-shifter afterlife in a state of permanent, unappeaseable arousal. I closed my eyes, opened my mouth and angrily pushed my tongue past his, tightening my grip in his hair and feeling it slide like ripped black silk across my palms. I flicked the tip of my tongue against the tip of his, then surged deeper before withdrawing slightly and biting down hard on his bottom lip. The rush of the creaking wings overhead was so loud now that their sound was all-enveloping, and despairingly I kissed Mikhail harder. He kissed me back, every muscle in his body rigid with need, his biceps straining against the sides of my breasts and his hands on my shoulders feeling like steel vises. Through his jeans I could feel the outline of him pressed hard against my thigh, and despite myself and the situation, I suddenly felt a blaze of heat run through me.

The world seemed to tip on its axis. The heat running through me turned instantaneously to ice and then to flames again. I felt dizzy and sick and as if something were terribly wrong with me, and I tried to wrench myself away from Mikhail.

He released me. I fell like a lead weight to the ground, but that was wrong, too, because the ground seemed closer than it should have been. I raised myself onto my hands and knees and took a deep, mind-clearing breath of air. Then I opened my eyes and saw Mikhail standing in front of me in wolf form.

"Run." His voice was a growl, but I heard it normally, not as if it were coming from inside my head. "Run like you've never run before. Don't wonder about anything, don't think, just *run!*"

Running had been a good idea sixty seconds ago, I thought as I began to race for the trees. I shot a glare at Mikhail, loping shoulder to shoulder with me, but he was looking back so I risked a glance back, too. The dark cloud of bats wheeled in a wide circle over the entrance to the well where we'd been standing a moment ago, then turned as a group and begin heading toward us, one massive bat slightly ahead of the rest. As the lead bat begin to close the gap between us I saw green fire flash from its eyes, and I nearly stumbled.

"Keep going!" Mikhail snarled. "We're nearly at the treeline, and the brethren are coming to meet us!"

I couldn't take in what he was saying. "The lead bat's got emerald eyes," I said, terror giving a rough edge to my voice. "Mikhail, it's Zena! And she's got a damn army backing her up!"

"We've got an army, too," he growled, jerking his muzzle at the trees. "Once we lose ourselves in the brethren, we're safe."

"Who the hell are the brethren?" I pictured an earnest group of door-to-door Bible-thumpers who had somehow gotten themselves stranded out here in the middle of nowhere. Then, through the tall grass that partially obscured my vision, I saw pinpricks of brilliant gold ahead of us by the trees. "A wolf pack?" I swallowed. "They understand I'm under your protection, right?"

Mikhail snapped his jaws close to my neck. I felt a sharp slicing sensation as his nip pierced my flesh. "If you don't pour on the speed, I'll rip your throat out myself rather than let that bitch take you down, so *move!*"

Maybe it was the shock of knowing he'd bitten me, or maybe it was just the fact that Zena was gaining on us. Whatever it was, I put on a burst of speed I didn't know I had in reserve, aware of a fetid rush of air bearing down on me and the creak of leather wings just feet above my head. Then I reached the protective stand of trees and was surrounded by a dozen or so wolves. I kept running, but now I was pressed in on all sides by the pack. I glimpsed Mikhail's lean, muscular shape pivot beside me and leap into the air, white fangs snapping closed inches away from the lead bat. Several wolves directed their attentions at the handful of other bats that had followed their mistress into the small forest and were dodging the low-hanging branches, their outsized wingspans liabilities now, rather than assets.

At some point I sensed we were no longer being pursued. The wolves flanking me reduced their speed to match mine, loping instead of racing through the trees, but although it seemed I'd been running forever, I felt no need to stop. In fact, I didn't want to stop, I realized as I nimbly scrambled up a small scree of fallen rocks onto the ridge of a hill and then down again into a shadowy valley. Through the branches overhead I could see a huge moon hanging in the velvety night sky, its reflection mirrored in the waters of a nearby stream. The sight of it seemed to add an edge of exhilaration to my relief at having escaped Zena and her hordes, and a wild, uninhibited joy ran through me. The grass underfoot was fragrant and soft. The night was warm. I felt bursting with energy, my pack had proved themselves to be loyal and brave companions and my mate was virile and ready to take me whenever I signalled my readiness.

Boy, was I one happy she-wolf.

I came to a skidding stop inches from the stream. The other wolves kept going, except for the black wolf with the silver-tipped ruff holding back at the edge of the water.

"Mikhail." I said his name without looking at him. I

tried to tell myself that my voice hadn't come out in a low, canine whine. "What did you do to me?"

"What I had to, to save your life." His voice was a growl—no, not a growl the way it was when he was in human form, but a *growl*. I could understand it as well as if he'd been speaking English. "You're under the radar now, as far as any vampires are concerned. You give off the scent of a wolf, not a human, and wolves aren't vamp prey."

I dipped my head toward the water. The moon's image floated like a golden lily pad on the surface of the stream but I wasn't in the mood for Zenlike beauty at the moment. I stared at the wavering reflection of a female wolf, her fur pale in the moonlight, and opened my mouth to speak. The wolf in the water opened her muzzle, showing the gleam of white teeth.

"Am I stuck like this?" I said/growled, still looking at my reflection and not at Mikhail.

"Would that be so bad?" I was sure I detected a note of wolfish amusement in his reply. "The night is warm, the grass is soft and your mate is virile and ready to—"

If I'd been in human form I would have punched his arm. As a wolf, I apparently had less of a sense of humor and more of a hair-trigger temper. I whirled around, my sudden move shattering my reflection into a mosaic, realizing from the strange sensation on the nape of my neck that my ruff had risen. I sprang toward Mikhail, my canines slashing at his shoulder.

"You should have *warned* me, you carrion-eater!" I didn't know where the insult had come from, but I sensed it was one of the worst things I could call him. "Maybe you're used to popping back and forth between human and animal, but I like having a heads-up as to which species I might be at any given moment! Now tell me—*am I stuck like this?*" I punctuated my question by ripping at his left flank. In the moonlight I saw him bare his teeth as he turned on me, his jaws closing on the fur at my throat. I rose up on my back legs, intending to twist out of his hold, but he knocked me to the ground with his muscled forelegs.

A second later I was lying on my belly, his jaws still clamped on my neck. "No," he said through a mouthful of my fur. "You change back the same way you became a wolf."

"By kissing you?" I let my anger trickle into my tone as I slanted my gaze backwards over my shoulder at him. "How do we manage that trick in our present forms?"

"We don't. You undergo the shift with me if we're physically intimate at the moment I begin to change." The amusement returned to his tone. "I thought you'd prefer to stay like this until we get back to the motel, in case Zena's left a couple of undead watching the Mini. As you've discovered, a wolf's stamina and speed and night vision are better than a human's. But if you want, we can shape-shift now."

"Get off me." When he didn't immediately move, I let a growl rise in my throat, and felt his jaws release their hold on my ruff and his body heat recede from my flanks. I leapt to my feet, intending to slash at him again, but when I spun around to confront him I wrinkled my nose in confusion. "What are you doing?" I asked with fresh suspicion.

His front feet were splayed out on the ground in front of him, the black and silver fur of his chest almost brushing the grass, while his hind quarters were in normal standing position. At my question he hesitated a moment and then suddenly tore sideways a few feet and took up the same stance, still staring at me. His teeth showed between his open jaws, but his lips weren't curled back in warning, and as I stiff-leggedly advanced on him he dashed out of reach again. His tail moved fractionally from one side to the other.

I ignored his maneuvers. "Not to be crude, but if I want to turn back into someone who can wear heels again you and I have to do it doggy-style, is that what you're telling me?"

"That's one way wolves are intimate with each other, sure." His tongue lolled out the side of his mouth as if he were grinning. Before I could anticipate his move, he dashed behind me, nipped lightly at my tail, and sped away again.

"What are the other ways?" I tucked my tail between my legs to keep it safe from this new, unpredictable Mikhail.

"You could let me groom you, we could fall asleep curled up together, we could open our souls in a group howl." Punctuating each possibility with a mock leap at me, he ended up with his nose touching mine, his lambent eyes only inches away from my glare. "But we've been wondering what it would be like to mate with each other since we first met, so let's go with that."

"We have?" My ears pricked forward alertly. "I mean, *you* have? You saw me as the enemy!"

"That didn't stop me from wondering." Suddenly he broke off contact with me and sped halfway up the hill. He stopped and looked back at me. "You don't have to make up your mind right away. Come on, let's play!"

Let's play? Was this the same Mikhail who'd spent the better part of a week glowering at me and acting like Darkheart's binding incantation had been a fate worse than death? And what about his admission just now that all along, his engine had raced a little hotter when he and I had been together?

"Maybe he shifts personalities as well as shapes," I growled under my breath as I saw him lope to the top of the hill and then whirl around again. I rolled my eyes heavenward in exasperation. "I've got enough problems trying to keep the vamp side of me from taking over. I'm in no mood to indulge in puppy-playtime with my *oboroten*, especially when Kat and Tash are out hunting—"

I stopped, my gaze fixing on the full moon. It was so *huge,* I thought, awestruck. And so...*golden.* It seemed to be shining directly on me, its magical beams drenching me in gilt spangles, the pull of its ancient power reaching straight into my body and running like quicksilver through my veins and sinews and muscles. I tried to look away, but I couldn't. It seemed to swell until it filled the indigo sky. A nameless desire shafted through me, and without knowing what I was doing or why I felt compelled to do it, I lifted my muzzle to the sky and let out a sobbing howl.

Weeks after this all happened, I made the mistake of telling Tash about my howling-at-the-moon performance. She gave a shudder and said, "Two words, sis—Un! Comfortable! I totally didn't need a permanent picture in my memory bank of my sister doing the wolf-girl thing at the moon."

I can see her point, but at the time my actions seemed perfectly natural to me. I don't know how long I howled, but when I finally dropped my muzzle and ran to join

Mikhail, all my inhibitions had fled. Following the silvered track of the moonlight, we raced across fields, through the trailer court and down dirt roads, taking the back way into Maplesburg. It was a run of about ten miles, but we stretched it into twice that. First Mikhail would circle behind me and try to nip my flank or my tail, then I would throw myself at him and we'd tumble in a pretend-fight. We treed a raccoon, drove a chained-up farm dog crazy with our scent until his barking woke the farmer, and when we got closer to the motel, tipped over some garbage cans outside a strip mall restaurant. When we finally made it to my palatial digs at the Park Vista, we were snuffling with laughter as we lurked in the shadows at the back of unit seven, and when I looked up at the small bathroom window I began to snuffle harder.

"You got any bright ideas about how we get in?" I asked Mikhail, my tail wagging in amusement. "That's latched from the inside. The front door's locked. And neither of us have opposable thumbs at the moment."

He touched the tip of his nose to mine, as he'd done in the forest. "Leaving aside the lack of opposable thumbs, how do you like my world, Crosse?" I heard his query only as a rumble coming from deep in his chest, but it was as understandable as if it had been put into words. His eyes seemed lit with gold fire. "Did it make you forget your human problems for a while?"

I dipped my head and lightly licked the side of his muzzle, my tail no longer wagging. "It made them recede, Mikey-baby. And becoming a wolf tonight saved me from going one-against-fifty with Zena and her creatures. That would have been a fight I couldn't win." I nuzzled his ear. "I like your world. But my mother tried to run from her destiny, and it caught up with her in the end. I can't stay a wolf forev—"

Dizziness caught me unawares. For the second time that night I closed my eyes as jarring sensations flicked through me. I felt strands of hair like rough silk under my fingertips, warm skin against my lips, and the solidity of Mikhail's biceps tightening around me as I adjusted to the unsettling feeling of standing upright on two legs and having clothes on again.

"I wish you'd warn me," I said shakily. "A girl likes to know when her world's about to be rocked."

"Too bad," Mikhail said, bending his head to mine.

I think I've already testified that the man can kiss, no? But that's like saying Rob Thomas can sing. Mikhail's tongue stroked the inner recesses of my lips and flicked against the roof of my mouth before retreating slightly. I felt his teeth close on my lip, then release it and lick the tiny sting away. His hands moved down my back to my rump. Spreading his fingers wide, he snugged me higher against him and made a frustrated sound deep in his throat. I let my palms slide along his shirt to his belt, and then to the straining hardness I could feel beneath his jeans.

"We should get a room," I whispered hoarsely.

"We have one," he breathed against my mouth. "All we have to do is get to it."

Making our way to the front door of the unit took a lot longer than it should have, what with me trying to unzip his jeans while we were edging around the corner of the unit still locked in an embrace, and Mikhail trying to reach under my top, unsnap my bra and peel my pants past my hips all at the same time. Luckily there was no one in the parking lot to see us, because when we finally fumbled my key in the door of number seven and got inside, we were both half-naked and there was a trail of hastily discarded clothing leading up to the unit.

"The first time I saw you in human form I thought, God, he's so *hot*," I said as he succeeded in getting my jeans off. "Well, actually, more like *hott*, with two *T*s. Maybe even three. *Hottt*. But then you turned out to be an asshole."

"I just thought, fuck, she's holding a gun on me and I've got a hard-on, what does that say about me? Was I really an asshole?" Mikhail ran his thumbs up the inside of my thighs.

"You dumped me in a graveyard at night," I reminded him, arching my neck and closing my eyes. I sank my fingers into his hair. "You've got a lot to make up for, Mikey-baby."

"I'm working on it," he said as he hooked a finger through the hip-band of my thong and dragged it down. "Hot with four *T*s," he rasped as he surveyed the little landing strip of neatly trimmed hair that was all Joyla, the brutally efficient Brazilian waxer I visited at the Beautiful You Salon, left on her willing victims, I mean clients. "You feel like satin all over," he muttered as he brought his mouth to Joyla's handiwork.

You know how in books they used to put three dots at the point where everything started to get hot and heavy? And then they'd pick up the story again with the lovers lying panting and exhausted in each other's arms? I used to think that was just the author drawing a discreet curtain over the wild monkey sex I was sure happened after the dot dot dot part, but now I think it's because, really, how do you describe going out of your mind?

Total rip-off if I don't try, though, so here goes.

The man brought the exact same talent that made him such a dreamy kisser to the lower area of my anatomy. His tongue teased me and invaded me by turns, and every time I thought he was going to let me go into full-blown Megan-goes-over-the-edge mode, he pulled back just enough to have me biting my bottom lip and practically begging him to play fair. At some point I found myself on the side of the bed, and in pre-orgasmic impatience I sneakily tried to get my own hand in on the action. Not missing a beat—okay, not missing a tantalizing lick—he trapped both my wrists with one hand and kept on driving me crazy.

Which meant that when he finally relented, I was *extremely* ready.

My hair felt damp. Oh, hell, to be honest it felt soaked. I'd lost my top somewhere on our striptease journey from the back of unit seven to the door, but my bra was still hanging off one shoulder, and my nipples looked like round pink pebbles. My fingers were raked through Mikhail's too-cool-for-school silver-chunked strands of hair and I felt like my grip on him was the only thing keeping me from spinning off the edge of the world as I let loose with an upwardly escalating series of gasping, whooping screams.

I know. Tough on the older couple in unit eight and a slam-bang audio performance for the single guy in unit six, but I was way past the point of worrying about motel decorum by then. And when I eventually drifted back to something resembling sanity, I had something bigger to focus my attention on.

"Oh my," I croaked, my throat raspy from hitting high C so many times in the past few minutes. "I mean, your jeans fit tight in all the right places and a girl's gaze just naturally drifts to the zipper area to check out a male's merchandise, so I kind of had a clue, but…" I lay back on the bed with an anticipatory purr. "Something tells me I'm going to be howling at the moon for a third time tonight."

"Something tells me I'll be joining you," Mikhail said, his grin flashing in the light slatting through the chinks in the blinds at the room's single window.

He moved to the bed and straddled me, the muscles of his thighs taut against my hips. I wrapped my hands around his shaft, feeling the velvet-over-steel tension centered there, and slowly let my palms slide down along its length. Equally slowly, I let them move back up and then down again, this time cupping him and letting my fingertips stroke him further. In the half light I saw him close his eyes and tip his head back, the tendons in his neck tight, and heat began building again in me as I watched his reaction. The next time my palms moved upward, I pulled him closer and raised myself from the pillow. This time when my hands slid down his length, my mouth followed and I heard Mikhail's sharply indrawn breath as he felt me take him in.

Okay, I confess: I was as mean to him as he'd been to me. And he loved it. I could tell, because in between growling hoarsely that he'd known from the first I was heartless and now I was proving it at his expense, his voice would trail off into a strangled moan and his hands would tighten convulsively on my shoulders. Once in a while, just to be a total tease, I'd swirl my tongue around the tip of him *verrry* slowly, looking up at him through my lashes as innocently as if I was licking an ice-cream cone. I would see the gold glint of his half-closed eyes, the thick shadow of his lashes on his cheekbones, the erotic way he sank his teeth into his bottom lip, and my own control would threaten to break.

But his broke first.

"Now." The word sounded ragged, but since he accompanied it with action there was no mistaking its meaning. Grasping my hips, he lifted me toward him, his breathing a measured rasp. The next moment I felt him easing into me, and all of a sudden my control broke, too.

"Oh, God, yes," I whispered unevenly. "Let's rock, Mikey-baby." I clutched the rumpled sheets tightly with both hands as he moved gradually deeper into me, his gaze fixed on mine. Just when I was beginning to think I couldn't take anymore, he paused and then began withdrawing.

"This is completely against the rules," he said tightly. "I'm your *oboroten*. Taking care of you this way probably breaks some ancient law."

"Screw the ancient laws," I murmured, pulling him into me again. "But not until you do me first."

A crease of amusement briefly slashed his cheek and his eyes glowed a deeper hazel as he lowered himself to his braced arms and looked down at me, his movements hypnotically rhythmic and building in intensity. "Know what the second thing was that I thought when I saw you?" he breathed, his mouth brushing mine as he went in and out, in and out.

I shook my head from side to side on the pillow, my vision blurring and my whole body starting to burn. "No, what?" It was an effort to speak past the tiny explosions that seemed to be bubbling up through me.

"That if I ever found myself in your bed I'd be in big

trouble." Mikhail's tongue slipped between my lips and he began moving harder into me. "I think I was right."

In the part of my brain that was still capable of tracking, I decided I'd figure out what he meant later. Then even that small corner of my mind stopped thinking.

And now I really do have to fall back on the old dot dot dot, because there just aren't any words in the human language to describe how it felt to go all crazy/orgasmic/rocket blast/firestorm/melty with Mikhail Vostoroff. See what I mean? Maybe in wolfen I could convey how it felt, but I doubt it. We howled at the moon together. An hour later we howled again. Just before dawn—yeah, you guessed it—we howled as it slipped like a pale silver disc below the horizon.

And right after that Van called me on my cell phone and everything started falling apart.

Chapter 16

"You got what you deserve, you tramp," Tash said in disgust as Colette finished slathering her with mud and drew the edges of a silvery heat-retaining sheet around her. With a melodious, "Enjoy, ladies," Colette left the treatment room and Tash went on, "A total hotty like Van Ryder makes it clear he's serious about you and you let him think you feel the same, but the next night when he finally gets you on your cell phone you're doing the wild thing with a shape-shifter." She lifted one of the cucumber slices that covered her eyes. "The man turns into a *wolf*," she said with heavy emphasis. "He's not completely *human*. What were you thinking?"

It was the afternoon after my howling-at-the-moon marathon with Mikhail, and my sisters and I were at the Beautiful You Salon and Spa—mainly for Kat's benefit, since she looked like a wreck and wanly admitted she felt like one, too. "I staked two vamps last night," she'd told me in a faint voice when I'd phoned the house this morning to ask her to drive me to my stranded Mini. "Grandfather made it official that I'm this generation's Daughter. He insists that as I grow into the role I'll find it easier to carry out my duties, but honestly, Meg, everytime I kill an undead I feel like I'm being torn in two. We're going out again tonight and I'm so stressed my neck muscles feel like they're tied into knots. I've booked a massage and a treatment, and Tash has, too. Want to join us?"

"I'm a teensy bit achy myself," I'd confessed, congratulating her on her Daughter of Lilith status and deciding to wait until I saw her to divulge the reason for the ridden-hard-and-put-up-wet impression I gave when I tried to walk at any pace faster than a hobble. During our white tea soaks I spilled the whole story. I'd opted for a honey mask while I was soaking and my eyelids were stickily glued shut, so I didn't see Tash's increasingly outraged expression or Kat's concerned one as I dished about Mikhail's kissing and other techniques, Van's inopportune phone call in which he'd guessed that his phone call had been, well, inopportune, and Mikhail's reversion to asshole when he'd realized who'd called. But when I finally fell silent I sensed my sisters weren't exactly with me on this one, especially when Tash exploded, and her reaming-out of me made it plain that she and Kat thought I'd crossed a line. She'd shut up when Colette had come to escort us to the mud-wrap room, but now she picked up where she'd left off.

"Where's Mikhail now?" Her tone was thin.

"Outside in the parking lot." I began to shrug but my mud-casing had dried to the consistency of cement. "Like Darkheart says, a strong vamp like Zena's not restricted to the night as long as she avoids direct sun, but I don't really expect her to show up without her cheering section. Anyway, with Mikhail's ability to sense my emotions, he'd know if I was in danger so he decided it wasn't necessary for him to accompany me in." I tried to smile, but ditto on the mud-thing as before. "It feels strange not having him two feet away, glaring at me."

"What right does he have to be mad?" Kat asked. "I have to agree with Tash. If there's an injured party in all this, it's Van, not Mikhail. You felt a real connection with Detective Gorgeous, and as far as I can tell, with Mikhail it was all about the sizzling sex."

"I know," I admitted. "And Mikey-baby knows, too."

"That you *used* him?" Tash's voice rose to a squeak. "Omigod, no wonder he doesn't want to be around you anymore than he has to. Manimal or not, his ego must be totally trashed."

"Don't call him that!" I said sharply. "He's a man who's sometimes a wolf, okay? And who could read my mind when I was talking to Van and feeling incredibly guilty about standing him up for a night of multiple orgasms with Mikhail," I muttered.

Kat's eyes widened. "*Multiple* org—" She stopped herself. "You felt guilty. Did you also feel a twinge of regret?"

I nodded as much as my mud-pack would allow. "All I could think was that if I escape this vamp curse and actually have a future, Van's the kind of guy I could see sharing it with me. When he realized I was with someone,

I suddenly knew I'd jeopardized something that might turn out to be solid for a one-night stand."

"Well, if Mikhail read all that from your mind, sis, all I can say is why didn't you just kick the poor guy in the nuts while you were at it," Tash declared. "I can't blame you for seeing Van as serious boyfriend material and Mikhail as just a roll in the hay to see what it would be like with a shape-shifter, but talk about being a ball-breaking bitch. And now you've lost both of them."

I gave her an irritated look, but since she'd replaced her cucumber slices it was wasted on her. "Not exactly," I said. "I told you, Van's one-in-a-million. I phoned him back while Mikhail was in the shower and said I'd been a jerk but that I really wanted a chance to make it up to him. I'm seeing him tonight for dinner, and then he's coming vamp-hunting with us."

"Smooth, sweetie, very smooth," Kat said admiringly. "And with Mikhail carrying out his *oboroten* duties at a distance now, you and your yummy detective might have a chance to sneak in a smooch or two between stakings. We usually don't leave the house until ten, so you'll have time to mend your fences with him over dinner someplace romantic, like that new French bistro—"

"Uh, there might be a teensy problem with the dinner-and-a-staking date, sis," Tash said in a small voice. "At least for tonight. Why don't you reschedule for tomorrow?"

"What didn't you understand about me just telling you how I almost screwed things up completely with the man?" I asked. "Of course I'm not going to blow him off with some lame request for a rain check." Tash had removed her cucumber slices, and her eyes met mine with a guileless look I knew only too well. I sat up, my mud cracking off in huge chunks. "With you, *teensy problem* usually translates as *catastrophe*. What did you do, brat?"

Before she could answer, the door to the treatment room swung open to reveal a group of women, all clad in white terry robes and all wearing Kabuki-like masks of the spa's special seaweed and mallow-blossom detoxifying facial. It was impossible to recognize them under the paste, but when the woman in front spoke her affected tone immediately gave her identity away.

It was Mandy Broyhill and her posse. And my sisters and I were as trapped as the citizens of Pompeii in our hardened mud.

"Well, well, the faaabulous Crosse triplets," announced Mandy, advancing on us. She snapped her fingers at her fellow Kabuki actors and obediently they all came crowding into the room. "Take a good look at them, girls," she ordered, leveling a poisonously bright stare at us. "They snatched Maplesburg's three most eligible bachelors right out from under our noses and then found themselves standing at the altar with egg on their faces when their fiancés didn't show." She lowered her voice confidentially. "I don't care what the police say, darlings, everyone who matters in this town *knows* you were jilted."

Beside me I saw Kat struggling to break free of her silvery Mylar blanket, but Mandy continued. "Any other three girls would go into the Dumped Brides Protection Plan and disappear forever…or at least keep their heads down and hope that the scandal blew over in a decade or two. But what do the Crosse sisters do?" Dramatically she turned to her audience. "They throw a belated reception party for Megan! And instead of having it at the country club where everyone else has their reception, they pick the sleaziest venue they can find—the Hot Box Club!"

"Don't forget the male strippers!" one of her entourage squeaked excitedly. Mandy froze her with a look.

"With. Male. Strippers," she said, her tone low and measured. "I nearly *died* when I got my e-mailed invitation this morning! How incredibly trashy, I told myself. How brazen! Do they really expect anyone in our crowd to show up to celebrate the fact that the Crosse girls had a narrow escape at the altar?"

I decided to grab the opportunity to do some damage control. "Of course not, Mandy," I said placatingly. "You're right, the whole thing's just too trashy for words. But I think you should know that Kat and I didn't have any part in—"

"You bet your *ass* I'm coming!" screamed Mandy, her Kabuki mask splitting into a delighted grin. "We all are! What an inspired idea—a big, drunken bash for girls only, to show the men in this town that we don't need them to have one hell of a good time! Megan, Kat, Tashya—I never would have suspected it, but you ladies have *balls!* See you tonight at the Hot Box…and tell the strippers you've hired that I get the first lap dance!"

With a waggle of her fingers and an airy, "Toodles," Mandy turned to the door. Her posse parted in front of her like the Red Sea in front of Moses, and she swept out.

"Before you kill me, hear me out," Tash said rapidly as the door closed. "You're about to turn vamp any day now, Megan, and we haven't had any luck in finding Zena so we can stake her and save you. Well, you've seen her twice, but the first time you only broke her hold on you by somehow linking with Mikhail's mind and growling at her, and the second time you were outnumbered."

My fury at her was momentarily diverted. "What do you mean, I linked minds with Mikhail?"

She looked exasperated. "Well, duh. Where else would that growl have come from? On some level he's probably psychically attuned to you all the time, whether the two of you are consciously aware of it or not."

"This is because of what Darkheart said last night!" Kat broke in, her voice shaking with anger. "Don't try to tell us it's because you're worried about Megan turning vamp, when what's really eating away at you is the fact that Grandfather officially presented me with Mom's stake and swore me in as this generation's Daughter of Lilith. This whole farce of a reception party's a trap for Zena, and you're baiting it with a roomful of tipsy women, a bunch of male strippers and the Crosse sisters, knowing she won't be able to stay away from such a tempting combination. All so you get a chance to stake her and prove to Grandfather he chose the wrong sister!"

Her mud-wrap cracking like plaster, she slipped off the table and walked to the corner of the room where her purse sat on a shelf. Opening it, she pulled out the silver-bound stake I'd seen her use on Maisel a week ago and threw it at Tash. "If you want it so badly, it's yours! From the start I said I didn't want Mom's life—the killings, the loneliness, the knowledge that I'll never be able to have a normal existence, because the fate of the whole damn world rests on the shoulders of the Daughters! But you wouldn't believe me, and now you've set up this confrontation with Zena! What if I blow it? What if I don't kill her, and she finishes what she started with Megan!"

Kat was falling apart before my very eyes, I realized in dismay. Inspiration struck me. "You forgot one important detail, Tash—the Hot Box is a crime scene," I said coldly. In my second phone conversation this morning with Van, I'd learned that his PCP story was now the officially accepted theory for what had happened, and I went on, "I don't know who you spoke to at the club when you made your last-minute booking, but there's no way the police will let the place open for business two nights after a supposed drug riot. You'd better start calling everyone you invited and tell them my so-called reception's been cancelled."

"The Hot Box will be open for business tonight. I cleared it with Detective Ryder himself," Tash said, not meeting my eyes. "Although he might have gotten the impression that the plan to trap Zena was yours," she muttered. "The only way I could convince him to go along with the reception idea was to tell him you were terrified that time was running out for you."

I stared at her. Then I hopped off my table and went for her. "You're *unbelievable!*" I hissed as I began shaking her. Her terry turban fell off and her red-gold curls began bouncing on her mud-smeared shoulders. "It's always all about you, Tash, and the hell with everyone else! The man I'm interested in is standing in the way of your plans? No problem, you just lie to him and pin the lie on me! You think Zena might be tempted by the thought of a bunch of new victims—hey, you e-mail every female we know and invite them to a party! But what's really low is the way you're forcing Kat into a confrontation she's terrified she won't win. I don't care who you have to apologize to— you're calling off that party right now!"

I punctuated my last sentence with a final hard shake before I released her. Tash glared at me pugnaciously, but then her chin began to quiver and her shoulders slumped. Tears slowly filled her china-blue eyes. "I felt that Kat becoming the Daughter made her closer to Mom, somehow, and I was so jealous I couldn't stand it. But I know that's no excuse for what I did. I'll explain to Van you didn't know anything about this, Meg, and then I'll phone Mandy and tell her there's not going to be a party. I didn't mean to be so horrible to you, Kat," she sniffled. "Please don't stay mad."

"I'm not," Kat said slowly. She walked over to where she'd tossed her stake and picked it up. She raised her gaze to Tash and me. "We're not canceling the Hot Box bash. No matter what your reasons were for arranging it, Tashya, it's a good plan—one that I should have come up with myself, as a Daughter of Lilith. We've been letting Zena jerk us around like a bunch of puppets on strings, reacting to her instead of making her react to us. It's time we forced her out into the open."

"No, it's not," I said swiftly. "You said it yourself, Kat, you still haven't fully grown into your role as a Daughter and everytime you stake a vamp it takes its toll on you. I won't let you do this!"

Now, here's the thing: even though we're triplets there's never been any doubt as to who's the eldest of us, and whenever I'd taken a firm stand in the past, Kat had backed down. But as I saw the unshakeable resolve in her sapphire gaze, I knew our relationship had changed. She wasn't my sister anymore, she was a Daughter of Lilith.

"And I won't risk you turning vamp just because I'm too

frightened to accept the inheritance Mom passed on to me," she answered. "This is what my life's about now, Megan, and I'd better get used to it. Don't fight me on this."

Isn't it funny how sometimes the words coming out of your mouth can have absolutely nothing to do with what you're really saying? That's what happened to me as I watched Kat wrap her grip more tightly around her stake while she waited for my reply.

"Okay," I said heavily. "The Hot Box bash goes on as planned."

As I say, isn't it funny? Those were the words I spoke to her, but what I was really saying was goodbye. And what makes it funnier is that even as I did, I knew Kat had already gone from me....

There were three of us in the Mini as I drove through the deepening dusk to the Hot Box club that evening, and Van wasn't one of the three. That fact alone didn't account for the reckless clashing of gears and jackrabbit acceleration I was indulging in. Beside me, Darkheart checked his seat belt.

"Is not necessary to drive like Nikolai Fomenko," he said, bracing himself as I came to a stop at a red light.

"Who's he?" I said, my tone anything but interested.

"Russian race driver." Darkheart was thrown back in his seat as the light changed and the Mini jumped forward.

"Never heard of him," I said, shifting from first into fourth without bothering with the intermediate gears. From the back passenger seat came a low growl.

"What happened at house was upsetting, *da,* but does not mean change in you will definitely come tonight." Darkheart's hand rested briefly on my knee as he spoke.

I spoke through tense lips. "When I tried to walk into the house, I felt like I'd slammed into a brick wall. I'd say that's a clear indication of imminent vamp-hood, wouldn't you?"

The scene had been replaying in my mind for the past hour, and now it did again. I saw myself getting out of the Mini just as Van's unmarked sedan pulled into the circular drive in front of the Crosse mansion. Since Mikhail had ignored me all day I didn't feel bad about leaving him to extricate his six feet four inches from the Mini while I ran to meet Van.

"You could have met me at the Hot Box," I said, feeling all girlish and breathless as he laced my fingers through his. "I'm just here to change into something drop-dead sexy and then we can leave. And talking about drop-dead sexy…"

He was wearing a charcoal Zegna three-button suit. His shirt was creamy white, his cuff links gleamed silver under the porchlights and his tie was perfectly knotted. Impulsively, I gave him a kiss on his cheek just as Tash opened the door.

"Remember what I said about making it up to you?" I gave him a sultry look as I turned to walk into the house. "Maybe I can start later tonight, if you know what I mean—"

The next moment I was sprawled on my tush, tears welling up in my eyes and my nose feeling like someone had just whacked it with a baseball bat. Out of the corner of my eye I saw Mikhail take the front steps at a bound as he came toward me, but Van was already pulling me to my feet.

"I think you're going to have to formally invite Megan in," he said with a strained smile at Tash.

"Invite her in?" Tash's mouth formed an O of comprehension. "Oh, invite her *in*." She looked at me with something like pity, but then her gaze sharpened. "Uh, come on in, you guys. Except this is a one-time-only pass, Megan. Sorry, but I've got to take some precautions in case you come back later tonight all fangy and looking for blood."

It hadn't been a great start to the evening. And when Mikhail had told me that his at-a-distance bodyguarding of me didn't include being driven in another car while I went with Van to the club, and *I* told *him* that I wasn't going to have him riding shotgun with with the two of us, and then Darkheart butted in and suggested Van take his own car and—well, you get the picture. I'd received proof positive that my change to vamp was nearly complete, plus I'd ended up chauffeuring Darkheart and Mikhail while Tash and Kat rode with my date.

By the time I swerved into the Hot Box's packed parking lot and stopped at the entrance, the atmosphere in the Mini was funereal. Although Darkheart hadn't said as much I knew he was worried for Kat, and as he opened the passenger door to get out, I saw the strain on his features. Suddenly I felt ashamed. For the past week I'd been rivaling Tash in the it's-all-about-me category, I reflected, and it was time I snapped out of it.

"Kat's the Daughter. She was born for this." As he'd done earlier to me, I briefly touched my hand to Darkheart's knee as he started to exit the car. "She may have trouble handling some aspects of her legacy, but so did Mom."

"*Da,* is what I am remembering," he said in a low tone as he got out of the Mini.

"I guess that wasn't the best point to make," I said under my breath as I headed for a parking space. I glanced into the rearview mirror at Mikhail, who was looking out the window at the arriving crowds of women.

Many of the faces were unfamiliar to me and I realized that Tash had either sent out a mass e-mail or the prospect of male strippers had tempted party-crashers. But the guest list wasn't my main concern at the moment. As I saw a space and inserted the Mini into it, I opened my mouth to speak.

"Don't." Mikhail's single-word sentence forestalled what I'd been about to say. Before I could reply, he was out of the Mini. I took the keys from the ignition and got out, too.

"Don't what?"

"Don't apologize for how you feel."

Like Van, he was dressed for the occasion, although I had no idea how he'd produced appropriate attire on such short notice. His suit and tie were midnight black against the snowy contrast of his white shirt, and as I looked at him I had the totally unworthy impulse to push him up against the Mini and indulge in a quickie before heading into the Hot Box. His gaze flared at me.

"I'm your *oboroten,* not your tame fuck, Crosse. Like I say, you don't have to apologize for the way you feel about Ryder. What happened between you and me didn't come with a Valentine's card, it was just physical, and I don't have a problem with that. What I do have a problem with is that for an instant when you were on the phone with him this morning, you couldn't believe you'd done it with a shape-shifter."

"That's not true!" My denial was automatic.

"Yeah, it is," he said steadily. "Ryder's human. I'm part of the darkness that's invaded your life. You don't mind slumming in the darkness once in a while just for a thrill, but as far as you're concerned it doesn't compare to the normal world." His jaw tightened. "I don't think of myself as completely human, either. Only difference is, I don't see my wolf side as making me less than equal to someone like Ryder."

If everything he'd said had been totally untrue, I probably would have reacted with justified anger. But there was a smidge of truth in it.

Which meant that I didn't react with mere anger, but with towering fury.

"You got that right, Mikey-baby!" I spat out. "Your wolf side isn't what makes you less than Van—it's your personality that does! Whatever the hell I did to deserve having you tied to me, I wish I could somehow take it back because I can't take any more of your constant pissiness!" I glared at him. "I don't want you as my *oboroten!* I don't want your protection, I don't want to be bound to you by some stupid ancient contract, I just want to be *free* of you, understand?"

A sharp shock ran through me, as if I'd stuck a fork into a toaster. I jumped, and saw Mikhail give a sudden start, as well.

I stared at him. "Did I just do what I think I did?" I asked incredulously. "What about having to say it in Aramaic?"

Mikhail's gaze narrowed. "Anton does everything the old-fashioned way, even when he doesn't have to. My guess is he didn't tell you how to break the contract between us because he knew you would, the first chance you got."

"So you can walk away from me now?" I said slowly.

"I don't know." He held my gaze. "The only way to find out is for me to try."

For a heartbeat longer he looked at me. Then he turned and began striding between the parked cars toward the entrance. He reached the double doors of the Hot Box and went into the club.

Mikhail Vostoroff wasn't my *oboroten* anymore. He hadn't even looked back.

Chapter 17

"At least the evening hasn't been a total bust," Tash said glumly to Kat and me.

It was after midnight and although our nonreception reception was still going full blast, of Zena there'd been no sign. I caught sight of Van standing in line at the bar and smiled at him before turning my attention to Tash. "How do you figure that?"

She nodded toward a Chanel-clad brunette sitting with a group near the stage. A buff fireman, stripped down to boots and not much else, was gyrating in front of the brunette while she avidly stuffed five-dollar bills between his suspenders and his oiled chest. "I'll never be intimidated by Mandy Broyhill again. By my count, that's her tenth lap dance of the night."

"I don't blame her," Kat drawled. "Those strippers you hired are so hot I'm surprised the sprinklers haven't come on."

"The only part of this I personally arranged was the balloons," Tash said with a glance at the festively beribboned globes held aloft near the ceiling by a mesh net. "I left everything else up to the club, including hiring the talent. Even though they were just as fooled by their new Russian boss-lady as the general public was, the remaining staff's worried about losing their jobs, what with the club's owner missing and the ongoing police investigation. The day manager was only too happy to accommodate us." She sighed. "I thought this was such a great idea. I should have known Zena would realize it was a trap."

"She could still show up." Kat waved away a passing drinks waiter. "If the bitch does show, I don't want my skills impaired, whether by alcohol or anything else, sweetie," she said in response to my raised eyebrows. "That's why I wore this." She took a step, the thigh-high slit in her ice-blue silk sheath parting to show a tanned length of leg. She frowned in mock disapproval at my black DSquared dress with its top to bottom zip and then at Tashya's apricot Escada confection. "You two look yummy, but those outfits aren't exactly staking wear."

"You sound as if you'd welcome a confrontation," I said. "No offense, Kat, but that's not exactly the impression you gave earlier. I mean, you made it clear you wouldn't back down from her if the two of you met, but now—"

"Now I sound like I'm looking forward to it?" She tipped her head to one side. "Maybe I am. I did a lot of thinking today and I realized how stupid I've been, tearing myself up everytime I make a kill. They're vamps. They have to be eliminated. That's going to be my attitude from now on."

"Works for me," Van said as he joined us. He handed me

a celery-garnished drink. "One virgin Mary, as ordered. And you have no idea what I suffered through to get it," he added.

I patted his arm. "I saw the hordes of females at the bar. Just be glad you're not wearing suspenders and rubber boots."

"I might as well have been," he informed me. "I got my ass pinched four times while I was waiting in line."

"*Da,* I felt pinch, too." Darkheart had made his way through the crowd and now he looked indignantly over his shoulder at an elegant older woman with cropped silver hair whom I recognized as Liz Dixon, a local art gallery owner. She waggled her fingers at him and he spun back to face us. "*Amerikanec* women are much bolder than in Russia," he sputtered. "Where is Mikhail?"

I kept my expression neutral. I'd told Van that I'd broken the bond between me and Mikhail, but I hadn't yet shared that information with Darkheart or my sisters. "Why, did you want to talk to him about something?"

He shook his head. "*Nyet.* Is only I begin to have bad feeling about all this. Probably nothing," he muttered.

"*Definitely* nothing," Kat asserted. She patted her thigh. "I've got my handy-dandy vamp-sticker, and if Zena crashes our party I'm sending her to hell. What's to worry about?"

"And even though I'm not the official Daughter, I'm perfectly willing to send a bunch of her vamp buddies to the hot place with her," Tash said complacently. "Besides which, I've got a little surprise prepared."

"The vial of holy water I saw you tuck into your evening bag?" Kat said with a smile. "Good thinking. We make quite a kick-ass team, no?"

I know Tash answered her. I seem to remember seeing the worried look in Darkheart's eagle gaze fade, to be replaced with one of affectionate pride. I was aware that beside me, Van made a small joke, and of my sisters and Darkheart laughing at it, but none of that was important compared to the sickening revelation that swept over me.

The moment I'd been dreading for so long had come at last, I realized in icy horror. I'd just turned vamp.

Kat had made a mistake telling me where she kept her stake, I thought with detached calculation. In less than a second I could be upon her, knocking her to the floor and disarming her. After that, it would be easy to get to Tash. My gaze flicked to my youngest sister, and for a split second I realized I felt nothing toward her but a cold emptiness.

A wave of dizziness passed over me and hastily I raised my drink to my lips, but as I saw the thick red tomato juice in the glass I suddenly felt as if I was going to be sick.

"We've been here for hours and I still haven't made the acquaintance of the formidable Ms. Broyhill," Van declared, taking me by the elbow. "If you'll excuse us, folks, Megan and I are going to make nice with the guests."

"Van, I'm not up to small talk at the moment," I said shakily as he led me through the crowd. "I—I feel a little nauseous. I probably should have eaten something before—"

"Cut the crap, Megan." His tone was sharp with concern. "Something happened to you just now while we were talking with your sisters and your grandfather. That's why I made an excuse to get you alone. What's the matter?"

"I've turned." I had to force the words out. "You shouldn't be near me, I'm not safe to be around. Please go."

"Like hell." He scanned the room. Then he nodded

toward a door I hadn't noticed before, not far from the stage. "Let's get you out of this crowd."

I felt too stricken to protest, but as we closed the door behind us and the noise of the music and merrymakers was suddenly muffled, I pulled my elbow from his grip. Van stood aside to let me precede him up the short flight of stairs in front of us, but I shook my head. "I once told you what I planned to do if I ever turned, and now it's time to put that plan into effect." I raised my hand to touch his cheek, but then I withdrew it. "I don't even trust myself to touch you," I whispered, feeling the tears start to my eyes. "When I looked at my sisters it took all my control not to throw myself on them and attack them…and I don't know how long my control can last. Just say goodbye and let me walk away from you, Van, *please*."

"Not this risk-taker, honey." He gave me a tight smile. "I told you two nights ago how I felt about you, Megan. Nothing's changed for me. We're going to deal with this problem together." He tipped my chin up so that my gaze couldn't avoid his. "It's just a matter of time before Kat destroys Zena, right? As long as we make it impossible for you to take first blood before she's dusted, the curse will lift with her death."

"That's one theory," I said, hope rising in me despite myself. "What are you proposing?"

"Up these stairs is an office. While we were going over the crime scene here I used it as a coordination post, and it's still off-limits to the Hot Box staff so you'll be alone in there." A corner of his mouth lifted. "I left some odds and ends behind, including a pair of cuffs. I know this isn't how we'd hoped to use them, but if Zena doesn't show up tonight,

I'm sure your grandfather can think of another way we can contain you for the next few days until she's staked."

"Said containment to include a whole bunch of wild garlic, holy water and crucifixes?" I tried to smile but the tears that had been brimming in my eyes splashed over. "Oh, Van—it just might work!" I moved in closer to press a kiss to his lips. "How did I ever get lucky enough to meet someone like you? I didn't plan to tell you like this, but I think I'm falling—"

Kill him now while he's vulnerable! The terrible thought tore through my mind with such cold intensity that I reeled backwards from Van. I could tell from his alarmed gaze that my horror was mirrored in my eyes.

"You'd better secure me right away," I said through numb lips as I pushed past him to the stairs. "When you have, find Mikhail and tell him to stand guard over me. He's the only one here who won't have any problem killing me if I manage to free myself from the cuffs."

The location of the Hot Box's office had been chosen for a specific reason, I thought half an hour later as I sat at a metal desk, my left wrist encircled by a steel cuff. The other end of the cuff had been snapped closed through an iron ring on the door of a massive, old-fashioned safe. My movements were limited, but I'd been able to reach the curtains that stretched the length of the wall in front of the desk and pull them aside to reveal a long window that looked down on the main floor of the club. From here, a suspicious manager could watch the bartender to make sure all sales were rung in, and also have a good view of the tables where the lap dances took place.

But I didn't care about the bartender or the strippers. I just wanted to see Van escorting Mikhail through the crowd, and so far I hadn't. I'd spotted him when I'd first opened the curtains and looked down on the floor below. He'd been talking with Kat and I'd seen her shake her head. From her he'd gone to Darkheart, who'd gestured with a shrug toward the exit in an apparent guess as to where Mikhail might be. I'd watched Van make his way out of the room, but that had been fifteen minutes ago and he hadn't reappeared.

There were two possible reasons for his non-appearance with Mikhail: either he hadn't yet found my former *oboroten,* or else he had, and Mikhail had refused to cooperate. I hoped it was the first, not the second reason, but as I remembered the bitter words we'd exchanged upon our arrival my heart sunk.

Mikhail had thought I'd seen his wolf side as making him less than equal…to a man like Van, and to myself. And there'd been a sliver of truth in that, I admitted with shame, just as there'd been a sliver of truth in Tash's assertion that I'd slept with him just to see how hot his wild side was.

"Well, I definitely got the answer to that question," I muttered unhappily under my breath while staring through the window at the stage as the lights dimmed to announce a new stripper. "But although I never thought I'd hear myself say it, mind-blowing orgasms aren't the only thing a girl looks for in a relationship. Sometimes she just wants someone to be there for her, to share the moment with, to be human for God's sake! And that's what Van—*wow!*" My jaw dropped as I saw the G-string-clad Adonises who were strutting onto the stage.

Okay, you're probably thinking, *damn*, girlfriend—you just turned into a vampire, plus only a moment ago you were all, sex is dandy but there's more in life than the horizontal mambo. Now you're taking a time-out to drool over a troupe of male strippers? And to that admittedly justified criticism, all I can say is you had to be there to see those living dreams parading around on the Hot Box stage. Their bodies were oiled so that the amber spotlights gleamed off their pecs, their biceps, their six-pack abs. Every single man jack among them had a chiselly jaw, luscious lips and a butt you could bounce a dime on, although any woman who wastes her time bouncing dimes when confronted with a delectable hard body needs to get her priorities straight, in my opinion. But none of the hormone-charged females in the audience was thinking of small change. I saw Mandy Broyhill standing on the seat of her chair waving a thick sheaf of bills, and then others in the crowd were doing the same.

Suddenly it all seemed wrong to me—the shimmering perfection of the men on stage, the fever-pitch of desire in the audience, the cluster of waiters standing at the back of the room as if waiting for a signal. A staccato drumroll came over the sound system, a brilliant white spotlight illuminated the curtained entrance to the stage, and a woman dressed in a scanty version of a circus ringmaster's costume walked into the spotlight, her hair rippling like living fire down her back.

At the same time, Van entered the room. As I saw his gaze sweep over the men on stage and then harden on the red-haired mistress of ceremonies, I knew my *oboroten*'s absence had just dropped to second place on his list of problems.

"Are we all here for good time, ladies?" Zena purred, giving the whip in her hand a playful *crack!* Despite the pane of glass between us, I could hear her perfectly thanks to the audio feed piped into the office. The speakers on the desk in front of me almost vibrated off as the audience's roar of agreement surged through them, and Zena's red lips curved cruelly. "Then let games *begin!*" she screamed as the pulsing beat of a rap song began booming over the sound system and the vamp strippers began to leap off the stage into the crowd.

At that point the action went split-screen. Since I wasn't watching a movie and the events unfolding in front of me were all happening at once in a jumble of lights and bodies and movement, when I think back on that night all I see in my mind are a handful of images ripped from a larger, confusing scene. My gaze instinctively sought out Kat and I saw a flash of ice-blue move swiftly through the press of laughing women. Relief flooded me as I realized she'd recognized the strippers as vamps, even if those around her didn't realize the danger they were in. Then my breath caught in my throat as I glimpsed Mandy Broyhill, still waving her bills in the air, leap onto a nearly naked vamp. The next moment one of her posse, a mousy-looking blond woman, wrenched Mandy off her prize and triumphantly ran her hands over the stripper's carved abs.

I saw the vamp's fangs lengthen. From her ignominious position on the floor where she'd fallen, Mandy's furious expression froze and I guessed she'd glimpsed his metamorphosis, too. But the mousy blonde, unaware that the buff body she was caressing belonged to an undead creep, squealed in excitement as the stripper lowered his mouth to her neck.

Then Kat was upon him, pushing the blonde aside. Her stake sliced through the air as the snarling *vampyr* turned to attack her, her unerring aim plunging the yew-wood blade through his oiled pec into his heart. Kat swayed, but held her stake steady as the vampire, chiseled jaw and all, disintegrated.

"Dammit, Kat, don't stand there waiting around for him to dust!" I tried to get closer to the window but the cuff yanked me back. "Stake in, stake out, and get ready for the next—"

As if my warning had reached her, she whirled around just in time to nail the vamp coming at her from behind. I caught a glimpse of her white face before my attention was diverted.

"Omigod, it wasn't the Mai Tais!" Mandy bent down and wrenched off one of her shoes before facing a vampire who was attempting to seize her. As his fangs lengthened she dodged out of his way, her expression a mixture of fury and unwilling comprehension. "I *did* see what I just thought I saw! You're a…you're a…" She swallowed. Then her chin jutted out and she reared back like a Yankee pitcher and slammed her shoe against his chest. I shook my head in mingled admiration and dread.

"Kitten heels, Broyhill. Not only a cop-out fashion choice, but totally not long enough to pierce the heart," I muttered tensely. "You should have gone with stilettos this evening."

"Heads up, ladies, party favors coming down! Grab some and protect yourselves!"

The shrill cry cut through the pandemonium that now

filled the Hot Box. I looked in the direction of the voice and saw Tash standing by the entrance to the room, her upraised arm jerking a rope that snaked up the wall to the ceiling. The net above parted and the gaily-colored balloons it had been tethering began floating down upon the crowd…along with a rain of more solid objects clattering floorward—stakes, garlic and crosses. A stake fell on the table beside Mandy just as the vamp she'd tried to dust came for her and I saw her lunge desperately for it. She retrieved it, turned to the vamp, and drove Tash's party-favor stake hard into his chest.

From my own experience with Dean, I know there's nothing like a girl's first successful staking to sweep the final shreds of doubt from her mind. Mandy stared down at the pile of dust at her feet before whirling to the rest of her dumbfounded posse. "What are you all standing around for? Grab a stake!" she screamed. "And if I see anyone shirking, you'll never eat lunch in this town again!"

Whether galvanized into action by Mandy's threat or by their own sense of self-preservation, women all over the room started scrambling for the party favors my sister had supplied. Tash herself began laying about her with a will, her technique enthusiastic, if not as polished as Kat's. The brat was doing her best, I thought, swallowing past the sudden lump of love and fear in my throat. Her party-favor idea had been sheer genius, but it was all too obvious she wasn't a Daughter of Lilith. That title belonged to Kat, who never missed, never underestimated her opponents and who was even now dealing yet another of Zena's Chippendale-wannabes a death blow.

I spared a glance at the fiery-haired queen *vampyr*, who

was watching the action from her vantage point on the stage. She didn't seem worried that several of her undead boy-toys had fallen in action, I noted with a stab of suspicion.

"Granddaughter!"

Darkheart's cry of alarm broke into my worries about Zena. Kat was staggering backwards from the vampire she'd just staked as if she, not he, were the one who'd been dealt a mortal blow. Only Darkheart's steadying arm around her shoulders kept her from losing her balance. I waited for Kat to recover, but instead she did something that turned my blood to ice.

Raising our mother's stake high above her head, she flung it violently from her. It went flying over the crowd and hit the far wall where it splintered and broke before falling in two useless pieces onto the floor.

She collapsed into Darkheart's arms, her eyelids fluttering closed. On the stage, Zena began screaming with laughter. And looking down on them all, I was suddenly filled with a numbing sense of shock.

By doing what no Daughter would do—destroying her stake and retreating from the fight—Kat had just proved she hadn't inherited our mother's title. Tash was barely holding her own. That left only one Crosse triplet who could kill vamps with a cold and efficient zeal, who felt a savage satisfaction in battle, and who was capable of going up against Zena.

I was that triplet. And I was handcuffed to half a ton of iron, with no possibility of escape.

Mikhail, I need you! The cry reverberated through my mind with the intensity of a scream as I struggled against the steel band that encircled my wrist. A wave of nausea hit me as one of my frenzied attempts came close to dislocating my left shoulder, and again I silently screamed out the psychic call—not to the man I'd fallen in love with and who had the key to the cuffs that held me, but to the shape-shifter I'd sent from my life. In desperation I bent my head and began gnawing at my wrist, hoping the slickness of my own blood would help the cuff slide free. In the part of my brain that wasn't maddened with desperation, I knew that calling to Mikhail instead of Van didn't make any sense.

"But neither does the fact that I'm both a vamp *and* the only female in this generation of my family who got some of Mom's abilities, even though the vampness will eventually win out," I muttered, one foot braced against the heavy bulk of the old-fashioned safe as I strained to drag my hand free. Steel slid through blood and then jammed against the trapezium bone below the first knuckle of my thumb. "And that could happen at any moment. I'm showing all the symptoms, including my inability to enter the house without an invitation. There's just no other way to explain the changes in me."

"I always knew we'd find something to agree on." I jerked my head around to see Mikhail standing in the doorway, the partially open door obscuring his full view of me. His eyes took on a sudden lupine light. "I smell blood."

He stepped into the room and stopped dead. Then he was at my side and shrugging out of his shirt. "Who did this to you?" he asked tightly, tearing a strip of fabric and pressing it to my ragged flesh. Instantly the white material became crimson.

"I did it to myself. I don't have time to explain everything, but Van cuffed me at my request and now I have to get free." I ripped off the bandage he'd just applied and leveled a flat stare at him. "I need you to kiss me."

From his harsh intake of breath I knew he understood what was behind my request. "You wouldn't have put yourself in this position unless you knew you were about to turn. Do you really think all you have to do is ask and I'll set you free?"

I glanced with barely concealed impatience at the fight taking place below and then met his eyes again. "You kiss me while you begin to shape-shift. I start turning into a wolf with you, and as soon as you hear the cuff fall from my foreleg you reverse the shift and we're human again. Yes, I think you'd do that for me." I took a breath. "Even though there's no longer a bond between us."

His expression unreadable, he took me into his arms. "You broke the one that tied me to you as your *oboroten,* but what happened between us last night forged a new chain for me."

"What happened between us last night was that we had incredible sex. Neither one of us saw it as a commitment." I regretted the words as soon as they left my mouth but I didn't have time to rephrase them. I lifted my face for his kiss, relieved he wasn't fighting me on this, at least.

"That's all you saw it as, us having sex?" Mikhail's hold on me tightened as if I'd just confirmed a suspicion he'd harbored for a long time. "Most of what I sensed about you the night we met was right, sweetheart. I smelled danger and pain coming off you so thickly it was as if you were surrounded by a icy fog…and at the center of that fog was an even icier core. But I made two mistakes."

His mouth opened on mine. His lashes swept down, shuttering the gold of his eyes, and his tongue moved slowly inside me before he eased back, his breath warm on my lips. "I thought the coldness I sensed in you meant you bore Zena's mark. I forgot that there's one being even colder than a vampire."

I needed to *fight*, I thought. Why couldn't dual shape-shifting be a simple wham-bam-thank-you-ma'am affair instead of all this soul-sharing and intimacy? Frustration made my tone curt. "What could be colder than a vamp?"

"The Daughter who lives to kill them," he said, his mouth moving to mine again. *"You."*

This time he kissed me without holding back. Immediately I felt the wildness spilling from him into me, the powerful sensations of the shift mingling with the shock of his impossible statement. As if from a long way away I heard the clang of metal against metal. An agonizing pain lanced through me and I guessed we were reversing the change we'd half completed.

Then it was over. Mikhail's mouth lifted from mine and involuntarily I glanced through the window at the scene below, my undamaged right hand already retrieving my stake from inside the front of my dress. I turned to him. "I'm not the Daughter, Mikhail. After arguing away all the other evidence for me being a vamp I'm still left with the fact that I couldn't enter the house tonight. I hate knowing that I carry Zena's mark, but since I do, I'll use its darkness against her and her kind while I can. Let's go."

"I can do more damage in wolf form. I'll join you as soon as I've shifted." He looked at me, his gaze molten. "Take care the darkness doesn't turn on you," he added.

But I was already out the door.

Chapter 18

I love the smell of vamp-dust in the morning. After my near-shape-shift with Mikhail, my senses were still wolfishly heightened as I strode onto the Hot Box floor. I stood for a moment, feeling a Zenlike calm settle over me—which was ironic, since the situation around me was anything but.

Zena was no longer on the stage. Hoping to glimpse her, I saw instead a ferocious-looking female climb out from underneath a table, a stake in either hand and her face smeared with grime. Her outfit consisted of a string of matched pearls around her neck, a silk blouse and a pink Chanel jacket. From her waist down all she had on were a pair of beige pantyhose and kitten-heeled shoes.

"Mandy?" I murmured disbelievingly. The reason for

her no-skirt look became obvious as she ran from one table to the next.

"Now I've seen everything," I said under my breath, averting my gaze to the rest of the room. Overturned tables and chairs were everywhere and the floor was a minefield of broken glass, popped balloons, and fruit slices from spilled cocktails. Burly vamps had taken up positions at the exits, but instead of the usual bouncer duty of removing troublemakers from the room, they were obviously there to prevent anyone from leaving.

The confused free-for-all I'd witnessed from upstairs had evolved into several pitched battles. One was taking place in the bar area where Kat had fallen, and my breath caught in my throat as I saw Van grappling so closely with a vamp that the two of them looked as if they were engaged in a grim dance. Even as I started forward, Van made a sudden move. The next moment his dance partner was dust and no longer blocking my view.

"God, *no!*" As I whispered the automatic words of denial my heart contracted. The prone figure of Kat was laid out on the bar's marble-topped counter, looking like a body on a mortuary slab. Then I saw Liz Dixon at the bar sink wringing out a damp towel. She handed it to Darkheart, who placed it on Kat's forehead before reaching for her wrist and glancing at the bar clock on the wall beside him.

I let out a relieved breath. The fact that Kat was still unconscious was worrying, but Darkheart and Liz were monitoring her condition and Van was providing protection. As hard as it was to take my attention from her, I needed to assess the situation in the rest of the room.

The Maplesburg contingent were holding their own so

far, judging from the scattered piles of vamp-ash I could see. Not only were the thirty or so vamps in the room heavily outnumbered, but Tash's stake-drop had obviously caught them off-balance by arming the women they'd assumed would be easy prey. Some of Zena's boys had adjusted their tactics, however. Like jackals hanging around an antelope herd, they kept to the fringes of the crowd and watched for any woman standing alone.

Which was why I hadn't jumped into the fray as soon as I'd stepped into the room. Even before I'd seen Mandy, I'd glimpsed the five gorgeous hunks heading purposefully my way and had decided that if they wanted to save me the trouble of hunting them down individually, I'd let them. Out of the corner of my eye I saw them move apart with the obvious intention of surrounding me when they were close enough and I quickly dropped my gaze, hoping I looked like a woman paralysed with terror instead of one who was about to seriously turn the tables on their planned clustersuck of me.

My terrified act was convincing enough to fool Zena's boy-toys. Unfortunately, it also fooled Tash.

I'd been holding my stake so that it was concealed from the approaching vamps. As I discreetly adjusted my grip and felt the leather-and-ivory handle snug into my palm, through my lowered lashes I saw a blur of apricot swing over the heads of the crowd.

"Don't worry, Meg, I'm coming!" Tash yelled as the rope I'd seen her pull earlier to release the balloons arced closer, with her clinging to it. "Your asses are totally *mine!*" she added to the five undead strippers.

Okay, how do I put this in a nice way? It would be

bitchy to suggest that Tash looked like an Escada-clad Tarzan as she sailed through the air on her vine, I mean, rope. So I'll just say that I wondered what Darkheart had been thinking when he'd devoted hours of practice to teaching my sister the finer points of rope-swinging and back-flips, when what vamp-killing came down to was facing and staking the bastards. Which was what I'd been about to do before Tash threw me off my game, I might add.

The vamp nearest me had surfer-boy good looks enhanced by the *glamyr* he was projecting. His Malibu-blue gaze traveled over me in a way that was supposed to distract me with thoughts of him and me doing it on a beach, and to make sure I didn't miss his point he slowly licked his lips. Since, in my experience, beach sex makes about as much sense as handing your partner a sandpaper condom, I decided instead to take surfer-vamp's lip-licking as a sign that he wanted to be the first in line to taste my stake.

I started to oblige him, and of course, Tash chose that exact moment to let go of her rope.

I was halfway into my lunge at the vamp, my upper arm and shoulder locked and my backhand thrust already slicing my fisted weapon toward him, when she landed between us. I had an instant's glimpse of her startled face and an even briefer glimpse of surfer-vamp's as he saw the unexpected get-out-of-Hell-free card fate had just dropped on him. Pulling her to him, he aimed his fangs at her neck as she tried to shove him away. I didn't have time to think, so I just acted.

Tash's yell of pain mingled with surfer-vamp's scream of rage as my stake sliced through the web of skin between her thumb and her outspread hand and buried itself in his heart. A thrill of satisfaction rushed through me with the same icy heat as a shot of vodka. In one smooth motion I wrenched my stake free from both the now-disintegrating vamp and Tash's hand, and pivoted instantly to impale it in the chest of my next target. I was in the zone now, my mind filled with a cold clarity that shut out all distractions and focused only on the essentials—like the fact that a snarling black-and-silver wolf had just taken down one of the two nearest vampires. "Thanks, Mikhail," I murmured, turning my full attention to the other vamp. "Stay out of my way, Tash," I added in the same detached tone as I stiff-armed her aside and drove my stake into my current target.

Since Mikhail was keeping vamp number four occupied, as I pulled my stake free I tossed it into my left hand and caught it with the ivory blade facing toward my wrist, which was still braceleted with blood from my struggle with the handcuffs. Without turning around, I executed a backward thrust at the undead who was about to attack me from behind before moving toward the one struggling with Mikhail and dusting him, too.

I scanned the room. "Over there, Mikhail—those seven *vampyrs* fighting with Mandy and her posse. We'll clean out that hornet's nest next." Mikhail raced ahead of me and I followed, my thoughts so focused that when Tash planted herself in front of me I barely registered her presence. Without breaking stride I moved around her, but I found myself being jerked backward as her hand clamped around my arm.

"I thought you could use my help." Tash's face was pale as I turned to face her. "In return, you sliced a stake through my hand and then knocked me to the floor as I was about to take down one of the vamps that were trying to kill you."

"Now isn't a good time for this," I said briefly, removing her hand from my arm. "Have you seen Zena? The last I saw, she was on the stage but she's—"

I broke off in midsentence, my attention caught by the sight of one of the Hot Box waiters crashing into a nearby table and falling to his knees. His uniform of black pants and white shirt was torn and bloodied, and as he got to his feet and staggered toward us his movements were clumsy with panic.

"You've got to help me get out of here!" He had none of the *glamyred* gorgeousness of the stripper vamps but he was good-looking in a boy-next-door way, although right now his soft brown eyes were wide with terror. "I keep hoping this is a nightmare, but it's not, is it? The vampires are *real!*"

Some of the color came back to Tash's face and her strained expression softened. "Totally real, unfortunately, but that doesn't mean we're defenseless against them. The first thing to do is arm yourself with a stake. Do you have one?"

"No." The young waiter looked sick. "I wouldn't know how to use one if I did."

"It's easy." She patted his arm. "Come on, I'll—"

"Excuse us a minute," I said politely to the waiter. I looked at Tashya. "Can we talk, sis?"

She took a step toward me. "I thought you said it wasn't a good time," she said coolly. "If it's about Zena—"

"It's not," I said as I quickly moved past her and slammed my stake into the waiter's chest. Immediately his soft brown eyes turned a blazing red and his jaws flew open as if he still thought he had a chance to use his fangs on me. I waited until he began to dust and then turned to see Tash staring at me.

"How did you know he was a vamp?" she asked, her voice hoarse with shock. "He seemed so...so *nice!*"

I shrugged. "That's what triggered my alarm bells. He was too good to be true, so I knew he couldn't be what he seemed."

She shook her head. "The way you fought those vamps...even while you were killing them, it was like you saw them and you as being in the same secret club that nobody else could join. And as for staking someone on the basis of a suspicion—what if you'd been *wrong?*" She took a step back. "You're not the sister I know anymore, Megan, so who are you? *What* are you?"

The fear in her eyes told me she knew the answer to her question as well as I did, and that a door had just slammed shut between us. I felt a sudden aching need to be in Van's arms, but when I spoke I made sure there was no trace of vulnerability in my voice. "I'm our mother's daughter, and tonight I'm going to take down the bitch who destroyed her. If you don't approve of how I do that, maybe you should stay away from me."

Tough Megan Crosse, striding away from her sister without looking back. A real kick-ass bitch, with the narrowed gaze of a woman who knows that sometimes a girl's gotta do what a girl's gotta do.

Yeah, right.

Zena had torn my sisters from me and there was only one way to deaden the pain screaming through me. I took care of three vampires in the first ninety seconds of joining Mandy's fight. I let another get close enough to graze me with his fangs before shoving my stake into him with such force that I had to wait for him to dust before I could pull it out, but as soon as I did I spun around and used it on the vamp Mikhail had by the throat. I felt the pain rising up in me again, but when I raced across the room to join a new battle I felt it recede.

How many *vampyrs* did I dust over the next hour? I honestly don't know, but if I'd been cutting notches on my stake I would have ended up with a toothpick. I was aware that their numbers were visibly thinning, and at some point I noticed most of the women who'd been alongside me earlier had retreated to the bar area, which seemed to have been turned into an impromptu field hospital with Van and Tash guarding its perimeter. But with every kill I made I felt less connected to what was happening outside my immediate zone of combat. Even the fact that I hadn't glimpsed Zena since she'd unleashed her gang of undead strippers on us no longer struck me as suspicious.

And before anyone pipes up with the money question, let me say that, yes, Virginia, I really *do* know how unbelievable that seems. My prime target had apparently vanished into thin air and I wasn't worried? The only explanation for that is unacceptable to me—that on some subconscious level, I guessed Zena would appear when the time was right and that everything was unfolding just as she'd planned. It's hard enough to live with the knowledge that I was Zena's puppet that night, but I won't believe I was her willing puppet.

At the time, all that mattered to me was taking down any and all undead comers, so when one of the vamp bouncers made a move for me I blocked Mikhail as he tried to assist me.

"I can handle this," I said as I ducked to avoid the vamp's fist. Under his short-sleeved white knit shirt his muscles looked as though they'd been hewn by a rock-hammer into the approximate shape of a human torso. His charcoal polyester slacks were cinched with a belt around his flat stomach, but strained over his massive thighs and his weight-lifter's butt. "Steroids much?" I asked the bouncer as I dodged another blow.

From a few feet away I heard a growl rumble from Mikhail's throat and I felt bouncer-vamp's foot graze my chin as I jerked my head back from his kick. I risked a glance in Mikhail's direction and briefly met his angry golden stare. "Feels like old times, Mikey-baby, with you growling and glaring at me." I directed my attention back to the bouncer and almost slipped as I stepped on a half circle of sliced orange. "But how about we do the memory-lane thing when I'm not going one-on-one with King Kong here, okay?" I saw my chance and slipped under the vamp's next punch, but his reaction was faster than I expected. Before I could aim my stake at the tiny alligator stitched on the left breast of his shirt, he pulled his punch and almost caught me in a crushing bear-hug. I dropped to the floor and rolled out of his reach before jumping to my feet again.

You want to tell me why you're deliberately prolonging this fight? Mikhail's voice was suddenly in my head, the ominous edge in his tone coming through loud and clear. Grabbing a chair with both hands while I held my stake between my teeth, I smashed it across the bouncer's face.

As he rushed me I sidestepped past him and wrapped my grip around my stake again.

"I'm not." Bouncer-vamp glided suddenly sideways and I danced out of his range. "The first good opportunity I get, I'll stake him."

The hell you will—you're trying to stay in the kill-zone for as long as you can. What are you using it to escape from?

"Fuck you, Vostoroff." I took a step toward Mikhail and sensed the undead bouncer rush up behind me. I spun on my heel. "You, too, hell bait," I said as I thrust my stake into his barrel chest. He disintegrated and I turned back to Mikhail. "So I was playing the extended-mix version with King Kong, so what? You know, Mikey-baby, I'm beginning to understand the whole seduction-of-being-a-vamp thing. You can call it the darkness if you want, but what you and Tash don't get is that it's one hell of a *rush*. Sorry if that blows your theory of me being a Daughter—"

The rest of my sentence stuck in my throat as the room was plunged into total darkness. As a few screams rang out I felt Mikhail's solid bulk press against my leg and my hand dropped quickly to his ruff. "Someone plugged in a kettle and blew a fuse? Nope, that's just not working for me," I said tightly. "Something bad's about to happen, and since the bar's the most crowded area in the room that's probably the target. Can you see well enough in the dark to get us there?"

He was already moving. I threaded my fingers more securely through his ruff and followed his lead, my apprehension growing as I heard low moans coming from some of the women around me. Half an hour ago, most of them had been fighting vamps, so their courage wasn't a question, but there was an difference between an enemy you could see and an invisible, unknowable terror.

"Grandfather! Detective Ryder!" Tash's voice, high and clear, cut through the rising commotion only feet away from me. "Kat's not—"

"Aaaaaaahhhh!" A terrible sound suddenly filled the darkness, a harsh, guttural scream so all-enveloping that it seemed less like something audible and more like a solid element that instantly existed in the room. It stopped and picked up again at exactly the same level and intensity, as if it was one unending barrage that had been arbitrarily cut and spliced back together. It was the sound of someone staring into the smoking heart of hell, and there was no sanity in it at all.

I let go of Mikhail's fur and blundered forward. Again the scream battered against my eardrums, and I felt the madness in it seeping into my own brain as I slammed into something.

No, some*one*. Even before I was conscious of reacting, I had the point of my stake jammed into a shirtfront. A split-second later I realized there was a stake pressing into me. I froze, trying to blot out the scream long enough to think.

And then a light snapped on somewhere in the room and I found myself staring into Van's shocked face. Like a pair of explosives experts gingerly snipping through the last two wires of a bomb, we both lowered our stakes and took an unsteady step back. He exhaled shakily.

"Aaaaaaahhh!"

My gaze flew from him toward the direction of the scream. Only then did I realize that the light in the room came from a single cone of illumination focused down onto one of the chrome striptease poles on the stage. Two women stood inside the harshly brilliant circle. One had her back to me, but I didn't need to see her face to recognize the red hair rippling like flame down the back of the floor-length velvet gown. The other woman was standing against the pole facing the room, and although I could see her clearly, I doubted whether she saw anything. Her eyes were wide and darkly blank. The tendons in her neck stood out like cords. Her mouth was frozen open as the terrible scream kept coming from her, and the heavy chains that bound her to the pole cut into her tanned flesh so deeply that her ice-blue dress was spattered with blood.

It was Kat. Wrenching my horrified gaze from her, I whirled around and bent over. I straightened up, filled with a hatred more corrosive than the sickness that had just spilled from me. I took a step forward and felt Van's grip on my wrist.

"Let go of me," I said thickly.

I pulled free of his grasp. On the stage Zena shook back a red velvet sleeve from one ring-laden hand and half turned away from Kat. With sudden viciousness, she spun toward her again, the back of her hand smashing across my sister's face so powerfully that Kat's head snapped sideways like a rag doll's.

Her scream abruptly stopped and her head dropped to her chest, blood pouring from the ring slashes across her face. She sagged away from the pole, the cruel bite of the chains all that kept her upright, and I heard a collective gasp come from the women in the room. My heart turned to stone in my chest.

"She's killed her," Van said hoarsely.

"Bitch would not be so kind." Darkheart's voice was flat with pain. "She only silences her, so noise does not offend her ears. Stay where you are!" His sharp command was directed at me, but as Tash also moved forward on the other side of him, he clamped a hand on her shoulder.

"And continue to watch Kat being tortured?" she demanded hotly. "I don't think so. I'm going to take Zena down."

"Your sister will be dead before you can raise your stake." Darkheart's voice was a rasp. "This is her game and she will play it her way."

"Very good, old man!" Zena turned from Kat, her gaze immediately fixing on Darkheart as if there were no one else in the room. She brought her palms together for three slow claps that sounded jarringly loud in the silence that had fallen over the crowd. "Is game with rules, as you say. But you have already broken them, and now game is over." Her tone became almost sympathetic, and I felt my grip tighten on the stake at my side. "Is probably for the best. Your line has played out. Dzarchertzyn line—" She paused, for the first time turning her smile on the women in front of me. The group seemed to draw in among themselves. "But in America, is polite I use name easier on American tongue, *da?* Darkheart line was once formidable opponent against me and my kind, but now is not so. Your blood has thinned, old man. This is not your fault and I am not monster, to hold it against you."

Darkheart shook his head. "You do hold something against me," he said. "Whatever it is, release my granddaughter and take your vengeance on me."

Zena's mouth tightened to a red slash, the pretence of sweet reason she'd assumed falling away. "This *is* how I take my vengeance on you, Darkheart—by destroying what you love, as I did once before! Then you insulted me by sending a lapsed Daughter against me. Now you send a false Daughter, a mewling girl who does not even have the stomach to kill the trash I tossed at her tonight. Do you know where she is right now, old man? Do you know why she screams?" She drew herself up to her full height. "She is in *hell!* She is suffering alongside those few she killed, screaming at the same tortures. Every moment she is there is an eternity to her, Darkheart, and when I kill her I will make that eternity of hell real!"

Her sleeve fell away from her hand again as she spread her fingers, showing crimson nails. "You drove a stake through your daughter's beating heart, old man. I let you do same with granddaughter's when I tear it from her chest."

Zena began to turn toward Kat. Cursing myself for listening to Darkheart when he'd warned that any move on our part would cause Kat's death, I pushed urgently past him and Van just as Tash's voice rang out behind me.

"You skanky undead bitch, leave my sister out of this!"

Zena froze, her taloned hand outstretched toward Kat. "Skanky?" She shook her head in seeming confusion, her eyes taking on a flat red sheen. "Is unfamiliar *Americanic* word to me. Means what?"

"Look it up in the dictionary sometime," Tash retorted. "Except you won't be able to, because you'll be a big pile of ashes. You're all, 'I've been dissed because Darkheart sent a non-Daughter against me'?" Her voice quavered slightly. "Well, you're right—Kat obviously isn't a Daughter of Lilith, so I guess that must mean I am."

Mikhail stood in the shadows behind her and Van and Darkheart were nearby, but I only saw Tashya…and I suddenly knew it was the first time I truly was seeing her—not as my brat sister but as the woman she really was.

A dried trickle of blood ran from her tangled curls to her eyebrow and her lips were pressed together in a stubborn expression she'd worn dozens of times over the years during spats with Kat or me, always a signal that she was determined to take the fight to the limit even if she wasn't sure she'd win. Although her opponent in this fight was the queen vamp who'd destroyed our mother and put our sister in hell, Tash wasn't backing down this time, either.

She was so damn brave, so damn loyal, so damn… I saw her turn her back to the stage and my heart sank. "Oh, Tashie, you're so damn predictable," I said under my breath.

She snapped into a backflip and kept going, tumbling end over end through the parted crowd of women toward the stage. I stuck out my foot.

While she was still dazedly sorting out her limbs I walked over to her, extending my hand as Darkheart came toward us. As she stood to face me she snatched her fingers free from mine. "I can't believe you just did that, Megan!" she said furiously. "Who the hell do you think you *are?*"

"What I tried as hard as possible to convince myself I couldn't be, Tashie," I said flatly. "I'm a Daughter of Lilith."

Chapter 19

"You half suspected that earlier this evening, didn't you?" I asked Tash.

She opened her mouth, the words of denial ready to spill from her. Then her eyes met mine and she let out a breath. "It's so totally not fair," she said unevenly.

"I know it's not. You would have made a way better Daughter than me." I began to turn away. "But this is my fight, Tash."

"Stake you are carrying is unusual. Where did you get, Granddaughter?" Darkheart's tone was sharp.

"I stole it from Zena," I answered. "Why, is that another Daughter of Lilith rule I've gone and broken? Look, I know you probably can't believe I'm the—"

"Was not what I was going to say at all. Fits your hand like was made for you."

I looked past Darkheart to the gleam of gold eyes in the shadows behind him. "I'm getting used to the feel of it," I said shortly. Squaring my shoulders, I turned toward the stage.

Be with me. As I touched the leather-wrapped ivory to my lips, the words ran silently through my mind. I clamped the stake between my teeth and began to run, no longer thinking of anything or anyone but the task and the opponent ahead of me. I reached the stage and leapt onto it, landing in a half crouch facing Zena. Instantly I straightened, ready to strike.

"Was mistake not to let me take you easy way. Now you will be dying very hard, my darling."

Her voice came from behind me. As I spun around in disbelief, something smashed into the back of my legs. They gave way under me and I went sprawling full-length onto the floor.

"But life as Daughter is harder, so perhaps death is not so bad, *da?*"

I looked up in time to see the iron pipe in Zena's grip swing down at me and rolled sideways just as it crashed into the spot where I'd been, the force of the blow splitting the wood floor. I forced myself to my hands and knees, the pain in my legs fogging my thoughts. The pipe hadn't hit me, so why were my hands and arms spattered with blood? Another thick drop appeared on my braced arm and ran in a slow rivulet to the floor. The fogginess in my brain suddenly cleared and I turned my head, letting my gaze travel upward.

Kat sagged against the chains that bound her, her eyes closed. Blood spilled past her lips and dripped to the floor.

I stumbled to my feet and saw the length of iron blurring

toward me again, but instead of trying to avoid it I ran straight at Zena. My move was stupid enough to take her by surprise. As I slammed into her and drove her backwards, the pipe flew from her hands and clanked metallically to the edge of the stage. Jamming my stake in my belt, I grabbed it.

"*Release* her, you bitch!" My vision blinded by tears, I swung the pipe wildly in her direction, rage surging hotly through me as I felt it connect with her upraised arm. "Whatever you did to put her in the hell she's going through, reverse—"

My words were choked off as a tight band clamped around my neck, and I felt my feet abruptly leave the floor. I dropped the pipe, my hands flying to my throat to break free of the crushing pressure. As I felt myself rising higher, I looked down and realized Zena was one-handedly lifting me in the air with no visible effort whatsoever.

"Is as I tell old man," she hissed, clouds of red drifting across the green of her eyes like oil spreading over water. "Darkheart line is no longer threat. Angelica forgot she was Daughter when babies she loved were in danger, and you do same for sister. I wish often to have lived in time when my kind faced strong enemies, instead of weak and foolish girls!"

A loud roaring sound began to echo in my ears. My fingers were still clawing at my throat but there was no strength in them. In the growing blackness around me only Zena's white face stood out, tight with scorn.

"*She* knew her kind and mine were only mirror image of each other. She understood her strength came from dark side, and constant temptation not to fully embrace it. You carry her bone and her sinew, but you do not carry her blood!" Her lips pursed. The next moment I felt wetness trickling down my cheek.

The bitch had *spat* on me. Outrage pierced my fading consciousness enough for me to rasp out a question. "What are you talking about? Who's *she?*"

Her eyes widened briefly. Then she gave an incredulous laugh. "All the time I am thinking you know! Is why I believe cannot kill you without setting trap, but my fear is all for nothing! You call yourself her Daughter and do not even feel her power in your weapon?"

I was too far gone to feel her pluck my stake from my belt before it swam into my fading view. Zena held it with the tips of her fingers, as if she didn't feel comfortable touching it, and as my senses began to shut down the leather-strapped hilt and ivory blade swinging back and forth in front of my eyes blurred until it didn't look like a stake at all, but like a lithe figure moving swiftly against some unseen opponent.

And in the same way that I'd seen Tash's true nature, I suddenly saw my weapon for what it really was.

Her bone…her sinew. The lost relics of the original Lilith, missing for centuries… I brought my trembling fingers up to touch the stake, my lips moving inaudibly.

Lilith, be with me.

Zena tossed it aside and ran a contemptuous finger down my cheek, still holding me aloft with her other hand. "You made wrong choice, *nyet?*" she whispered, her lips close to mine. "I offered you pleasures with me, but you chose sisters and grandfather. Darkheart cannot save you, and as for sisters, one is dying and other is no match for me." She held her finger up so I could see the blood glistening on her razor-sharp nail, and slowly licked it. She touched my lips. "Die knowing you saved no one. I kill false Daughter next, then old man. And one with hair like golden roses shall be mine before this night ends."

She wanted me to die in pain. She'd seen my anguish over Kat and now she was tripling it, wringing every last drop of agony out of me while she watched the light leave my eyes and the breath leave my body…but she'd over-looked one thing.

I'm a hereditary Daughter of Lilith. And while I'm as emotional as the next girl, I need to be able to bury those emotions under an impervious glacier of ice when I'm fighting. It took me a while to understand that about myself and even longer to stop feeling like I should apologize for it, but now I'm totally okay with this part of me.

Of course, at the time that Zena was choking the life out of me, I hadn't figured all that out. All I knew was that the bitch's little head-game wasn't working on me and instead of feeling anguish, I felt a spark of cold anger. Her finger was still tracing my lips. I opened my mouth and bit down on it as hard as I could.

I guess as a vamp she was more used to biting than being bitten, because her scream sounded like a cross between a steam-whistle and a thousand cats getting their tails stepped on at once. She let go of my neck and I fell to the floor, gulping in as much oxygen as I could to make up for what I'd missed in the past few minutes. As my vision cleared I saw Tash and Darkheart and Van trying to battle their way through the crowd. Glimpsing the almost-hyp-notised blankness on the faces ringing the stage, I wondered briefly if Zena had somehow manipulated the crowd to form a wall of bodies. Then I saw my stake lying on the floor by Kat's chained figure about twenty feet away, and I shut my mind to everything else as I began crawling toward it.

Zena was still screaming. Queen *vampyr* though she was, she obviously wasn't impervious to the shock of seeing her finger hanging from her hand by a strip of flesh. I'd felt bone shatter when I'd bitten her, I thought with cold satisfaction as I dragged myself forward. It was partial payback for the ones I was pretty sure she'd broken in my legs.

But partial payback was all I was going to get, I realized a moment later as Zena's screams abruptly stopped.

"First I open you, neck to belly," she said in a thick, choked snarl. "Then each organ I slowly remove. You will pray for death a million times before it comes, Daughter of Lilith."

I heard her velvet skirt brushing the floor as she advanced upon me from behind, and knew there was no way I could cover the remaining distance to my stake in time. I'd failed everyone who'd been counting on me, I thought bleakly. Darkheart would pay for my failure with his life and Tash with her soul, but the price to Kat would be highest of all—an eternity in hell. I lifted my gaze to her battered face, knowing that this last sight of her would torture me more than any pain Zena could devise.

My heart seemed to stop in my chest. Kat's head still hung slackly down and blood still dripped slowly from her mouth, but one purpled and swollen eyelid was open a slit. A sapphire-blue eye, clouded and unfocused, rested dully on me as a faint, pain-filled whisper escaped her.

"Sweetie…kill the bitch!"

The toe of a blood-stained Jimmy Choo stiletto nudged forward to touch my fallen stake. Then it flicked weakly sideways, sending the weapon skittering across the floor to me. A sudden gout of scarlet gushed past Kat's lips and her eyelid closed as I wrapped my hand around the stake and felt the power of Lilith's bone and sinews against mine....

And entered fully into the kill-zone.

Everything seemed to happen instantly after that. My left leg felt broken. The realization passed through my mind as I rose swiftly to my feet, but only as a fact to be noted and dismissed. The pain was even less relevant, so I willed myself to ignore it as I pivoted to face Zena and lunged at her. I saw a flash of red velvet as she made a sudden sideways movement, received a quick impression of a second figure blurring across my line of vision, and disregarded both distractions as I completed my lunge at her and thrust my stake at her heart.

I froze, my gaze locked on melted-chocolate eyes that were only inches away. From the tip of my stake a fine red thread began slowly unravelling in the snowy white of Van's shirt-front.

"I fucked up, Megan." A muscle jumped at the side of his jaw as Zena's grip tightened on his upper arms, but he didn't turn his head to look at her standing behind him. "I was trying to get to her before she could finish you off."

Zena's smile was thin with triumph as she looked at me over Van's shoulder. "I tell you life as Daughter is hard, *nyet?* Now you see how hard is road you have chosen. Can destroy me only by killing man you love." Her smile became mocking. "Or maybe you do not love him? Then duty is regretful, but not impossible to carry out."

I glanced at her with loathing before looking at Van. The weapon I was holding was only carved bone and tanned sinew, I thought bleakly. How could it suddenly feel so damn heavy?

"I fell for you from the moment I first saw you," I told Van, letting my gaze dwell on his sexy mouth, the tiny half moon scar by his lip, his melting eyes.

With an abruptly powerful shove I thrust my stake through him and into Zena.

"But I think I always knew you were too good to be true," I said as his neck arched back in agony and his fangs extended in a death reflex. "The real clincher came tonight when I finally accepted I was the Daughter, not a vampire. I realized the reason why I couldn't enter my own home had to be because I was holding hands with a vamp at the time."

I've never been sure whether he heard my last words or not. He turned to dust, and I was left facing Zena.

She was looking down at the stake puncturing the left breast of her velvet bodice. "Is not fatal," she whispered. "Is like when Angelica tried to kill me, *da?*"

"*Nyet,* bitch." I smiled tightly at her. "I don't expect you to understand, but by finishing the job she started I feel like I've won back what you took from me when you killed her. Because of you I never knew Mom. Now that I'm following in her footsteps, I understand what her life was about."

She looked up at me, her gaze searing. "But road you are on is already different from Angelica's. Different and harder, my darling. To end of your days, you will be tortured with knowledge that man you loved was mine, never yours." The emerald of her eyes bloomed red. "Angelica was lucky enough to die without ever learning same about your father."

I stared at her. "You're lying." Around her white face her fiery hair began smouldering and then suddenly burst into real flame. Smoke began drifting from her parted red lips, and behind the red sheen of her once-green eyes I saw the hotter red of glowing coals. I started to grab her by the shoulder, but I jerked my hand away just in time to avoid the crackling flames that erupted from the velvet of her dress. "You're *lying!*" I repeated, my voice rising. She was completely enveloped in flame now, but behind the curtain of fire her lips curved into a secret smile. "You're already halfway to hell, bitch! Save yourself a few eternities of damnation by admitting you're lying about my father being one of your vamp lovers—"

The flames surrounding her suddenly rushed together. I had an instant's glimpse of her face, no longer smiling, but crushed and unrecognizable, and then the concentrated ball of fire seemed to consume itself like a sun going supernova. A moment later there was nothing but a few drifting motes of ash, so fragile that they dissipated before they reached the floor.

As I slowly replaced my stake in my belt, I was aware of the women near the stage moving aside to let Tash and Darkheart through. Behind me, I heard the clank of falling chains, and when I looked around I saw Kat, no longer bound to the striptease pole, lying crumpled on the floor. Her face was free of blood, and the eye that had been so badly swollen shut now looked normal. Tash rushed past me to her, but Darkheart paused.

"You did well, granddaughter, but inside is pain for detective, *da?*"

I shook my head. "He was working with her right up to

the end. Earlier this evening, my Daughter senses were telling me to stake him, but I persuaded myself that I was the danger, not him. Go tend to Kat."

He nodded slowly, but as he began to turn away I spoke again. "What she said…there was no way it could have been true, could it?"

"That your father turned *vampyr* at some point before his death?" Darkheart's gaze seemed more hooded than usual. "She was lying. David Crosse was good man and he loved your mother. Remember him that way, granddaughter."

I made my way outside by using the iron bar that Zena had smashed my leg with as a cane. As the Hot Box's front doors swung shut behind me, I hobbled around the building away from the lights that festooned the front of the club and eased myself to the ground. I saw moonlight glint on the silver-tipped black hair of the man approaching me, and closed my eyes.

"I keep thinking about that scar by his mouth," I said. I didn't open my eyes, but I could feel him watching me. "He told me he'd gotten it as a boy, when he jumped off a garage roof. I wish I'd asked him before he dusted if that part was true. I'd like to think some of the things he told me were."

"He was a vamp," Mikhail's voice was emotionless. "Every time you'd been with him I could smell it on you, even if I didn't know it came from him, and vamps lie like we breathe. He even killed his own kind to keep up the deception."

I opened my eyes. "Thank you, Dr. Phil," I said flatly. "I came out here to be alone, Mikey-baby. No offence, but can you give me some space for a while, maybe go mingle with the other females inside the club? I've heard that the first thing most people want to do when they narrowly escape death is to make love, so there's a good chance you could get lucky tonight."

"They don't remember that they narrowly escaped death." He looked over his shoulder at the parking lot, where women were heading for their cars. "They think they were at one hell of a great party. I wiped the rest of the evening from their minds."

"I should have guessed you had talents I didn't know about," I said without interest. "That doesn't mean you can't still get lucky, big guy."

"That's not in the cards for me now," Mikhail said. "I told you earlier tonight that I'd made two mistakes with you. My first was that I thought the coldness I sensed meant you'd received the mark of the vampire. I never did tell you what my second mistake was."

"But you're about to, right?" I looked up at him, my neck muscles throbbing. Everything in my body ached, I thought, but the physical pain was nothing compared to the emptiness I felt in my soul. "Okay, tell me. But then I'd just like to be alone, Mikhail. I've had enough of vamps and people for tonight."

"What happened between us wasn't just sex for me. I didn't intend it to be more, but by the time I realized what was happening to me, it was too late. For me it was a mating."

I exhaled. "Mating, sex—what's the difference?"

"The difference is that wolves mate for life," Mikhail shrugged. "It's just my bad luck that the mate I gave myself to is still in love with the vamp she had to kill tonight."

He turned and walked away, leaving me in the shadows. For a long moment I stared into the darkness around me.

Zena had said I'd made the wrong choice, but I'd never had one to make. I'd done everything I could to turn away from being a Daughter of Lilith, and like Angelica, in the end I'd realized there was no escaping my legacy. But the queen *vampyr* had been right about one thing: she'd said the road of a Daughter was a hard one. This was my first night walking that road, and already it was almost too hard to endure.

I closed my eyes to see a boy with a gaze like melted chocolate jump off a roof…and just for a moment, he flew like an angel.

Putting my arm around the silver-tipped ruff of the wolf who silently returned to sit beside me, I buried my face in his fur and let myself cry.

Epilogue

Kat says she doesn't remember much about that night. Tash says she remembers everything, especially the part where I was such a bitch. But apparently Mikhail's mind-zap or whatever he calls it worked, and none of the rest of the women, including Mandy Broyhill, who were at the Hot Box recall fighting vamps, dusting vamps or watching queen vamps go up in a big ball of flame.

It's just as well—I work better alone. That's not strictly true, since Mikhail's always with me in wolf form, and Tash and Darkheart often join me on my nightly excursions around Maplesburg, but although I can face the undead with no qualms, society girls in vamp-killing mode are just *too* scary.

What else? Well, Grammie and Popsie are still on their cruise, Darkheart's dating Liz Dixon—okay, I know I shouldn't say *ewww* and feel uncomfortable about my grandfather having a relationship with a woman, but *ewww*—and Tash has come up with the bright idea of us starting an investigative agency called Darkheart & Crosse to deal with suspected vamp-related cases. I'm not sure how that's going to work out, but for now I'm going along with it, mainly because Maplesburg still seems to have a sizeable undead population.

I haven't said anything to my sisters, but I've been worrying about that. I mean, this little town was vamp-free before Zena came, right? And when she died, the ones she created should have been released of her mark, leaving the local Daughter of Lilith without a job.

Except I keep staking them, night after night. And that makes me wonder whether the crackpot monk's theory that Darkheart rejected might not be true—the one that insisted the death of a queen *vampyr* doesn't lift her curse from her victims. I once thought my vision of stalking Kat and Tash meant that I was a vamp…but what if it really means one of them is?

Dear Lilith, I pray that the road never gets that hard.

* * * * *

A special treat for you from Harlequin Blaze!

Turn the page for a sneak preview of
DECADENT
by
New York Times *bestselling author*
Suzanne Forster

Available November 2006,
wherever series books are sold.

Harlequin Blaze—Your ultimate destination
for red-hot reads.
With six titles every month, you'll never guess
what you'll discover under the covers...

RUN, ALLY! Don't be fooled by him. He's evil. Don't let him touch you!

But as the forbidding figure came through the mists toward her, Ally knew she couldn't run. His features burned with dark malevolence, and his physical domination of everything around him seemed to hold her like a net.

She'd heard the tales. She knew all about the Wolverton legend and the ghost that haunted The Willows, an elegant old mansion lost by Micha Wolverton nearly a hundred years ago. According to folklore, the estate was stolen from the Wolvertons, and Micha was killed trying to reclaim it. His dying vow was to be reunited with the spirit of his beloved wife, who'd taken her life for reasons no one would speak of, except in whispers. But Ally had never put much stock in the fantasy. She didn't believe in ghosts.

Until now—

She still didn't understand what was happening. The figure had materialized out of the mist that lay thick on the damp cemetery soil. A cool breeze and silvery moonlight had played against the ancient stone of the crypts surrounding her, until they joined the mist, causing his body to thicken and solidify right before her eyes. That was when she realized she'd seen this man before. Or thought she had, at least.

His face was familiar. . . so familiar, yet she couldn't put it together. Not with him looming so near. She stepped back as he approached.

"Don't be afraid," he said. His voice wasn't what she expected. It didn't sound as if it were coming from beyond the grave. It was deep and sensual. Commanding.

"Who are you?" she managed.

"You should know. You summoned me."

"No, I didn't." She had no idea what he was talking about. Two minutes ago, she'd been crouching behind a moss-covered crypt, spying on the mansion that had once been The Willows, but was now Club Casablanca. And then this—

If he was Micha, he might be angry that she was trespassing on his property. "I'll go," she said. "I won't come back. I promise."

"You're not going anywhere."

Words snagged in her throat. "Wh-why not? What do you want?"

"If I wanted something, Ally, I'd take it. This is about need."

His words resonated as he moved within inches of her. She tried to back away, but her feet were useless. "And you need something from me?"

"Good guess." His tone burned with irony. "I need lips, soft and surrendered, a body limp with desire."

"My lips, my bod—?"

"Only yours."

"Why? Why me?" This couldn't be Micha. He didn't want any woman but Rose. He'd died trying to get back to her.

"Because you want that, too," he said.

Wanted what? A ghost of her own? She'd always found the legend impossibly romantic, but how could he have known that? How could he know anything about her? Besides, she'd sworn off inappropriate men, and what could be more inappropriate than a ghost? She shook her head again, still not willing to admit the truth. But her heart wouldn't play along. It clattered inside her chest. The mere thought of his kiss, his touch, terrified her. This wildness, it was fear, wasn't it?

When his fingertips touched her cheek, she flinched, expecting his flesh to be cold, lifeless. It was anything but that. His skin was smooth and hot, gentle, yet demanding. And while his dark brown eyes were filled with mystery and wonder, there was a sensitivity about them that threatened to disarm her if she looked too deeply.

"These lips are mine," he said, as if stating a universal fact that she was helpless to avoid. In truth, it was just that. She couldn't stop him.

And she didn't want to.

* * * * *